Under An Indifferent Heaven

SHARAD KESKAR

AuthorHouse™ UK
1663 Liberty Drive
Bloomington, IN 47403 USA
www.authorhouse.co.uk
Phone: 0800.197.4150

Cover Design by Jane Keskar.

Published by AuthorHouse 01/11/2016

ISBN: 978-1-5049-9495-8 (sc)
ISBN: 978-1-5049-9496-5 (hc)
ISBN: 978-1-5049-9497-2 (e)

Print information available on the last page.

This book is printed on acid-free paper.

To my sister Enid
for the sacrifices she made
and Jane
again and always

O call back yesterday, bid time return.
Shakespeare

Life must be understood backwards, but… it must be lived forwards.
Kierkegaard

ONE

We stood silently holding hands on the platform of Baroli Railway Station till the engine driver blew his warning whistle. The two short, sharp bleeps, followed by a prolonged shrill one, made us jump. More than that, it affected my mother strangely. Her whole body shuddered violently and I looked up at her. She turned to my uncle Ganesh and begged him to let us see my father. Uncle Ganesh, who was standing some distance away, keeping a close watch on us, shook his head and raised a forbidding hand.

Another blast of the whistle was followed by a loud clang as the train jerked forward, grinding its couplings. My mother screamed 'Devnath!' and, grasping my hand, dragged me towards the waiting train, only to find uncle Ganesh barring our way. He waved his hands and roared: 'Back! Go back!' His strong voice, distinct above the hubbub of plying hawkers, rushing passengers, and the clamour of well-wishers offering last minute farewells, was chilling.

My mother checked herself with a soft cry, took a deep breath and continued her walk towards the train in measured dignity. It was too late. The driver blew his valedictory whistle and with a whoosh of white steam the train gathered speed, taking my father away from us forever. At the time, I did not realise I would never see him again. I turned to my mother. She had covered her head with her sari and was calm again. To show loyalty to her, I seized her hand and glared hard at my uncle. His conduct struck me as strange and it troubled me not to be able to make sense of it. Where was father going? And why did uncle Ganesh prevent her from seeing him?

Confused and afraid, I tugged at my mother's arm as I flashed another angry look at him. But he had gone, lost in the chattering mass of people returning to their homes. The Baroli Railway Station was less than two years old and still a wonderful novelty to be talked about. My mother remained rooted on the platform staring at the space left by the departed train. I coughed. She ignored me. A moment later another engine, puffing smoke and steam, shunted backwards into the vacated space. It was only the second time I had seen a railway engine and still found it hard not to believe it was a living, breathing black monster. I recall asking my father, when he took me to see the new station, about the engine that had been put there, on display, for village folk to see. I was proud he knew so much about engines and the railways, so I plied him with questions just to watch village folk gape at him in wonder. Most of all I recalled the long walk back to Pali, our village, and asking him why there was no railway station there. He explained that India was full of villages like ours and that at present the Government was concentrating on linking only the big towns of India. Baroli, he said, was not a big town, but because it served as a link between Poona and the newly settled cantonment of Pultanpur, it was decided to build the station.

Pultanpur is where father worked as an accountant clerk or Munshi. It was why I saw so little of him. He stayed there during the week and came home to us on Saturday evenings, taking the early train back every Monday morning.

My eyes grew heavy. I was tired. It was barely light when my mother and I had set out to walk the three miles to Baroli Station; and now the thought of the walk back to Pali chilled me. I coughed and tugged at her sari. She squeezed my hand till it hurt. I tried freeing it, but she squeezed all the harder. Biting my lower lip, I dare not cry, though I cried easily. Instinctively I felt it was not a time to be myself. That for her sake I must bear up. Why, I couldn't think why? I was then six years old and the situation beyond me to resolve. I looked up tearfully. She loosened her grip but, when I tried to pull my hand away, she squeezed even harder than before. The pain made me buckle. I tugged in desperation. She released my hand. I pressed it between my knees to relieve the throbbing ache but, unable to contain myself, I broke down and bawled. She picked me up in her strong arms and with a soothing whisper cradled me against her ample bosom. Its yielding softness calmed me. I rested my head under her chin.

'Hungry,' I whimpered.

'You'll have to wait till we get home.' She kissed me. 'Did I hurt you?'

I moved my head away from her and nodded.

'Was it this hand?'

I nodded again.

She took it and kissed it. It went damp. I wiped it on my shirt and studied her face. It was wet. I raised my hand to touch her cheek. She put me down hurriedly. 'Don't!' she hissed. 'From now on they must never know...' She covered her head with her *pallu*, the loose end of her sari and, using a corner of it, dried her face. 'You must never talk about what you saw today. Not to anyone. It is our big secret. Promise me?'

I nodded without quite understanding why. 'But they're not here,' I whimpered.

My mother tapped my face lightly. 'Yes, they are. They haven't gone. There, in that stone building...the station building...they are there, waiting and watching...from the big window?'

'Uncle Ganesh?'

'Not just Ganesh uncle. All of them.' She sighed, looked at me and took me in her arms again. 'Do you know why we had to walk this morning to this station?'

I shook my head.

'They did not want us to be here.'

There was much I wanted to know, much I wanted to ask. To begin with, why father was away last Sunday and why was he on the train, today? But I couldn't. Her sad, tear-stained face froze the words in my mouth. It also angered me. 'Why do we have to be with them?'

My mother was silent for a moment. 'Because we have to,' she said.

I frowned. 'And why didn't father want us to go with him?'

'Hush! When did you...what makes you think he didn't? What makes you ask that?'

'I heard... something I heard father say. I can't remember when. Something he said made me feel...'

'Hush now. One day you will understand.' She jiggled and rocked me.

'*Daada* hits me. Not like you. He gets angry and hits very hard.'

'Learn not to ask too many questions. And try keeping away from him. You don't have to know everything.' She put me down. 'Oh, you are heavy!'

'And *Daadi* hits me with her fan.' I said, bent on strengthening my case. 'With the handle of her fan!' I emphasised the correction by adding: 'Crack! Crack!'

'Oh, my dear, dear child!' She bent over me and wiped my face with the open palm of her hand. 'Darling, there is nowhere else for us to stay!' She spoke softly. Years later I was to learn that she spoke beautiful Marathi, as was to be expected from a daughter of a Brahmin pundit. She looked at me and sighed. 'But doesn't *Daadi* pet you and give you sweets?'

'And she laughs even when I tell her it hurts.'

'Sweets? Oh, you're still thinking about her fan. I'll tell her not to. She listens to me. Not *Daada*, your grandfather. He won't listen, because I'm a woman. He can be so...' With a quick movement she buried her face into her sari *pallu*, and wept bitterly.

Someone came out of the stone building; a tall, thin, grey man, with a strong limp. His head was clean shaven, apart from a top-knot with its long, single twist of hair. It was my grandfather. He was looking about him angrily. Only his limp prevented him from rushing at my mother. I screamed and he checked himself within inches of her. 'Stop! At once!' He barked. 'I forbid it. Woman, have you no shame? Making scene in public. He was worthless. If I had my way, I would not have agreed to your marriage. It was my wife and greedy brother! They arranged it. Behind my back! They arranged your marriage.' He started to cough. The coughing gave him time to be reasonable. 'Of course, they couldn't know how foolish your husband would turn out to be. I knew. Clever people are trouble. They get mad ideas.'

My mother bent down to touch his feet. He stepped back. She fell forward on her hands. 'But *Mamanji*, I love him!'

'Stop, I say! Stand up. Come on! Up, on your feet!' Humbly my mother obeyed. 'Good, now listen. Forget him. He was a shame to his caste and he brought dishonour on all of us...on the whole family. I reasoned with the obstinate fool. He wouldn't change his mind; even after I got his brothers to give him a good thrashing!'

'Why? Mamanji, why?'

'Yes, I asked him. I wanted to know why! What is this obstinacy? I said. What's so special about this Christian *dharma*?'

'But you knew, *Mamanji*. He told you. You refused to listen.'

'What? What could he tell me? Nothing but foolishness.'

'He told you he hated our caste system... and the way we treat servants and the poor. He wanted to work alongside our farmers, but you would not let him.'

'Farming is for farmers. A Brahmin does not put his hand to the plough. Some of our new tenant farmers are low-caste. And you, how did you feel? You of highest caste Brahmin? Did you really want your husband to mix with the low and the untouchables? Why such degrading loyalty to a foolish man? Love, you say! Love is nothing. Not in the face of our time honoured caste system. That is God-given!'

'Oh, *Mamanji*! How can you say this of me? Three times I followed him round the sacred fire. I walked, tied to him, in submissive obedience to Hindu precepts; following round that fire, taking the oath of wifely duty. He led. I followed. He's my *nath*, my household god.'

'Not if he's lost his way. Are you going to follow him to *jehanum*? To hell?'

'*Hai Rey!* This is your son you are talking about! He is your flesh and blood! You named him Vasudev and on our wedding day you called me Rohini. Can't you forgive your own son?'

'No, and now you know why I chose Ramoo and Ganesh to manage our farm lands, and let your husband work for those Britishers. I let him do what he wanted, because he promised me he would maintain some dignity. I gave him a home, built him another room so he could bring up his family. And what does he do? He betrays me.'

'It is only in his mind that he sees things differently.'

'*Ha*, yes,' wheezed a short, fat woman, who approached, unobserved by either of them. But it took me a moment to recognise it was grandmother, my *Daadi*.

'Yes, yes,' she continued, 'just a mental change. I keep telling you. Why won't you listen? Your son may think what he likes. Have all sorts of strange thoughts and mad ideas, yet still he is Brahmin. Brahmins are twice born. Once a Brahmin always a Brahmin.'

The man stared at her, astonished. 'Be quiet, woman! How dare you speak to me like that? How dare to interrupt your husband!' As he glared at her, he brushed his full, white moustache, grunted, touched his forehead, on which was smeared, in sandalwood paste, the caste mark of a Vishnu devotee. Grandmother attempted to address him again.

'Not another word,' he fumed, 'I forbid it.'

She threw her hands up in despair, sank to the ground, squatting frog-like on her feet. Then she pressed the knuckles of her hands against the temples of her head and, rocking from side to side, uttered a low moan. 'Will I ever to see my son again? You've driven him from the house … never to return to me… Have you no heart?'

'You have two other sons and three daughters-in-law, deserving of your love and pride.'

'Pride! Your heartless pride stops at nothing. You can make a scene in public and I must be silent. Look, look? See the crowd you've gathered!'

The man turned upon the expanding circle of men, women and children, standing behind him, gaping. 'Hey! Hey! *Challo! Challo!* Move on. This is no *natak*. No street drama. Go, go! Get going! Get about your business.' The gathering stared mutely. Their silence was made all the more pointed by the stifled giggles of children hiding behind their elders. Slowly and with much reluctance the sullen circle broke up in little groups and dispersed.

Grandfather waited till they were far enough. 'Come along, woman,' he said gruffly.

My grandmother started to rise but fell back with a piercing scream. Sitting crossed-legged she began once again to rock from side to side and moaned plaintively.

The old man was taken aback. '*Arrey*! Karunabai, what is the matter?' His voice took on a tone of nervous concern.

'Are you blind? The boy! Where is the boy? He has disappeared. Run away. Gone! All this due to your shouting! You frightened the child. Now our Krishna is gone! God help us!'

I was terrified by the way *Daada* had so harshly treated my mother and decided to appeal to the only stranger I knew. So I stole away and hid under a vegetable stall that sold aubergines, onions, *karelas* and tomatoes and then took the first chance to dash into the office of Mr Chand, the stationmaster. To my utter disappointment he shook his head and held me back, saying it would be over, soon. 'Your *Daada* is not a bad man. He will cool down.' Then he gave me a piece of guava from a plate he had in front of him. 'Now, when you have eaten it, I'll give you this one shiny anna and later, when the ice-fruit man comes to the village, buy a nice red, juicy ice-*gola*. You should even have change to buy another one tomorrow.'

Taking the anna absently, a glance through the window made me aware of the turmoil taking place outside. Grandmother's alarm had so upset mother, she started to scream: 'Krishna! Oh my Krishna! Oh my dear Krishna! My heart! Where are you?' She then ran up to the small crowd, pleading to them as they backed away from her. 'Did you see my son, Krishna? Oh, tell me! Where is he? Where did he go?'

And, hobbling behind her came *Daada*, trying hard to calm her: 'Hush *beti*, hush daughter! Listen to me! Don't be making scene. I'll find him. He can't go far. People know he's my grandson. Let me talk to Karam Chand, Stationmaster, and when he...' He did not finish the sentence but turning round moved as fast as he could towards the Stationmaster's office and to me, with my mother and grandmother following him in a daze. On seeing them approaching, I panicked and began to cry.

'Enough now,' the stationmaster patted my head. 'Okay, all right, I will talk to your *Daada*. Everything will be okay.' He put his hairy arm round me, which smelt heavily of nicotine and sweat, and gave me an affectionate squeeze. I cringed and tried to push myself free as my *Daada* entered the room, advancing menacingly towards me. But mother rushed in, overtook him, and grabbing me in her arms, hugged me passionately.

My poor mother did not live long. Truly in love with my father, she pined for him, ate little, generally neglected herself and grew increasingly silent. Soon even her few smiles for me ceased. Then one day, about a year after father had left us, she was found lying on the floor of our room in a coma, clutching to her breast an old photograph of him. I watched stunned and helpless as they lifted her on a light stretcher, placed it on a bullock-cart and took her to the hospital, some miles away. She died before they got there.

It was 1881. I clearly recall the year, because the village schoolmaster always wrote the date on a blackened board for us to copy down on to our slates—the palindrome pattern of figures left its indelible image on my mind. Now without my mother to turn to for consolation and comfort, I began to fear for myself. But, her death had had a strange effect on my grandfather. He grew morose and spoke to me only when he was teaching me to read and do sums. Strangely, too, he seemed more kind, even patient. That may have been because I was a fast learner. Besides, I had taken my mother's advice to heart, giving him little cause to lose his temper. Yet, I was afraid of him. His health began to suffer and his cough grew severe, often forcing him to break into a hawking, choking fit, recovering only to clear his throat and expectorate violently.

The loss of my mother hurt me deeply. I turned into a quiet, sulking child. Then early one morning, about a year after her death, I awoke to the sound of loud voices. Getting out of bed, I crept to our window. The potted *tulsi* plant, which my mother religiously tended, was no longer on the sill. *Daadi* had removed it and taken over its care. Our rooms were separated from the main house by a small inner courtyard. I peered across it. It was still dark and all I could see were dancing shadows cast by the flickering flame of the earthen oil lamp that burned in the courtyard's little shrine to goddess Lakshmi. I listened. The voices rose and fell in a peculiar pattern. Those of my uncles, Ramoo and Ganesh, paid deference to their father but were raised to thwart *Daadi*'s feeble protests, while all three went quiet when grandfather spoke. And as I listened, an increasing sense of fear and concern came over me. I understood enough to know I was the subject of the whole commotion. *Daada*'s speech I could follow best. As always, he spoke with great deliberation and priestly clarity.

'Woman, can't you see, it is for the boy's own good. Have you listened to a word we have said? The boy's father, your son, has brought shame upon the family. That shame must be wiped out, forgotten. We must wipe the slate clean. Already many rumours are making life difficult for the men of the family.' He broke into a coughing fit. It lasted a few minutes. 'Laxman, my elder brother, in Mandi village, will have nothing to do with us if we don't set things right. You always respected him, did you not? Well, he and our high Brahmin pride had been shamed. Your son...'

'What is this?' *Daadi* interrupted in a high-pitched shriek. 'What is this, your son, your son? He is your son too! Is he not? You were at their wedding! You gave them your *arshidvar*, your blessings. And *ha*, such a beautiful daughter-in-law, you said. Couldn't take your eyes off her.'

'Enough woman! It was supposed to be an arranged marriage. How was I to know they were in love?' He paused and in that quiet moment I heard *Daadi* sobbing. 'Now, what is this? What is the point of crying? Accept it. Soon you'll understand. We do what must be done. Ramoo, now you are the eldest. Take your mother to your home. And Ganesh, you take charge of the boy. I'll go on *yatra* to Benares. There I will spend my final days in prayer and meditation, bathing each morning in *Ganga Mai*, Holy mother Ganges.' He sighed. 'I've spoken. Everything is to be done just the way I said.' There followed silence, broken by a sudden full-throated howling. It startled me to realise it was *Daada*, for it was so unlike him: 'O God! *Hai Ram* why? Why this? Why has this happened? O how I loved that boy! My first-born! My Vasudev!'

Daadi greeted this outburst with an ironic giggle. Uncle Ramoo broke in: 'Mother, please! This is not helping. And father, what is all this? Where's your pride? What's all this nonsense talk about Benares and becoming a *sannyasi*. It is not yet time. You are only fifty!'

'Forty-nine,' growled his father.

[...looking back I realise my grandfather was not really "old", and my big, strapping uncles were young men, as also my own father, who could not have been more than twenty-eight... So to a child, unfolding truths mean memories have to be constantly adjusted...]

Uncle Ramoo's intervention caused my grandfather to lose the thread of his lamentation and for a while no one spoke. Then I began to pick up a low muttering that made no sense to me. I was about to go back to bed when I was alerted not only by a renewed clarity in *Daada's* speech, but also by the irrelevance of what he was saying. 'White men, Ramoo, have polluted this country. We could have got rid of them. But no...because of the Sikhs. They betrayed us.'

'*Bapa*, what are you talking about?'

'*Arrey*, the Great Uprising. The *gora log*, the Britishers call it "mutiny". Nonsense, I say. If we Indians were united, we would have called it something grand...having got rid of the white enemy.'

I was familiar with grandfather's talk about the Indian Mutiny as it was his pet topic. It constantly stirred my curiosity even though no amount of explanation on my mother's part helped me to make sense of that historical event. For a long time it remained just a terrifying fairy tale of battles against a band of white rulers I had never seen and who, in my vivid imagination, were devils. But the shape of the tale was familiar enough for me to guess what *Daada* would say next.

'Ramoo, twenty-five, I was at the time. I wanted to go to Jhansi to fight alongside the Maharani... that brave, noble queen, hero of Jhansi. But you were newly born and, because our farm workers were being troublesome, my father refused to let me go.'

'But *Bapa*...' Ramoo waited till his father overcame another bout of coughing. '*Bapa*, you can't only blame the Sikhs. Many other Indians saw no reason to... almost all the Maharajas and most of South India, took no part. Yes, we were not united because, *Bapa*, it was an Army mutiny. It began with the sepoys... sepoy fighting sepoy. More Indians fought for the Brits. The Brits were so small in numbers, without Indians helping them, they had no chance.'

'Arrey, Ramoo, that is to India's lasting shame. We have never been united. United, we would have kicked out this British Raj and with them, the Christian Missionaries, who have destroyed our caste system... On top of all that, 1877, Vicktory, that English Rani, becomes Maharani of India.'

'Victoria. Anyway, *Bapa*, as the English say, "no point crying over spilt milk." Also, we don't see them. They are invisible. The Brits don't exist as far as village life is concerned. We are governed by elders of our own people. People like you. And simple village folk don't even know Brits are ruling India.'

'What do you mean?'

'I was talking to farmer, last week only. He asked if the Mughals were still ruling the country.' Ramoo laughed then checked himself. '*Arrey Bapa*, when has any Britisher come to this village?'

'You stupid owl! That is not the point... Anyway the Collector sahib, did he not come?'

'Yes, but that was three years ago.'

'What a big tamasha it was! He riding horseback, with Indian boot-licking slaves on camels; more horses and four-wheeled box-carriage... all done to make a big show. Mules also, carrying tents and big bundles of I don't know what. I took your elder brother, my boy Vasudeva, Krishna's father, to the meeting at temple grounds. And our shameless *panchayat*, village elders, treated this Englishman like some god. Giving him a special high-chair...'

'But *Bapa* you spoke highly of him. Sir Peter Finn, you said, was a just and honest man. Yes, I remember. You also said...'

'Stop! Not another word!' Grandfather growled. 'Maybe I was thinking of the days before the big uprising. When I was a boy these Britishers came, making no fuss, sometimes alone, spending time in villages and promising help with problems. Anyway, forget all that. We don't need them now. I can see you are impressed by the *gora* log, these white faced devils. Don't be impressed. Ha! See, Karunabai? Are you listening?'

'What listening? All my life I'm listening,' grandmother moaned.

'English corrupting this house. Milk spilling! Huh! Now Ramoo also talking and thinking like them. That is why, Ramoo, though you are now the eldest, I have asked Ganesh to...'

Again, Daada's voice turned confidential and it was hard to make out what was being said or why his mumbling was again followed by *Daadi's* plaintive wailing.

A tall shadow crossed the courtyard and before I could get back to bed and pretend to be asleep, uncle Ganesh entered my room. He took my arm and roughly hauled me up. I could have flown across the room if he had not held on to me, for Uncle Ganesh was a man of exceptional strength. As a wrestler, he had won the Baroli Wrestling Championship Prize, two years running. I stared at him shocked and trembling. 'Get dressed,' he growled, 'and stop gaping at me. Just shirt and shorts; hurry up!' He had with him a small gunny sack and while I dressed I saw him roughly shove into it the few remaining clothes I had in my room and an old pair of shoes. I pointed to the sack. 'Where you're going,' he said, 'you may need a spare set of clothes. And here, clean your teeth with this during the journey.' From the top pocket of his *kurta* he handed me a twig of the *neem* tree.

I took it. Facing the inevitable, a strange calm came over me. Since mother died I suffered the loneliness and neglect of an unwanted child and, in my unhappiness, I consoled myself with the thought that it would matter little to me to be anywhere but here; that a new life, away from such hostility would be preferable to my present situation. Increasingly there was less room for nostalgia and in its place I wondered about the outside world, placing hope in new friendships, new adventures and in the company of strangers, an imagined contentment. Such dreaming cheered me and, though I could not truly say how I felt, I was less fearful.

In my helpless defeat I was determined to find consolation and accept whatever fate had in store. 'But where are we going?' I asked, trying to hide feelings that were a mixture of tension and excitement.

'Don't ask questions. You'll soon see.'

I shrugged my shoulders, twice, for him not to miss my lack of concern.

'So,' Uncle Ganesh nudged me sharply with his elbow and gazed down at me. 'Your father wanted you to learn English, so that one day you will become a sahib and a slave.' His sarcasm and hostility was wasted on me. With one hand he held the sack and with the other he gripped both my hands and led me outdoors to the stable at the back of our house. He lifted me on to the front of his cart, sat me behind a pair of bullocks and raised a warning finger: 'Don't you move! Stay where you are.' He tossed the sack into the back of the cart and disappeared.

I knew the bullocks by name and greeted them. Hira and Moti responded by nodding their heads and swishing their tails. The tintinnabulation of the bells round their necks made me realise this was the sound that woke me and that Ramoo and Ganesh had travelled from their farms in this very cart to visit their father.

I turned to look back at my grandfather's house, wondering if I would ever see it again. The windows were shut but I heard *Daadi*'s muffled wails and thought of jumping down to knock on the window behind which I knew she would be. Too late! Uncle Ganesh returned, sprang up beside me and lifting the tails of the bullocks, clicked his tongue and goaded them with his toes. I turned to see if *Daada* or uncle Ramoo had come out to see us off. But we were alone and the only sound that broke the stillness of the air was the clicking of uncle Ganesh's tongue.

The bullocks seemed reluctant to move till another goad and a sharp kick up their backsides got them going at a steady pace. The brass tips on their horns picked up the pale morning light as their heads rolled from side to side. I watched fascinated, till with a jolt I realised that Ganesh uncle had avoided going through our part of Pali village. Instead, he turned into the large open area that had been allotted for new housing and expansion. Here the old, frail, wattle and mud huts were being replaced by new all-brick ones. As we passed through I decided, with wistful pride, that grandfather's house was as good as the best of these and not unlike the one next to the temple with its orange flag. Some evenings my mother took me to that temple but never inside it. She was happy to let me climb the tamarind tree that stood by the covered sacred well and once when the tree was in season she gave me a small packet of salt mixed with a little red chilli powder, to dip its sharp, green fruit into it before eating. I returned that day moaning, for my teeth were on edge. That indulgence was never repeated.

As I looked on, a woman carrying something in an open leaf bowl crossed our path and called out: 'Panditji!' A bald man, a string across this bare chest and wearing a white dhoti that barely covered his bow legs, came out of the temple and rang the brass bell which hung over its front entrance. He folded his hands, bowed and turned to approach the woman. Then I lost sight of them as our cart took a sudden turn to the left. I glanced at my uncle. He always wore his slim white turban with a long tail resting on his left shoulder, which now he swung across his face, covering his nose and mouth. Immediately, I knew why. We were trundling along the edge of the open field that the village used as a public latrine. He lifted my shirt. 'There, cover your nose.' As I did so, I spotted a woman and a girl squatting in the distance, staring at us with deep concentration. I pointed to them and for my pains received a sharp crack on my head. Slight as my uncle's backhanded clip was, I lurched forward and almost fell off the cart. 'Don't look! That is women's area,' he growled, but for the first time his lips betrayed a smile. 'Have you been this morning?'

I shook my head. 'You gave me no time,' I said sullenly, daring to add, 'and I haven't had breakfast.' He reached behind him, pulled out a white cloth bundle from under the tarpaulin, uncovered a round, flat, circle of thick barley bread, broke it in half, put a large lump of brown jaggery on it and handed it to me with a peremptory: 'Eat!'

I had noted, when he lifted the tarpaulin, a brass, screw-lidded pot in a reed basket.

'Go on! What are you looking at? Oh that! Buttermilk. We'll stop soon and have some. The bulls can do with some fodder too. See there, the hut next to the well. It's Narpat Singh's land. Once it was your *Daada's* property. You can go in the field there, there behind that bush. He'll bring you a *lota* of water to wash yourself.'

When we resumed our journey, at its start, I felt a sense of well-being and began to wonder if my Uncle's attitude had softened a little. I glanced up at him and ventured to ask again where we were going.

'You'll soon find out,' he said, maintaining a steady gaze ahead.

We travelled for miles along a treeless, deeply rutted cart track that cut through brown fields of golden maize and millet. It was a misty November morning and the start of the cool season. I shivered and complained about being cold. My uncle pointed to the red square blanket under my feet. I stared at the large black ants crawling all over it with horror and shook my head.

'Not long now,' he grunted and nodded towards the sun creeping over the horizon. 'Soon it'll warm up.'

I hugged myself and stamped my feet. He looked down. 'You're wearing your mother's Rajasthani sandals.' I crossed my legs and tucked in my feet. He laughed. 'Don't worry, you can keep them.' He yawned. 'Either she had small feet or you have large ones.' I pretended not to hear. He looked away and swore at the bullocks and raised his stick. I cringed, dreading to hear sharp cracks on the backs of Hira and Moti. But it was only a threat. The cattle bells rang out louder as they tossed their heads and quickened their pace. 'See,' my uncle swore, 'just the shadow of my stick gets them going, though the lazy sods will soon slow down again.'

Long hours later we entered a town, the sight of which brought back a ghostly memory; and as we passed the tall clock tower in the crowded bazaar, that dim memory struck me with the weight of an actual happening. Had I done this journey before? I couldn't think when and why. But it would have to have been with my father. I tried to recall that past journey. Only a vague vision of a pond and getting thoroughly wet returned. It made me shiver. I wondered if uncle Ganesh would know. I looked at his implacable face and decided not to ask.

We continued to the town's edge and after crossing a wide, sludge-filled drain, approached a large wall-enclosed compound and stopped in front of tall cast-iron gates. A huge, bearded man in a light grey-green turban came out and gestured menacingly with his heavy knotted staff, telling us to move on. My uncle drove the cart fifty yards ahead, sprang off it and, freeing the bullocks, tethered them under the shade of an old banyan tree. He lifted me down. 'That man is the chowkidar, watchman,' said my uncle, 'a Pathan. But he won't scare me,' he added, drawing himself to his full height. Then he picked up the sack and together we walked back to the gate. Before we got within sight of it, we were stopped by a young man with a clean shaven head. He wore a saffron vest and a *dhoti* that was little more than a loin cloth.

'Where are you taking the boy?' he asked.

'It's none of your business,' my uncle replied and waved him on.

'It is my business,' insisted the young man promptly. 'I know you. Are we not Vaishnavite Brahmins? And do you not know that the very shadow of that gate is pollution?'

'I will bathe seven times after I've escorted this boy to the Mission,' my uncle said through clenched teeth. 'Now be off, or you'll feel the back of my hand.'

'Why this aggressive behaviour? The boy's related to you, is he not?'

'No! No relation.' My uncle glowered at me with a sidelong glance. 'I am just doing a friend a personal favour.' And with another wave of his hand he dragged me to the gate.

Once again the burly Pathan barred our way, but now, much to my surprise, he seemed to shrink in size as my uncle confronted him. Peering past them and through the iron bars of the gate, I saw, in front of the gatehouse, a dappled grey pony feeding from a nosebag while a syce scraped his back. Next to them a *tonga* rested on its twin shafts. Then I looked up, and studied the brick arch over the gate. It was surmounted by a white cross; and as for the strange writing below it was, I later learned, the name of this Christian Mission School. I tugged at my uncle's hand and pointed to it. My uncle looked up, grunted and pushed me forward.

'This boy,' he said to the Pathan, 'for this school. It is in accordance with his father's wishes.'

For a moment the Pathan stared back blankly. Then signing us to wait, entered the gate-house to shortly emerge with a little man dressed in a white flowing *dhoti*, over which he wore a *kurta* or long white shirt and a black waistcoat. The Pathan spoke to my uncle and introduced the small wizened man. I heard the word "Munshi" and knew it meant that he was some sort of clerk or accountant, because my father also had that title. The Munshi tucked a purple stained pencil behind his ear, adjusted his black pillbox hat and gold-rimmed spectacles, and folding his hands to greet my uncle, wobbled his head. My uncle returned the salutation.

The Munshi dismissed the Pathan, studied me closely and speaking in Hindustani said to my uncle: 'How shall I address you, in Hindi or Marathi?'

'Marathi,' my uncle growled.

'I see. So, this boy is for enrolment; but were you not expected yesterday?'

My uncle nodded.

'Well, you will have to come in. There are papers to sign.'

My uncle visibly shrank back and shook his head.

'No signature, then no place for boy in school,' the Munshi said firmly.

'All right, all right,' uncle grumbled and as we passed through the gate he pointed to the sign above. 'St Thomas Mission School,' he said. Neither the name nor the fact that he stressed the aspirant meant anything to me; and I was never to know how and why he had any knowledge of English. I watched him sign his name, more than once, on two sheets of paper, at the places to which the Munshi indicated. When he had done all he had to do, to the Munshi's satisfaction, my uncle got up to leave and picking up the sack from the floor offered it to the Munshi. 'Some of his things...' The Munshi looked at it and rolled his head. 'Leave it there in that corner. It'll be collected.' Then he held out his skeletal hand to me. I stared at it in horror.

'*Chacha!*' I cried.

Uncle Ganesh relented. He turned back and knelt in front of me, gripped my shoulders and gave me a tight squeeze. 'You must not cry. There, you must be a brave boy. One day you will understand and forgive us. I am sorry it had to be this way. Don't cry.'

'I won't cry,' I said loudly and took the Munshi's hand defiantly.

The Munshi grinned, baring large prominent teeth. 'Good. I think the boy has the makings of a brave gentleman, if I may say so.' I looked up at him blankly.

'Speak to the boy in Marathi,' reminded my uncle.

'That I shall do. It poses no problem to me. I am educated man. I speak English, Bengali, Hindi, and Marathi also.'

'Good,' said my uncle. 'Now I will take my leave.'

'Visiting hours, every Saturday afternoon, between 2 and 5 p.m.'

'You will never see me again,' uncle Ganesh said firmly.

'That is most distressing, but none of my business. My duty is to inform you what is possible under the rules of this Mission. In truth, apart for one or two relatives, no one comes to visit. Sad to say this is indeed an orphanage.' The Munshi spread his hands and waited till my uncle passed through the gates. He then gazed down at me, arms akimbo, and chuckled merrily. 'Now,' he said, 'you and I go to big house. Meeting Padre sahib for first but not, I hope, last time. Now, I myself am Bengali. But here we all learn to speak English. Padre sahib is an Englishman, so, speaking English is essential to make life easy for all of us.'

I looked back at the sack that uncle Ganesh had left.

Again the Munshi chuckled. 'Never mind that! Our James will take it to the Hostel and leave it on your bed. Fear not, you will see it again.'

I frowned. 'Jay...who is...'

'You will meet him soon.' He led me down a long, earth-hardened path, through an avenue of kapok trees and pointed to the long building on our left. 'That is School,' he said, 'and on the other side, Chapel. Note the bell on the roof. Behind Chapel is Boarding house or the Hostel. James is in charge of boys in Hostel. Here all are Christians, worshiping Lord Jesus. You will soon learn about the Lord Jesus.'

I looked up at his forehead, which had a caste mark not unlike my *Daada's*, except his also had a dash of red powder. The Munshi noted my frown. 'Ah, now when I say all, not me, not the Pathan and also not some servants. No, we are not Christians.'

I was curious and sometime later found an opportunity to ask how, as a Hindu, he was happy to work for a Christian community. He explained that when it came to getting jobs, the British were only interested in qualifications and efficiency. He was comfortable with their formalities and that aloofness, which he believed was less to do with racial prejudice and more with respect for local customs. Also it suited Hindu sensitivities, because apart from their sense of fairness, the British tried, whenever possible, not to interfere with cultural traditions. Even missionaries, who set out to convert people they called "heathens", could not quite shed that British reserve.

We walked on till he stopped abruptly and pointed to a line of white painted bricks. 'No boys beyond this. Out of bounds! Beware!' The Munshi wagged a long bony finger close to my face. I nodded absently but my eyes were directed at a neat bungalow inside a low walled enclosure. 'Ah, that is house of Dr Jacob Rivers, the Revd Dr Jacob Rivers.' He repeated the name slowly and clearly. 'The great and good Padre sahib, who is Head of Mission.'

I stared at the house in wonder, never before having seen anything like it. Its steep roof was neatly red-tiled and sheltered a veranda, at the centre of which were three steps. On the top of those steps, leaning against a wooden pillar, was a small figure in a blue dress that reached down to a pair of open sandals. Over the dress was a frilly white pinafore. I gaped, tugging wildly at the Munshi's hand. '*Go-oody*?' I stammered.

'What! What? No, no. Not *guddiya*. Not doll. That is girl. I see, you have never seen white people before. That *missybaba*: Miss Esther Rivers, daughter of Rivers sahib; a most intelligent and clever young lady.'

Now, as I write of that ghost-like vision of Esther as first I saw her, a peculiar sensation stirs within me. I have never been able to dispel the myth-like quality of its original impact. Esther Rivers wore her long auburn hair in a fringe across her forehead and she studied me with sullen, red lips. In my astonishment I had raised a hand to point and for it received a sharp smack on the head. 'No! No pointing,' said the Munshi, 'it is most rude to point. We don't do that here.'

I thought the girl gave a squeak of disapproval. I can't be sure. But I do know that I looked up at the Munshi, hurt and surprised. His bony finger wagged again. 'Listen, take care. That is Padre Sahib's daughter. She is here on school holidays. Remember, that white line of bricks? Never cross it or enter the Rivers's compound. Never, unless Padre sahib say so.'

'School?' I asked, pointing to the school building.

'No, no. Her school in hill-station. A white lady and gentleman, from that school, take her there and bring her back for long holiday.'

'What is holiday?'

The Munshi laughed. 'Holiday is *chutti*, free time, no school, children go home to mummy and daddy.'

'*Daadi*?'

'No. Daddy, meaning father. How old are you? Never mind. You are eight. Miss Esther is twelve. Padre sahib and his lady, her daddy and mummy, last week on her birthday, gave sweets to all. After prayers in Chapel.'

'Chapel?'

'Enough questions now. This evening you will see Chapel.'

I looked back. The girl had gone and where she had stood there was a tall man in a white cassock. He was very fair with curly red hair and a neat red beard. He waved us in, speaking, I assumed, in English, but for my benefit the Munshi answered in Marathi. 'Yes, Padre sahib. This is the boy, Krishna. He understands Marathi. Krishna, this is Dr Rivers.'

I folded my hands, as in prayer, and bowed.

The tall man smiled. 'A clean, neat and polite young lad,' he said in fluent Marathi.

'Indeed, Padre sahib, the boy comes from a good Brahmin home.'

'Yes, I know. Welcome to St Thomas's. So, the boy is eight years old. Good, and tall for his age. Munshiji, the boy must be hungry.'

'But, sahib, it's late. Past lunch time.'

'Let the boy sit down here.' He pointed to the steps and added in English: 'Sister Agnes will find some biscuits and a glass of milk.'

Somehow I understood what was said. I was hungry. I rushed to the steps and sat down.

The tall man laughed and the Munshi rolled his head. 'See sahib, there was no need for me to translate. It is a child's survival instinct, is it not, sahib?'

The Padre nodded. 'Indeed, Mr Das Gupta, hunger like water finds its own level. However, clearly the boy is extremely intelligent. You may go now. I'll look at the register later. This boy is a special case. I will explain all that later.'

The Munshi bowed, gestured me to wait and left. He was halfway down the avenue of kapok trees when a sudden gust of wind gathered up his white dhoti in a billow that revealed his spindly legs, white socks and highly polished black leather shoes.

I turned to find myself alone and now this sense of isolation in new surroundings hit me with a heightened sense of being abandoned. I began to cry as all my pent up unhappiness drove itself home. Sobbing bitterly, I failed to notice that the tall man was back and sitting by my side.

'There's no cause to cry,' he said, laying a hand on my shoulder. 'Look what Sister Agnes has for you.' I looked up to see a pale, round face with merry blue eyes. I sniffed, wiped my face with my hands and my hands on my shirt, then folded them and bowed deeply. 'This is Sister Agnes,' he explained. 'She is my wife.'

Sister Agnes wore a long grey skirt and a plain, long sleeved white blouse. Round her neck was a silver chain bearing a plain black cross. In her right hand was a glass of milk. I sprang up to take it, but she moved back and mumbled. The tall man nodded, took the glass and, before giving it to me, warned me to drink it slowly. Then he held out a plate. On it was a collection of pale brown squares. Some had white and pink blobs on them, others were sandwiched together by a creamy yellow filling. I studied them.

'Biskoot,' said the man with an encouraging smile. I knew what that meant. Mother used that word for biscuits she prepared as an occasional treat. But her biscuits were roughly diamond shaped, deep fried and sprinkled with powdered sugar before she stored them in a large earthen jar. Her father, who died when I was two years old, had worked as a clerk and interpreter for an English businessman. As a child, mother was often invited to play with the Englishman's daughter and almost as often stayed on for tea. She did not like English food, but adored cakes and puddings. Mother even picked up a little English and wanted to teach me what little she knew, but my grandfather forbade her.

'Go on,' coaxed the tall man, interrupting my thoughts. The biscuits looked too perfect to be edible and for a moment longer I continued to gape at them. Besides I was used to eating alone and away from being watched. So I took the plate and glass of milk and attempted to move into the far end of the open veranda. But the tall man stopped me with a stern shake of his head.

'I know Brahmin men eat alone. Not here. Here you'll be eating with a lot of other boys at a long table. Here we live, eat and study together like one big family. Do you understand?'

I nodded thoughtfully.

'So, stay here. Good lad, now go ahead, eat.'

I bit into the biscuits with some trepidation. Finding them delicious, I started to gobble them up. Again Sister Agnes mumbled and the tall man immediately restrained me. 'Eat slowly or you will be sick. Slow! There's no need to rush!'

Something in the look he gave me called for immediate obedience and clearly it was futile to pretend I did not understand. I stared and passed the back of my hand across my mouth.

[For years after that day I never saw those biscuits again. The school daily diet being, almost unrelievedly, rice and lentils with a blob of hot mango pickle. But Sunday afternoon dinners were a special treat of a lamb curry dish, which the boys saw as their reward for sitting through Matins and a long sermon. At first, as a vegetarian, I missed out on this treat, but soon, pressed by pangs of hunger and inspired by the look of sheer delight on the faces of the boys, I gave in and joined them in their delight of this weekly repast.]

'Now, after you've eaten, wait there,' the tall man pointed to a wooden bench under a jujube tree. 'I'm going to the office but I'll send James. He'll show you round the school, hostel and the lavatories...especially the lavatories...how to make use of them. Here, no one goes out in the open. Afterwards, he will bring you to the Munshiji's office.'

He made as if to leave, hesitated, and stroking his beard thoughtfully studied me. Then he opened his mouth as if to speak, changed his mind, bent down, ruffled my hair and discovering the Brahmin pigtail at the back of my head, gave it a playful tug. He chuckled, went indoors and promptly emerged wearing a pith helmet. I saw him stomp down the kapok avenue, his pale feet shod in rope sandals. I watched, till his tall figure, shimmering in the haze, vanished out of sight. Turning to the bench under the jujube tree, I found it occupied by the girl with the long auburn hair. She beckoned. I hesitated, then approached and as my shadow fell on her smiling face, all screwed up and flushed in the hot bright sun, it relaxed. Her brown eyes were startlingly golden, and beautiful. She talked rapidly. I gaped, trying hard to understand. She stopped, pointed to herself and said: 'Esther.' Then she pointed to me. I correctly assumed she was asking my name. 'Krishna,' I said.

'Kis-na...Chris...Like Christ, yes. But you are Michael.' She nodded. 'Yes, Michael.'

We stared at each other for a while in silence. Then she pointed to the sky, blew down the front of her pinafore and fanned her face with her hands. 'It's hot.'

It was the hottest part of the afternoon and hazarding another wild guess I nodded, pulled my shirt forward and blew down it. ''Ot, 'ot,' I tried mimicking.

She giggled. I wondered if she knew how much hotter it was a few months ago. Just then the woman in the long grey dress came out and addressed me in Marathi: 'Where is Dr Rivers?' I frowned. 'The Padre sahib?' I was about to speak when she waved a hand and pointed. 'Never mind, there's James. You must go with him.'

I turned and saw a dark young man, with curly, wild hair and heavy features. He approached the house, came up to the white line of bricks, stopped there and waited till I joined him.

'My name is James,' he said. 'Call me James.'

'James,' I said, surprised at my ability to get it right the first time.

He held out a hand but I shook my head and took a step back. James smiled, shrugged his shoulders and nodded, briefly studied me with arms akimbo, then waved me on to follow him.

He moved with a swift animal-like spring in his step and I found it necessary to break into a run to keep up with him. But he had the patience of a good guide. We walked together, or almost together, as he briefly indicated landmarks with wide sweeps of his hand. He explained there was a lot to see and learn but not enough time for him to show me round all of it, but I was not to worry, because later, Munshi Gupta, would complete the tour. And he, James, was always around for help and advice. He spoke Marathi with an unfamiliar accent, but gradually I had no difficulty understanding him.

James grinned at my gasps of wonder, for I had never seen buildings of such size and solid structure. He pointed to the Chapel, the kitchen behind it, and the dining hall. 'This evening you will see the inside of these buildings. They belonged to the Government's army. But when the army moved to Pultanpur, they gave it to the Mission. First I will take you to the hostel and the wash room, which is in that long building there, the one with the big windows.'

'And that,' I asked pointing to a long, low building, with small windows just below the roof, and looking very like a railway carriage I had seen at Baroli Station.

'That is the latrine. We'll start there. Do you need to go?' I shook my head.

As we entered the building, I covered my nose with my arm expecting to be met with a strong stench. But apart from knowing it was a latrine, it was not unpleasant to be there. The windows, high up near the low ceiling, were a row of five, small, square openings. Below them was a long, strong wooden platform, with six circular holes. James climbed up and sat on his haunches to demonstrate their obvious use, then sprang down and led me to the far corner where there was a pile of sand, a large galvanised steel tub full of water and two rather battered aluminium mugs floating in it. Sticking out in the pile of sand was a shovel with a short handle. 'Everyone,' James said, 'using the latrine must take a mug of water to wash themselves and then pour a shovel full of sand down the hole. Any boy not doing this gets punished by having to fetch water, from the pump outside, to fill the tub. And that's for a full week.'

Half the height of the wall opposite was covered with a metal sheet and where it met the floor at ground level was a gutter that led outside the building. 'What is that for?'

James looked at me inquiringly. 'It's the urinal, what else,' he said, 'and the gutter goes out to a *howdy*, that is a septic tank.'

'Sep...'I began.

'You'll learn what that means later. But Dr Rivers, sahib, takes great care to keep this place clean, so that no boy is exposed to bad germs that will make him sick. That is why, after use, boys must splash water into that gutter. The sweepers clean the gutter and empty the tank when it gets full...every two days.'

We left the building and moved to the hostel. On our way there James pointed to the pump next to a covered well. It had a zinc bucket under it.

'We have two wells,' he said, 'this one for the boys. There is a larger well near the kitchen.'

'Where does the sand come from?' I asked.

'From the banks of the river. Mr Gupta will show you the river. Once a month bullock carts come round to the back of the latrine, one with fresh sand and two for taking away the old used soil. That's when we all go away and picnic on the river bank... Do you know picnic? No? It is fun and games; and we have *puris* and potato vegetable...a change from the daily lentil and rice.'

The hostel was a very large room divided almost in half by a wooden partition. On our side of the partition were twenty-four narrow, rope-strung cots, twelve on each side of the room. On the side opposite the four windows was a plain yellow wall in the centre of which was a crucifix. Facing the entrance to this dormitory was a low bamboo slatted screen behind which was a single bed. 'That is my bed,' said James, 'and your cot is at this end, near mine. What's the matter?'

I had uttered an involuntary squeak at the sight of my gunny sack on the bed. 'It's my bag,' I said. 'The one my uncle packed for me.'

'What is in it?'

'A shirt, a singlet, and a pair of shoes...but he packed the wrong shirt in a hurry. It's got a big hole in it. And the shoes, they are old and too tight.'

'Most of the boys go bare foot. Also, soon, you'll wear school uniform, grey shirt and shorts, as soon as the tailor makes them...two of each. You must look after them with care. Wear one, wash one. D'you understand?' James waited for my nod. 'Now, there, that side of the wooden partition is the washroom. I'll show that to you later and explain how to use it. Now we have to get back to Mr Gupta's office. On the way I'll take you to the Baptismal pond...but before that, you must see the school classrooms.'

There were two classrooms, one slightly larger than the other. The smaller, furnished with a dais, two chairs and a low table had, spread in front of it, two plain, dun coloured cotton carpets. But what caught my eye were the three walls that faced the dais. They were covered in brightly painted posters of everyday objects: fruits, flowers, animals, each picture with a clear prominent symbol, which I correctly guessed must refer to a letter of the English alphabet. I checked with James and he confirmed that they were English sound letters. 'Those pictures,' he added, 'were drawn and painted by Sister Agnes. She is a wonderful artist.'

We entered the bigger classroom. Here a table and chair faced four rows of small student desks. The walls were bare except for the one behind the chair. It was painted a mat black with numbers chalked in columns, which could not be anything other than Arithmetic tables. Some of the figures were certainly like those I had learned from Motiram, my village teacher. 'When I first came to this Mission, five years ago,' James said, 'there were no desks or benches. We sat cross-legged on the floor with slates on our laps. But Padre Rivers is good man. Always asking Government for money and making friends of people who will help the Mission. The boys still use slates, but do you see these holes in the desks? One day Rivers sahib is going to fill them with small china inkpots. Soon Padre sahib wants to see boys using pen and ink on paper.'

When James left me at the Gate Office, I found Dr Rivers seated in front of a table. On his right sat the Munshi with a dipping ink pen poised over a large register. And after each entry he stamped the register with a blotting pad. Next to him was a high stool. The Munshi patted the stool and told me to sit down. 'Now, Krishna, listen well to what Padre sahib telling. He knows about you and lots about your father.'

Dr Rivers leaned forward. His eyes were a deeper brown than Esther's and as I looked into them, the lucid saintliness of his personality struck me. 'Now,' he said, 'give me your hands.' I did without hesitation, and as I did so, recalled, with a twinge of regret, ignoring James, when he had offered his hand. That young man's dark and wild appearance repelled me. But now, as Dr Rivers took my hands in his, all the caste qualms of my Brahmin upbringing seemed to leave me and, in its place, came a determination to overcome them.

'Tell me,' Dr Rivers continued, 'do you remember the day your father left you? Left you and your mother...that day, nearly two years ago, at Baroli Station?' He spoke in clear, fluent but rather deliberate Marathi.

I thought hard. How could I ever forget that day! But I hesitated over an answer.

'I was there, with your father. You would have seen us had you been allowed to. You must have wondered why you were not allowed to see your father. And why he was going away?'

I imagined I knew, but in truth I never really did; and since they were my own conclusions, drawn from all the bits and pieces I had overheard from the many confrontations my father had with his father and brothers, I decided not to express them. I shook my head.

'Your father,' continued Dr Rivers, 'was a Hindu from the highest caste, the priestly Brahmin caste. He was a bright, clever young man...I'm sure you're bright and clever too, so you ought to know, before you were born, before he married your mother, I met your father and got to know him well. He wanted to read books. He taught himself English and I lent him English books to read. This one in particular... it's that part of the

Bible, which is about Jesus.' He pointed to the picture high on the wall behind him. It was of a full figure of a man in a white robe, radiant with outstretched hands. 'That is Jesus. Your father wanted to learn about Christ. That is the other name for Jesus. And when he returned this book he asked to become a Christian. He did. Do you understand what I am saying?'

I frowned and shook my head vigorously.

'Go back and sit on that stool.' Dr Rivers waited till I did, then he sat back and sighed. After a short pause he leaned forward. 'Never mind! Did James take you around? Did he show you the dormitory…that big room with beds in it?'

I nodded.

'Good. And you know where your bed is? Now, did you see the pond, the white baptismal pond?'

I nodded again, but turned a puzzled look at him, then at the Munshi and back to him.

'Baptism. That is how people become Christian,' said the Munshi. 'Dipping in water.'

'To wash away what we were,' added the Doctor. 'Washing away the past to become a new person with a new name to be a member of Christ and a child of God.' He looked at me and sighed again. 'Just for now, all you need to know is that your father became a Christian and was given the Christian name, John. And when you were about three years old, he brought you to our pond, here, to be baptised. You may not remember but it was on the ninth of October and he wanted you to be called Michael.'

'There, Michael,' the Munshi smiled his wide toothy grin. 'Now going to Padre sahib. Go.'

Obediently I went and stood next to Dr Rivers. Pointing to myself, I stammered: 'Mike…I am Mike…Mike?'

'Yes,' said Dr Rivers, putting an arm around me. 'Mike will do. And you can call me Father Jacob or Father Rivers, or just Father.'

There were tears in my eyes. 'Father Ja…' I began.

'Just Father will do. Or Padre, as Mr Gupta says.'

'Where is my father?' I asked rapidly in Marathi. 'Will I see him?'

Dr Rivers took both my hands in his. 'Your father wanted to preach the Gospel, the good news, about Jesus. That made your grandfather and uncles very angry. Also, they did not want the Brahmins of Pali village to know that your father was now a Christian; and because John your father was well known, I knew it would be dangerous if he worked in the Baroli District. So I sent him to my friend in Poona, to join a Christian community—a family like ours here. Michael do you understand what I am saying?'

After some thought, I nodded. 'I know Poona. My mother's town…Is my father in Poona?'

'No. He had to leave. You see, the Indian Christians of that community are not high caste Hindus like your father; and knowing that John, your father, was a Brahmin, they treated him badly, insulting him and calling him bad names. So my friend decided to send him away. And because your father wanted to be like me, a priest, my friend sent your father to Aberdeen, far away, in another country, Scotland.'

Mr Gupta got up and placed a globe in front of Dr Rivers. 'This,' said the Doctor, with one hand on the globe, 'is the Earth. This is India, where we are. And this,' he turned the globe, 'is Scotland. See how far it is…over these seas.' Father Jacob looked at me and traced his fingers over the pink and blue of the globe. 'It gets very cold in Scotland. And while he was there, your father got very ill. He died in January, last year.'

I gaped. What could I to say? I knew so little of my father. Having seen so little of him, I found it hard even to remember his face. He stayed away during the week and came home late on Friday to be off again by the last train on Sunday. I thought hard for something to say and, tentatively touching the globe, pointed to Dr Rivers. 'Scotland? Father, you?'

'No, I'm from here, England. Scotland is there, north of England. England too, gets cold, but Scotland is colder. Michael, I'm sorry. When you are older I'll tell you more about your father and how much he loved you and your mother. I promised him I would take care of you, if for any reason your mother was not able. I will keep that promise. You have nothing to fear or worry about.'

We studied each other. I began to grasp much of what he said…to feel special and more at home, for I was the son of a friend of Dr Rivers. But with understanding came anger, and it felt right to be angry. With so much to take in, where and how to begin…to whom should I direct my anger?

'Maybe you should be angry with me,' Dr Rivers said intuitively, opening his hands.

I stared, speechless.

'But,' Dr Rivers continued, 'to keep my promise to John, after your mother died, I had to tell your family you were a baptised Christian. I knew it would force them to send you here and I wanted that.' He reached out for my hands. 'Now, Michael, at their baptism, Christians have godparents. People who promise, before God, to guide you. At your baptism, there was only Sister Agnes and me…so we are your…O and one more, Esther, my daughter. She didn't have to be, boys usually have two godfathers and one godmother, but she wanted to be a godparent, even though she was then just under eight years old. Your father liked the idea of one child wanting to take care of another.'

Doctor Rivers rose to leave the Munshi's office. I held on to him. 'No, no, you stay with Mr Das Gupta. He will tell you more than James told you about this place. About things you need to know. Knowing a place helps strangers to feel at home and he'll do a good job of it, because his Marathi is better than mine. Go to him for any questions you have and want answers.'

'Father-Sir, is he also another god-father?'

Dr Rivers laughed, as also did the Munshi. 'I think, it would be best if you call me "Sir", just Sir. All the other boys do. So that will be fair. The boys must not feel I am favouring you in any way. Now, Mr Gupta is not a Christian; and not being a Christian he can't be a god-father. But he's the best person for advice. James too, when he's around…James is head of the Hostel. He is there to look after the boys outside the classroom.'

Tears welled in my eyes. I started to whimper.

'Now, now, there is no need for that. No one here will harm you. Stay with Mr Gupta, he is a teller of tales and is good company. Talk to him. Tell him all your worries. I think you are a fast learner. Afterwards, when it is time for Mr Gupta to leave, he will take you to the dining hall for the evening meal. Then James will take over.'

Das Gupta sprang up with an unexpected alacrity. 'Not to worry, Padre sahib, he will soon know the ins and outs. Or do I mean the ropes?'

Dr Rivers smiled. 'Thank you, though I wish you'd drop the *sahib*. It ties me to a conduct of my fellow countrymen which, indeed, I do not share.' This was said to Mr Gupta in English, but I am able to record it here because I asked Gupta when Dr Rivers had left us. Gupta told me, adding: 'However, he always will be my "sahib", out of sheer respect. You, my boy, are so lucky to have such a saintly man as your guru.'

'What is gooroo?'

'Teacher, simply that. As such, I respect him. Good Hindus respect holy men. Remember that. Now Krishna, sorry, I should say Michael or Mike. We must be clear about names from the start. Your full name, as recorded here, is Michael Balaram. Balaram is your family name. Padre sahib fully respects people's dignity. He would like you to keep your Brahmin surname.'

'Munshiji,' I asked, in a spurt of irrelevant curiosity, 'why is James so black and ugly?'

Das Gupta drew himself up and glared hard at me. 'Are there no Bheels in Pali village?'

'What are Bheels?'

'Bheels? Bheels are tribal people. Ancient people, leading simple lives in small settlements, in open country. This was their land long before it ever became ours. Most Bheels look like James. You haven't seen them because your Pali is a Brahmin village. But you must never again talk like that. It is wrong to make personal remarks. If you were older I would have given you a *thapard*, or as English people say "you would have felt my backhand". Not, of course, Dr Rivers or his good wife, Sister Agnes. They are far too good for this world, but they have given me full permission to do so.' Gupta raised a hand. I ducked and cowered. He laughed.

'But Sir said, I should tell you my worries.'

The Munshi grunted. 'I hope you will get on with James and respect him.'

'Yes, I will. I want to be his friend. His bed is next to mine.'

'Good. Now, why are you frowning? Is there is something else you want to ask?"

'Where do *you* sleep?'

'At home. Every evening I leave promptly at six. Not Sunday. Sunday is a holiday, the best day for everyone. Then, I'm at home, resting.'

'Where...?'

'All you boys also have rest day on Sunday after morning chapel. A good meal and games... Sometimes boys go for outing or picnic by river, or swimming and bathing by the waterfall...with James and Rivers sahib.'

'Yes, James told me. Told me about picnic. But where, Guptaji, where is your home?'

'Rambagh. It will be the town you passed through, when you came with your uncle.'

'But that is far away.'

'No, it's just over a mile away. It will seem far by bullock cart. But Padre sahib kindly lets me take the *tonga*. Sometimes I walk. Come now, we should begin our tour of the Mission.'

'But I have been round with James!'

'That was only School round. This one is to show you those parts that are out of bounds to you and all boys...like the servants' quarters and the river edge, where *dhobis* wash clothes...'

'What does it means...out of bounds?'

'Meaning, not allowed; being against Mission rules...But no one breaks rules here. Boys stay together helping each other, telling each other what is good, what is right. You will see the fields where boys learn to grow herbs, onions, chillies, carrots, coriander; vegetables; also *bhindi* and beans, potatoes and pumpkin.' Mr Gupta ushered me out and locked his office. 'When we get back, if we have time, I'll take you to meet chowkidar, Waleed Khan and Namdeo, the syce. If not, sometime as soon as we can.'

'Saayce?'

'Yes, syce, he looks after the horse. He is also *tonga* driver. Now hold my hand… oh, did James tell you about the dormitory bed rules?'

'Bed rules? About making our beds?'

'No, the more important one…that boys must not sit on the beds of other boys.'

'Yes. James told me.'

'Did he tell you why?'

'No. But, I like that rule. I'm a Brahmin. Guptaji…'

'Ah! I like this "Guptaji". It is most polite.' The Munshi beamed. 'Yes, Michael?'

'Guptaji, you were here when I was bap…bap…when I became Christian.'

'No, but I met your father. He was most handsome man. Like a stage actor. He could have played Rama or Laxman in that great *Ram Lila* drama. In Rambagh, you know, every October we get travelling players. They put on drama. Stories from *Ramayana* and *Mahabharata*… But, no, I was not here when you…You see, I've been here four years. But when I first came, I was most disappointed. Shocked to see Padre sahib and his mem doing much work that should be done by servants. English families I've known have many servants. No less than ten, fourteen, even eighteen. They won't lift finger to work or even get up to fetch a glass of water.' Gupta stopped, looked around him and stretched his arms. 'Here we have one horse, they had stables. And, not just one tonga but four-wheel carriages as well. But I learned a most valuable lesson from Padre sahib. "I am not *lat* sahib," he tells me. "I do all I can for myself and only employ those servants I have to or can't do without. And I don't make them work like slaves." So, you will see Padre sahib keeping one personal servant, *khansama*, that is a cook; no bearer, no boy.'

We started to move again, walking between the bungalow and some low huts in the distance. 'For all other work,' continued the Munshi, 'Padre sahib uses school staff: chowkidar, syce, two sweepers, two dhobis and a *darzee* or school tailor. His *khansama* prepares English dishes, but most times Padre sahib eat with the boys…when Padre sahib has guests staying in his *bungla* he is not able to eat with the boys. Also is another *khansama*, cooking for boys only. All servants here are menfolk.'

'But I see women there. There, outside those houses.'

'Those are family quarters. Three… one each for the two cooks and one for chowkidar. Far behind them, are two more, for the two sweepers.

Namdeo, the syce, he also lives in Rambagh. All this area is out of bounds to the boys. Remember the line of white bricks? It comes round to where we are. Now we cross it to get to the river.' Gupta stopped abruptly, pulling me back by a hand on my shoulder. He turned me round and with a wide sweep of one hand indicated: 'All this you see is Mission Property. Yes, Mission Property.'

'James said the army was here.'

'Once, for some time, till the cantonment was built in Pultanpur. Now it's for our Mission.'

We walked on and I sensed a measure of pride in Mr Gupta's stride. Soon the dry ground turned damp, grassy and soft underfoot. On our right, at some distance were two mango trees. Below one of them, seated on a broad cane chair and singing to herself, was a dark woman with white curly hair. She wore a plain blue dress, a red, patterned scarf round her neck, and as she sang, in a rather high-pitched voice, she waved her ample arms, making the glass bangles on them jangle. Mr Gupta stopped and again held me back. 'Let us choose this path, I do not wish to meet that lady, at least not today.'

'She lives here?'

'Yes. See those three houses behind the Padre sahib's *bungla*? The English say bungalow… one is kitchen, large middle one is the godown, where all food stores are kept, and the smaller one has two rooms, which is now her home. She is Rosie Almeida, and she was Miss Esther's ayah. Now no need for ayah any more, but Padre sahib, being kind man, he not sending her away. He let her stay on. Now she sits there, singing songs that mothers sing to babies.'

'My *Daadi* sang Marathi songs to me. Is she singing English?'

'Yes. English. Lullabies they call it. Singing to Esther maybe, when Esther was baby.'

'Is she Christian, also?'

'Yes.'

'So she comes to Chapel, here?'

'No, she Roman Catholic. Going to Catholic Church in Pultanpur. Pultanpur is Army town. You know army? Sojers marching left, right, left…' Mr Gupta did a rather comic marching act.

I nodded. 'Pandit Motiram, our village teacher, made us march when he said we were lazy. I can army march,' I said with more nods, and swinging my arms and stamping my feet.

'Good. Stop, stop. Pultanpur is big Military Cantonment not far from here. Lots of English people live there. Army live in Cantonment and English homes in the Civil Lines. There, also, two schools. St Anselm,

Catholic School and St Peter, Church of England School. After three years boys from here go there, to St Peters. Good teaching. Good beating also. Any wrong do, getting cane on bottom.' Gupta tapped me lightly on the bottom. We laughed. 'This Mission is St Thomas,' he continued, 'we here are in middle. Rambagh this side, Pultanpur that side.'

Then I remembered. 'Pultanpur? Guptaji, I know Pultanpur. My father was there.'

'I know. He was Munshi, like me. But you have not been to Pultanpur.'

'No. Will I go there like the other boys?'

'Maybe. But when the time comes it would be better if you went to Bishop Weston School for boys, in Harzaribagh. It is far from here but not far from Calcutta. Better than Pultanpur.'

'Why? Because of less beating on the bottom?'

Mr Gupta laughed. 'Clever boy!' He patted me on the head. 'As I said, our Padre is kind. No beating with cane...once time only...when three boys stole food from godown. Chowkidar catch them and he let Chowkidar beat with cane. Boys respect Padre sahib. Those three boys caught their ears and touched Padre sahib's feet, saying sorry. Stop! Here you walk behind me.'

We walked on earth walls that separated the cabbage plots from the green gram ones, till we reached the river. Gupta let me take off my sandals and paddle in the brown waters and while I did that he pointed to three smooth, sloping slabs of grey rock.

'*Dhobis* washing clothes on those stones there. Mission has two *dhobis*. They live on other side of river.'

I looked across the river bed. It was fairly wide. A high sandbank in the middle divided the river course into two streams. The farther one was broader but shallower and on its nearer bank were two moving black objects. I pointed.

Mr Gupta removed his glasses. 'For distance, Michael, I see better without these.' He stared for a while. 'Those are two buffaloes. They provide milk for the Mission. Sufficient for tea, not enough for drinking. But good Padre sahib, always thinking how to make life good for Mission. So he bought a cow. Also, Esther, not liking buffalo milk...See that man, adjusting his *dhoti*, his name Mohan, our milkman. He is Namdeo's son, milkman caring for buffaloes and dairy farm. In all that land there will also be a fruit orchard. Guava trees, tamarind, lime, tomatoes... His wife and a son aged fifteen also work on farm. Look behind him, those trees... four *neem* trees in a line... Where are you looking? Not there! There, to the left, on other side of river. They sell the fruit in Rambagh. And give money for Mission.'

'Guava...what guava is?'

'Fruit. *Amrood.* Very tasty.'

'I like *amrood.*'

'In good season, any extra mangoes, guavas, boys get dinner time. Why you laugh?'

A prancing pony had appeared from nowhere, making the startled Mohan jump up and trip over his *dhoti.* Again I pointed.

'Yes, funny. Pony, baby horse...one day it will pull tonga...second tonga. Come, now.'

It was time to return and on the way back Gupta said he wouldn't be in the Mission Office for the next two days. I asked why. He tut-tutted. 'Why! Have you forgotten! So soon! It is the great festival of Lights. Diwali! Who did your family pray to? I know Marathi folk make much of the god Ganesh.'

'Yes,' I answered. 'But for Diwali, goddess Lakshmi.'

'Well, for us Bengalis, the goddess Durga and her other self, Mother Kali, matters most.' Gupta stopped abruptly. 'Why you look at me like that?'

That mark on your forehead. It is like my *Daada's.* You are Brahmin.'

'Indeed, I am.' Mr Gupta drew himself up with pride.

'Why are Brahmins so special?'

'Have you not had the sacred thread ceremony? No? Of course not, you couldn't have, but you have heard of Lord Brahma, the Creator, who with Lords Shiva and Vishnu are the three great gods, the Hindu Trinity. Brahmins, the highest caste, sprang from Lord Brahma's mouth. The second, warrior caste, came from his arms, the third, *bania* caste, from his stomach. From his feet came *Sudras.* They are the labourers, there to serve the three higher classes.'

'And the Bheels?'

'Bheels are tribal people. No caste, sometimes we say pariah. But I have learned a beautiful lesson from Padre sahib. We are all the children of God. Besides, I now follow Buddhism, so all this talk of gods and castes are of no matter to me; and should not be to anyone else.'

'Then why do you wear that mark on your forehead?'

The Munshi stopped and stared down at me. 'Oh, very sharp! Too clever for your own good, too clever for your age. You want to know everything. One day it will get you into serious trouble. Never mind. I was like you. Asking many questions.' He put a hand on my shoulder. 'And I suppose I talk too much. Once I asked Dr Rivers if that was so. No matter, he said, we have nothing to hide. Well, if you must know, I wear this mark to hide behind it. People keep away from Brahmins. That suits me fine.'

He laughed. 'And look at you. You still have your *chhoti*, your Brahmanic twisted lock of hair.'

I felt that twisted tail at the back of my head and nodded.

'Soon you will lose it. The *nahee*, that is the school barber, is due in two weeks. Every two months he comes to crop the heads of the boys.' Mr Gupta's bony fingers ran through my hair and he giggled. 'All this will have to go.'

'All of it?' I looked up with alarm.

Mr Gupta relented. 'No. But you have to thank Sister Agnes for that. Schools, like ours, believe in shaving the heads of the boys, to save time and money and boys did not have to worry about combs and mirrors. But our kind Sister Agnes, she said it makes the boys look as if they are in prison, or have been punished. So, just short back and sides, no shaving.'

'I don't have a comb. My uncle...'

'James will get you one. Combs are kept soaking in jars of medical stuff to stop the spread of lice. Did you not see them next to the two small mirrors in the washroom?'

I shook my head.

'So, James did not have time to take you to washroom? He will, later this evening.' Gupta looked at me thoughtfully. 'You are lucky to be here. I know of other Mission Schools where boys are treated harshly. Dr Rivers and his lady are too kind...always thinking of some way to help the boys. Help them to grow up happy and healthy.'

It was still light when he left me at the dining hall to join the other boys for the evening meal; and there we parted. The boys were standing in two groups. I was not invited to join either of them. I began to shiver, not because it was getting dark and cold, but alone I was afraid and I longed to run after Gupta. I knew that was foolish. I hugged myself and looking round found James next to me, a picture of primitive tranquillity. His large wild eyes and perfect set of teeth flashed in the darkness. Strangely the sight of him calmed me. Instinctively I searched for his hand. He gave mine a brief squeeze, told me to stay by him and warned me that always before dinner there were prayers in the Chapel. Calling for silence, he made the boys assemble outside the Chapel and took a roll-call, not by names but by numbers. Earlier he had told me that the Mission kept a Roll of twenty-five, never more or less and that I was number twenty-five. He addressed the boys: 'this is Michael, number twenty-five.'

The announcement created murmurs and muttering till once again he authoritatively called for silence. A bell rang three times and I noticed for the first time, above the low gable, over the Chapel door, a bronze bell, larger than the one we have over the entrance to our temple in Pali. James told me to note how the boy rang the bell. 'One day I'll ask you to do it,' he said.

We filed into the Chapel in silence. It was a square room with a raised wooden platform at one end. Behind the platform a tall painted screen depicted a Shepherd in a long white robe and shawl that half covered a head of curly red-brown hair. The figure held in his right hand a shepherd's crook, while his left carried a lamb. I guessed the figure was Jesus, because of the bright yellow circle behind his head. In front of the screen and placed centrally on the wooden table, was a gleaming brass cross. Also on the platform, to the left of the table, was a bench on which sat Dr Jacob Rivers, wearing a green robe with a purple cross and looking fatherly with Esther sitting next to him. Opposite them, to the right of the table, was Sister Agnes. She was sitting cross-legged on the floor, with a harmonium in front of her. We sat down in three rows, below the platform, on a carpet of coir matting. There was so much I wanted to ask James, but he hushed my every attempt to speak.

Father Jacob greeted us and read a long passage from a big black book. Though the reading was in Marathi it made little sense to me and my eyes wandered back to the screen, when to my amazement my attention was riveted by it. For the tender look on the face of Jesus was that of my mother and its effect was a deep consolation that also left me a little confused.

The reading was followed by prayers and a hymn, which the boys knew by heart and which was accompanied by Sister Agnes on her harmonium. After the hymn we were asked to stand for Father Jacob's blessing. As he drew a cross in the air I recalled those festive occasions when my mother blessed me with a circling flame and a dab of red powder on my forehead. I would have wept had I not looked back at the screen and saw her so clearly comforting me in words I couldn't hear.

After chapel James introduced me to Luke, a boy who could not have been much older than me. 'Luke will sit with you at meal times and guide you till you no longer need his help.'

We entered an inverted L-shaped dining hall, where along its length were two long wooden tables with benches on either side. Luke said the boys could sit where they liked, twelve at each table. Near the entrance was a small shelf with a pile of aluminium plates, which were picked up by the boys as they entered in an orderly manner, and moved in a queue to be served by James and the cook, who, Luke told me was a Muslim named Husain. Both James and Husain wore white cloth caps and they stood facing us, at the far end, behind two steaming cauldrons on a large iron table. Some distance away from this table was a large drum next to a washing up sink. It took me some time to recognise James, not because the white cloth cap hid his fuzzy hair, but because he was dwarfed by big Husain.

I told Luke I was used to sitting on the floor for meals. He said, until recently, that was how they ate, on the floor and from knitted leaf plates. 'But Padre wanted us to sit at table and learn to eat off plates. So, when he was able, he bought the wood and, with the help of Husain, James and the Chowkidar, made the tables and benches. As for the plates, I was told, that Padre sahib paid for them himself. We've had them for the past year or so. Now, soon he hopes to teach us to use forks and spoons. Dr Rivers is very kind man.'

At the end of the meal, James blew a whistle and we stood up to say Grace, which again the boys knew by heart. Then we formed a queue holding our plates, to empty any leftovers into the drum; and continued in the queue to wash our plates at the sink and stack them on the shelf as we left the Hall.

On our way back to the hostel, I saw Namdeo, the syce, lighting a large oil lamp, which was hanging from a tall cast iron lamp post and which, with the help of a pulley, he raised up to its horizontal arm at the very top. The lamp post was at least fifteen feet high and the lamp cast a good light over the path and much of the area that led to the hostel and latrine.

Before entering the dormitory, James lit two hurricane lanterns and led us indoors. He then took me to the wash-room at the end of the dormitory and stood me next to a long, shallow zinc trough fixed, at waist-level, on cast-iron brackets. Four brass taps, immediately above it, enabled four boys at a time to gargle and wash, while used water ran from it down a waste pipe. Nearby, on a small metal shelf were three cakes of red soap and an earthen bowl containing a powdered mixture of charcoal and salt. James showed me how to clean my teeth by putting some of this powder on the palm of one hand and, by wetting and dipping into it, use the forefinger of the other hand to massage teeth and gums. He then led me back to my bed and handed me a blue nightshirt. It was far too large and made me look ludicrous. James laughed helplessly. But when the boys joined in, he immediately scolded them into silence. 'Don't worry,' he said, 'the School *darzee* will make new ones to fit you. But that will take some time.'

I sat down on the edge of my bed. It was a narrow, rope-strung cot with a thin mattress and an almost threadbare rough cotton sheet for a cover. There was a small pillow. Oddly, its soft, yielding comfort made me shiver and want to cry. In so short a time my world had changed so completely. I was being asked to accept a new God, new rituals and strange worship in song and prayer, all of which meant nothing to me. In vain I sought strength from Father Jacob's words to me, after Chapel, just before we set off to come here. Taking me aside he said: 'Michael, you begin a new life in a new world. Open your heart to welcome all that is new. Make it your own.' He then asked if there was anything I enjoyed doing. 'School,' I said. 'I like teachers.' He was pleased to hear that and explained that the Mission school was a small one. 'Only three subjects are taught: Arithmetic by Mr Das Gupta, English and the Bible by Sister Agnes and me. I hope to build a shed and get a carpenter to teach the boys woodwork. Study hard, make good progress and after three years I will send you to St Stephen's. It is a good Church school in Ranchipur near Calcutta. Now run along and join the others. James is waiting for you.'

A shadow loomed over me. I looked up with a start. It was James. 'There are two lanterns in the latrine,' he said. 'Go now, because after half an hour they will be turned off.'

When I got back he gave me a small enamel mug. 'This for your morning cup of tea… now, every morning at eight, the Chowkidar strikes a gong for one whole minute. That's when boys get up, wash and get dressed… You have to be quick because you have only half-hour, thirty minutes. Then I blow a whistle for boys to form a line outside the dormitory with these mugs.' He hung the mug from the metal hook that was fixed to the wooden leg-post by my pillow.

In time I was to discover how important it was not to miss the morning cup of tea. The cook Husain would arrive with a great steaming kettle of watery, sweet, milky tea, which he splashed into our mugs. James would then give each of us a hard, brown biscuit that one could only eat by dunking it in the hot tea. To miss it meant going without sustenance till the first school break at ten o'clock.

James asked if I had a book to read. I shook my head.

'I could lend you one of Bible stories,' he said, 'but it's in English. Tomorrow I'll find one in Marathi. Can you read Marathi?'

'Yes,' I said with a vigorous nod, 'my *Daada* taught me.'

'Good. In the meantime this is for you. It is an English "ABC" book with pictures. Esther sent it for you.'

I flipped through its pages in the dim light and, when James left, put it under my pillow. As my bed was at one end of the dormitory, I could look down its entire length. There arose a low buzz as some boys crept into bed and started to read. Others went about their business till the final batch came out of the washroom. James lowered the lights and as he went past me into his private corner, he called out in English: 'Goodnight boys!' 'Goodnight!' chorused the boys, also in English. Then all went quiet and an eerie silence descended.

'Goodnight,' I whispered to myself and shut my eyes. I could not sleep. Raising my head I discovered my bed was near a small, low window. I waited till it was safe to move, then crept to the window and peeped through a hole in its jute curtain. Through trees, silhouetted against a dark sky, I picked out the shimmer of Diwali lights coming from the direction of Rambagh and imagined a house outlined by lights from tiny clay oil-lamps and wondered if there was a Mrs Gupta. Returning to bed, I lay down, trying hard to block memories of the way we celebrated Diwali in grandfather's house... the many lamps I helped mother to light on our flat rooftop... *Daadi* lifting the lid of a large steel box full of the delicious sweets she cooked in pure *ghee*. The green pistachio and orange carrot halva... rich creamy cubes of *burfi*, many covered in silverfoil. Oh, and saffron-rich *jelabies*, for which she was famed throughout Pali and Baroli... And fireworks, yes, fireworks outside the Temple... sparklers, crackers and glittering fountains of coloured lights, lighting up the smiling faces of happy children... the fun of it all, laughter, their merry laughter...

I buried my head in my pillow to shut out the sounds of distant fireworks now coming across the still night air and choked at the thought of being shut away in this dark, silent island, cut off from all those joys of Diwali. To fight back tears, I summoned all my resentment at the way my family had so heartlessly treated me, but quickly realised it was pointless; that it would be more sensible never to look back. I rolled on to my back and stared up into the darkness. 'When you can't fall asleep,' mother would say, 'think of a black sky without stars.' I tried and failed, till a uniquely soporific sound filled my ears. It came from Walid Khan the watchman, calling out '*khabadar*' in deep, low-pitched tones as he patrolled the area outside the gates of the Mission Compound. And after each call he struck the ground three times with his heavy staff, beating a monotonous rhythm...tap, tap, tap...

TWO

When and how Esther took on the task of being my tutor nagged me till years later, after tactful inquisition and speculation, I made a record of what I believe occurred. It may not be an actual record but my increasingly close and candid relationship with Esther and her father, satisfies me as to its truth. Looking back, that intimacy shed light and understanding. I saw it all clearly, with the privilege of knowing about Dr Rivers' frequent habit of kneeling in prayer before he took any momentous decision. In my case he confessed it helped him to accept the inevitable; that much as he wished it otherwise, he was helpless to prevent me becoming one of that peculiar band of displaced citizens, a by-product of the British Raj…

This then is that extract from my incomplete, unpublished and affectionate biography of Dr Jacob Rivers.

[Miss Esther Rivers was bored. The long school holidays left her little to do in a community directed solely at Christian enlightenment and the elementary education of derelict boys. 'Dad, isn't there something useful I could be doing?'

'Well, I thought you were helping Mother. She's been working on the banners and repairing the chasuble I'll be wearing when Bishop Robinson visits us in summer. Mum doesn't get much spare time.'

'I've tried to help. Mum's a perfectionist. She unpicks all my stitching, starts all over again, and sends me off to read a book.'

'That's a good way to spend time. You like reading.'

'I do, but there's little left…I mean, most of the books left, you don't want me to read.'

'There's nothing wrong in them, it's just that, for now, they're far too grown-up for you.'

'Well then.'

'And now I'm at a loss what to say. What about drawing? You used to...'

'Hush, daddy! Listen, I've thought of something I can usefully do. Mum thinks it's a good idea too. When I volunteered to be Michael's god-parent, I wasn't just saying it for fun. I could be helping the boy. I could be helping him with his English. I could also give him some of my old school primers.'

'You have already. James told me you had...'

'He shouldn't have.'

'Never mind, but I can't really agree to anything more than just you lending him books. It wouldn't be fair to the other boys.'

'But Michael is special. You promised his father to...besides I'm his god-mother.'

'You're a child, not much older than Michael.'

'I'm four, nearly five years older. Clever for my age...you're always saying that.'

'What about fairness? I mean it's giving him special attention over the other boys.'

'Better one than none. It's only for the next three years and during holidays only. O please daddy! Wednesday and Thursday afternoons, in the veranda, while you and mum are resting.'

'All right, I'll tell Michael. I've discovered he's a bright lad, keen and hard working.'

'Thank you, daddy. Today's Wednesday, we can start tomorrow. Mum's got a double-size teacher's slate for me and a small one for Michael. So he won't have to carry his around.'

'I see, so you two have been scheming behind my back. By the way, how long is it before you get back to Tara House?'

'Five weeks. Daddy, why is the Bishop, what's his name...?'

'Bishop Cyril Robinson.'

'Why is he visiting?'

'For the Confirmation Service. Five boys are to be confirmed.'

'Oh yes, I should have guessed. Mum has been taking the Confirmation Class.'

'The Bishop has been coming here every year since he was appointed. That'll be four years, now. You miss him because you are away when he turns up. This year he's a little early. But you'll still miss him. Confirmation, you know all about it! Last year you were confirmed at Tara House School Chapel, by Hardy, your favourite Bishop.'

'Remind me, what's a chasu... ?'

'Chasuble? It's what a priest, celebrating Eucharist, wears over his alb and stole. Albs, if you don't already know, are worn over cassocks. Wearing that and the chasuble, I'll probably faint with the heat, but old Robinson, bless him, is a great one for vestments. He's a High Anglican, which reminds me, I must get the local carpenter to repair that throne-like chair he brought with him last year but couldn't use. Bullock carts are not kind to grand old carved, walnut chairs. It's the second time I've been reminded about it. By the Bishop, I mean. Now run along.'

'But mummy says you're not happy when the Bishop visits.'

'She told you that? Did she say why?'

'No, not really, but I can guess. Is it because he's "High"?'

'I'm never really comfortable about fancy vestments, fuss and ceremony. You see I'm part of the Christian Missionary Society and we are what the Bishop would call "Low Church".'

'Yes. I see. And Daddy, thank you. You won't forget to tell Michael?'

'I won't.' He smiled as he watched Esther skip gleefully away. How hard it was to say no to her. Mature beyond her years, she reminded him of his mother, whom he had adored. But as he studied Esther's retreating figure his smile turned to a frown. Am I doing right by Michael? That boy's language and thinking will soon be rooted in English and Christianity. There was no escaping that. He will have to take on this new life before he finds himself. Was that so bad? Few lives are without upheavals. In his own childhood he knew pain and loneliness and till the age of thirteen his mother was his only companion. His father had died when he was three and since has remained just a black and white image of the kindly face he saw on his mother's bedside table. And then, after University he turned down a promised professorship to dedicate his life to a vocation that astonished his friends. Now, here he stood, a missionary, pledged to intrude into lives that happily could do without his input. But, as his mother said: "It is what Christ asks of you. Christianity is not just a religion. It is a Path, the only Path, laid by God Himself…a Path to travel on, even if it leads over the edge to martyrdom." Less than a month later, quite without much warning, she died in his arms, whispering mysteriously: "only distress has meaning". As he closed the eyes of her never-to-be forgotten face—for in Esther it lived on—he stayed intrigued by those words till, years later, in Central India, while unpacking, Agnes held up his father's old photograph, which had fallen from its frame. On the back, written by what could only be in his father's hand, words by Paracelsus: *Privilege and lineage pale into nothingness, only distress has meaning.* And he would never know why his mother kept this a 'secret' from him.

With determined strides he walked towards the schoolrooms and, passing the Chapel, faintly heard his wife practising carols and hymns for the approaching Christmas Season. He smiled as the old harmonium struck a false note. Poor Agnes! He will press the Bishop again. The hope of getting the pedal organ for the Chapel was a faint one, but surely Robinson could arrange for a new harmonium. For a moment he toyed with the idea of joining Agnes but changed his mind as a fresh thought on Michael's future rose. It was unfair to compare Michael's childhood with his own. His fatherless childhood was compensated by the love of a doting mother and by an education that was not a cultural upheaval. In Michael's case, the trauma of being torn from an orthodox Hindu home, at an impressionable age, would leave its imprint. No child's mind is a blank slate. Father Jacob knelt on the ground and prayed for guidance...]

Later that evening, after prayers in the Chapel, Dr Rivers addressed the boys.

'I have news for you,' he said. 'I shall say it in Marathi as most of you speak or understand Marathi. James will explain to the three who don't. First, tell me: Are you all happy here?'

'Yes, Sir!' chorused the boys.

'Good. As you know, despite the few resources at St Thomas's, we grown-ups—and that does not mean just Sister Agnes, Mr Gupta, James and I, but also the staff and helpers here...all of us want to make your life and learning, here at St Thomas, as comfortable as possible. And I am happy to see how well you get on with each other. How you willingly help each other, without envy. Envy is a sin. We cannot all be equal. God has given us talents, some more, some less, as in the parable Jesus told. Some people are born in rich homes, many more of us in poor ones. Life in this world isn't fair, so it may seem unfair for us to be giving more help to some and not to others. But by helping the talented, we hope that they in turn will help to make the world a better place for all of us. So we give special help to those who need it. But I am happy to see most of you get on well in your own happy ways without much help. Contentment is God's gift and very great blessing. Theo, you and Philip get extra lessons from Mr Gupta because you are good in Maths and we hope, in the future, you will do great things for the good of all. Some singers among you are chosen by Sister Agnes for our Choir. They get extra practice. Others of you get extra help in games and wrestling from Walid Khan, our chowkidar, and so on...Oh that reminds me, Joshua...don't stand up, keep sitting ...the *mali* tells me you have done good work in the kitchen garden. *Shabash!* Well done! I'm pleased to hear that. Now, as you know, we have a new boy. He needs help in learning English…Michael, come here.'

After some hesitation I got up and stood next to Father Jacob. 'This is Michael.' He put his hands on my shoulders and turned me to face the boys. 'Michael's father died recently. He was a good friend of mine. In memory of that friendship, I want all of us to help Michael in learning English. I will be helping him. Two days in the week, for a while, Michael will spend some time at my bungalow. Yes, the bungalow is out of bounds to boys, but as you know, in special cases, I break that rule. For some time Michael will be a special case.'

The boys cheered and clapped their hands and I wondered what they saw in me that made their support so spontaneous.

'Well done, boys! This is good to see. As I said, envy is a sin. Without envy we are blessed with the riches of Christian love and kindness. Remember St Paul's letter about Charity?'

"Yes" chorused the boys in unison, and Luke raised his hand. 'Sir, sir!'

Dr Rivers nodded encouragingly.

'Sir, chapter thirteen. First Epistle to the Cori – cor…I can't say it.'

'Corinthians. Well done Luke.' Father Jacob clapped and we joined in. 'Good. That is a wonderful letter and Sister Agnes has copied that letter in simple Marathi. I will read it to you, here, tomorrow evening. Remember, in the eyes of God, each one of us is special. So, in the end, no one gains or loses. Never forget that. That is all. James, lead the boys out.'

And, as we lined up, I looked at Luke with envy. I wanted so much to be the knowing one; so much to be the one who had the answers; so much to be praised and admired…

My lessons in English, under Esther's serious guidance, saw me keen to succeed. Then on the day after the first lesson, Gupta sent for me during the morning recess, where in the small playground next to the Gate Office, we are served a light snack. I had started to look forward to this meal more than any other, even though its unremitting and identical daily fare consisted of lightly cooked bean sprouts, spiced with chilli, salt and lime juice. It was served in neat little bowls made of intertwined pipal leaves. When done with, we threw these leaf bowls into a large steel barrel at the far corner of this playground. Thoughtfully, Gupta waited till I had eaten and then entering the Gate Office I found him in earnest conversation with Walid Khan. He turned to greet me with a wide smile and a roll of his head. 'I've just told Walid, our watchman, that you have permission to cross the line of white bricks between three and four every Wednesday and

Thursday afternoons. But, only on those days, otherwise the rule strictly stands.'

I nodded and was about to leave, when I turned back to ask if he had had a happy Diwali.

'Thank you. That was kind of you to ask.'

'And did your wife prepare a special dish?'

'Mrs Gupta? There is no Mrs Gupta. There never was a Mrs Gupta.'

I was a curious boy and quickly gathered, along with the other boys, that the loquacious Mr Gupta was easily tempted into telling stories and I soon learned that, given a captive audience, people who live alone, are easily drawn into sharing their thoughts. 'Did you light a *chirag* and a joss-stick before goddess Durga?' I asked.

Mr Gupta laughed. 'Michael, my boy, I should scold you for asking questions that are none of your business, but I do believe I have been open with you from the moment we were together from that first tour of the Mission Compound. It would, therefore, be unreasonable for me to be offended by your questions.'

At this early stage, I could not always keep up with Gupta's verbal facility. But I pretended to understand. Fortunately his expressive manner of speaking made the gist of his statements easy to guess. 'You see,' he continued, 'we Bengalis...'

The school bell rang, marking the end of the break. I was about to run out when Mr Gupta stopped me. 'That's all right. You may walk with me. I am taking your next class lesson. Now, as I was saying, Bengalis indeed worship Durga, Kali; but, Bengali though I am, I follow another way, a noble path. Have you heard the name Gautama Buddha? Don't make a face, boy. I do not expect you to know of the Lord Buddha.'

'But Guptaji, I have, but not of path...what is path?'

'Noble path...means his teachings. Buddha taught his followers how to live in peace with the world and with oneself. It is not easy to explain to a young lad. But for many years I have been his disciple. I was seventeen when I visited Bodh Gaya and sat under the very tree where Lord Buddha found enlightenment.'

'What is that? What he found?'

'Not now. You need to be a little older to understand. It is something so big...the answers to all life's problems. Giving *shanti*, peace...something like what the Padre sahib has found.'

'I want to find peace. Can I be like you? Is Padre Rivers also a Bud...'

Mr Gupta stopped and looked hard at me. 'Enough Michael, you're a Christian now. Find your peace there, like Padre sahib. Mind you, Dr Rivers is a great scholar. He knows a lot...all about Lord Buddha and about Hindu books. Come now, enough of this chit chat, walk a little faster.' Gupta put an arm round my shoulder and pushed me along. 'Michael, first you have a lot of living and learning to do. I've said before and I say again, you are a most clever boy, and so you have a great future.'

I looked up at Gupta, smugly grateful. It was clear, from remarks by those around me, that I was a bright lad and increasingly there appeared to be a concerted effort on the part of my elders to concentrate on the advancement of my education. James was told to speak to me in English and use Marathi only if communication failed. Quickly, I began to pick up English words from overheard conversations. But when I think about the rapid progress I was making, I must admit that, young as she was, Esther was a naturally good teacher and took her role seriously, though at times, a mistake by me sent her into a fit of giggles. Of course, I did not mind because, grateful for what she was doing, I strove hard to succeed. Sometimes her mother sat with us and helped with the lessons but for much of the time we were left to ourselves. Those sessions with Sister Agnes were a great help. From her Marathi translations I could follow Esther more closely, so that, by the last lesson, before Esther was due to go back to her school, we were able to converse and understand each other adequately.

I was determined to read and master sounds of the English alphabet and surprised mother and daughter by my innate ability to reproduce their shapes on my slate with accuracy. Script shapes always did fascinate me and I was sorry to have to wipe my slate clean before each new lesson. Esther noted that and at the end of our last session she gave me a book of names with pictures, a thin exercise book and a lead pencil. 'Michael, this is an old exercise book of mine,' she said flicking through its pages, 'but there are many blank pages for you to write on. Practice writing letters and words in it. I'll see them when I'm back.' She got up and stood behind me. I felt a gentle pat on my head and heard a shy giggle. 'You've got pretty eyes,' she said quickly, 'and long eyelashes,' and leaning forward put her face close to mine and with a finger pointed to her cheek. I stared at it, but before I understood what was expected, she straightened herself and ran inside. I waited. She did not return…

I waited awhile and then, as I picked up what she had given me, a new, deep aching sense of desolation gripped me. The thought of a long interval before I would see Esther again stirred in me a sensation I had never felt before; a yearning to be with someone, someone who meant more to me than just a kind stranger, left me unsettled. I thought of my grandmother, of those times of sincere love, when she would hug me and give me sweets. Surely she would take me back, hide and protect me! And I would refuse to leave her side… I began to wonder if escape from here was possible. I was sure I could squeeze through the turnstile by the Main Gates, make a left turn and set out on the trek back to Pali… or was it a right turn? No, it had to be left. The shady *chenar* tree, where uncle Ganesh tethered his bullocks, was on the right. Yes, yes, we had arrived from Rambagh and Mr Gupta had confirmed that was on the left. Obsessed by the thought of seeing *Daadi* again, I omitted to weigh the chances of making a successful escape and in my excitement I grew restless.

For much of that night sleep eluded me. A nervous tension kept me awake till after much tossing I fell asleep. In the morning I was woken by being shaken vigorously. I opened my eyes and started at the sight of a big curly head silhouetted against the white morning light. Cold and feverish I tried to pull the bedcover over me, but couldn't. The dark apparition stopped me. It was James and I realised he was holding the bedcover with one hand and shaking me with the other. A bout of shivering overcame me. James released his hold and reached out to touch my face and forehead. 'It's okay Michael,' he said, 'stay in bed. You've got fever. I tell Mr Gupta.'

I went back to sleep after James left me but woke again to find Mr Gupta standing by the side of my bed. 'Mike, my boy, James tells me you are ill. No cause for worry, I believe you are, as English say; "a bit under the weather". Let me check. Do you see what I am holding?' I gazed at what looked like a glass pencil and shook my head. 'It is a thermometer. It will tell me if you have fever. Open your mouth. Keep this under your tongue. Gently, it's glass, don't bite it!'

A moment later he removed it and holding it horizontally stared at it. 'Normal, no fever, but I think I will take you to our Sick Bay. Just in case. Making doubly sure'

'Sick bay? Guptaji, what is…'

'Shabash! Well done! Speaking in English now. Very good! Sick Bay is for boys who are sick. Special place with five beds. Did I not show it to you on that first tour of the Mission?'

I raised my head and rested on one elbow. 'No, Mr Gupta.'

'Yes, I remember now. I did not take you there because one of the boys had *choti mata.*'

I looked up at him inquiringly.

'That is chicken pox… no, no. I mean measles. It is most catching. And so, Sick Bay was out of bounds. No boys allowed that day. But now is okay.'

'Catching? What is catching?'

'It means, if I have measles and you come near me, you also will get the measles. But most serious it is to catch *mata*, the small-pox. Oh, God!'

Gupta stuck his tongue out and solemnly rocked his head. 'No hope then. You must know about *mata*, small-pox?'

I nodded.

'My boy, in this country, many such cases in village life... but, now British Raj send people to vaccinate in those villages. You must have mark to show you were vaccinated as baby.'

I pulled up my shirt sleeve, stared at the top of my arm and nodded again.

'When we go to the Sick Bay, you will meet Miss Enid Tolly. Tall English lady.'

'That why name Tolly?'

'What? No, no. That...' Gupta broke into laughter. 'No, not Tolly for tall, it is her name. All boys are afraid of her. But she is most kind. She is nurse, paid by Government PWD, and working for the Chief Civil Surgeon in Pultanpur.'

'PWD?' I screwed up my face.

'Public Works Department. And Surgeon? Do you know surgeon? Well, he is most clever man, who...' Gupta leaned over me, criss-crossed my stomach, 'will cut you up.'

What Mr Gupta called the Sick Bay turned out to be a square, box-like, grey stone building on the far corner of the Mission Compound, beyond the servant's quarters. It had an airy, wide veranda overlooking a garden that consisted of a lawn edged by beds of flowering plants. Bright rows of hollyhocks lined three sides of its perimeter, while pansies, sweet peas and dahlias made an English statement that pointedly excluded the ubiquitous Indian marigold. 'When there are no boys to nurse,' Gupta said, 'Miss Tolly spends her time gardening.'

In one corner of the wide veranda, I noticed a strange three-wheeled contraption. Pointing to it, I expressed my surprise.

'That Miss Tolly's tricycle. Tri is meaning three, three wheels. She comes here, to Sick Bay every morning for two hours only, then on this trike (she calls this big cycle a trike) back to the Pultanpur Cantonment Hospital. There Miss Tolly makes report to Chief Civil Surgeon.'

We entered the veranda and passed through double doors into a long room with large, high meshed windows that Gupta explained were shut to keep out insects and mosquitos. Inside the room were five tubular-steel beds, three opposite the doors and two alongside it. These were widely spaced, neatly covered with blue-grey counterpanes and each had a small bedside locker. Two more doors were set in the two gloss-white painted walls at either end of the room's length. They were shut. Gupta went to one of them, knocked gently and waited. There was no answer. He took out a hob watch from his waistcoat pocket and consulted it. 'No, we are not too late.'

I pointed to the other door. Gupta shook his head. 'That is bathroom, this is Miss Tolly's office.' He knocked again, more firmly. The door swept open. A tall lady filled its frame. 'I heard you the first time Das Gupta.' Then she looked down at me. 'What have we here?'

'This is Michael.' Gupta spoke with a tension in his voice. 'I fear he has caught something, some illness.'

'Come here, boy!' said Miss Tolly.

I looked at her unsettling tight mouth and froze. She seemed to have no lips. Then I noted her merry grey eyes, broad pale face and her distinctly maternal look. 'Come here, I shan't eat you, though you look a tasty morsel.'

I went up to her. Miss Tolly cupped my face in her hands and looked searchingly into my eyes. Then she felt my forehead. 'He's all right. No temperature.'

'Indeed, I myself took the trouble to check with thermometer. Yes, normal showing, but...'

'Good man, Das Gupta. Well, there's nothing that a good rest won't cure.' Miss Tolly held my shoulders. 'You missed on your sleep last night. Did you not?'

I nodded and smiled guiltily.

'You haven't being doing anything you shouldn't, eh? Playing with yourself? Naughty.'

'Thank you, Miss Tolly,' I said, not understanding and out of sheer politeness.

'Oh, bless the child!'

'The boy is learning English and making fast progress,' Das Gupta rolled his head.

'I can believe that. He sounds the words he knows rather well.'

'Miss Esther, she giving him lessons, but now her school holiday over.'

'And where is Dr Rivers? I saw him getting into the tonga as I came in this morning. Poor Agnes, I suppose she is monitoring both the Junior and Senior classes.'

'Precisely, Miss Tolly. Dr Rivers was on his way to Rambagh, where there have been fears of a plague epidemic.'

'Cholera, Das Gupta, Cholera.'

'Indeed, Miss Tolly, I stand corrected.'

'That is why, next week we will be inoculating the whole Mission here.'

'Oh dear,' said Das Gupta, rolling his head.

'You're lucky to have Dr Rivers,' Miss Tolly said turning to me. 'He takes good care of the health of the Mission. Well, now, run along both of you so I can spend sometime in the garden, 'afore I go.' Miss Tolly threw her head back and laughed.

Gupta rolled his head. 'You know Madam the boy showed some interest in your tricycle.'

'Indeed. Well, come with me and have a closer look.'

We accompanied Miss Tolly to the veranda and stopped in front of her tricycle. 'I'm proud of my trike, Mr Gupta. That what it's called, trike.'

'Can one get this in India? I have not seen another like this.'

'I'd be surprised. This came all the way from England. Bill, my brother, twin brother, who works for the Leicester Tricycle Company, came here three years ago and he brought this with him. It was his present for me. It can be folded, don't ask me how. It took a long time getting here. He had to collect it at the Bombay Docks, then transport it by train and bullock cart till after a hard journey it reached Pultanpur. It arrived as a big parcel of bits and pieces. Then, my sweet, generous brother put it together. He knew as a nurse I'd find the trike useful. Note the storage box between the two back wheels.'

'That metal store box is a most clever idea, Miss Tolly. India can do with a company making such useful things. Also bicycles. Dr Rivers told me he had one when in Oxford.'

'A bone shaker no doubt. Mind you, about that time they did start to fit pneumatic tyres to some of the later models. But, with British enterprise it won't be long before India gets them.'

'Indeed, madam, as Napoleon said the English are a nation of shopkeepers.'

'Napoleon was an incorrigible ass.'

Mr Gupta rolled his head. 'I like that word, incorrigible.'

'As I was saying, already there is a company in Calcutta, making rickshaws, that also plans to assemble trikes and cycles. I know, because Bill, my brother, returned to Bombay to catch the boat to Calcutta, which was transporting the necessary goods and equipment.'

'Does your brother know Calcutta?'

'No, but he will, since he had to spend six months advising his Bengali friend. He talked a lot about Mr Aaron Mazumdar, who visited his company in Leicester. I gather Mr Mazumdar had previously spent time as an apprentice in Coventry.'

'But, I expect these things will be expensive.'

'Indeed, Gupta. This trike of mine cost Bill £18 in Leicester.'

'So your brother Bill, he was killing two birds with one stone.'

'What on earth do you mean?'

'I mean, meeting you and also his friend in Calcutta, with goods and presents.'

'I see. Droll, very droll, Gupta. Now you must excuse me. I must attend to my garden.'

Back at the Gate Office, Gupta asked me to sit quietly on the floor by his desk and, from the deep shelf behind him, removed what looked like a large register with a red cloth cover. 'Now, Michael, are you feeling better? Mind you, Miss Tolly has answered that question. So, you rest here while I fill this register. After that I will take you to the dinner hall for your *bhojan*. Then you must join the afternoon school programme.'

What Gupta called *bhojan* was our midday meal, which was, almost invariably, either a thick porridge of coarse semolina and treacle, with a mug of hot, sweet tea, or boiled spinach mixed with mango pickle, spread on a thick cornmeal *chapatti*, followed by a drink of buttermilk. In either event it was not a meal I cared about, preferring the morning snack of spiced chickpeas or the evening suppers of rice and lentil curry; and, of course, the special Sunday dinners...but, best of all, the picnic fare of *puris* and hot potato vegetable, when its aroma of garlic, chilli and cumin made ones mouth water...

'I think,' Gupta interrupted my thoughts, 'you should tell me why you did not sleep well last night, Michael?'

I sighed. 'I don't know,' I said, quickly adding, 'Guptaji, can I help you? I like doing sums. Give me some work to do.'

'It is not anything you can help me with.'

'What are you writing in that book?'

'You know Michael, you ask too many questions. But it is good to know things. Clever boys are curious, as indeed you are clever and good at doing sums. Someday, soon, you could do my job.' Gupta laughed. 'You could be the youngest Munshi of this Mission School. No, not now. Keep sitting there...I am filling the Sickness Register. I note down here about each boy who was reported sick; why he went to the Sick Bay; what sickness he had. And then, I note down Miss Tolly's comments, what she said.'

'Why? Why write about something that is *khatum*, finished, over.'

'Because, we must. One day you will know why it is the right thing to do. Good Dr Rivers is a man who wants to know all that happens here. All about welfare of whole Mission...you know what "welfare" means?'

I shook my head.

'It means caring for people. Dr Rivers caring for all, you and me... All of us, learning and working here. Padre sahib is good man, but he also works for people who ask him about how the Mission is doing. They want to see the books, so, we keep many such books, registers, in which we write about everyday life here… reports and *hisabs*, which means, stories or accounts, of problems and worries.'

'History stories? Like Father Rivers telling us about King Alfred the Great, of England?'

'Yes, Alfred and the burning of cakes; but we would not know that story if someone had not first written it down. Yes, now be quiet till I have finished this.'

Mr Gupta pulled his spectacles to the end of his nose, picked up his pen, wiped its nib on a piece of blotting paper and with a wry squint began to write. I waited till he put down his pen, closed the red book and returned it to its place on the shelf. He then dusted his hands, sat down and turned on me a benevolent smile.

'Guptaji, what happened to the boy who was ill?'

Das Gupta's smile disappeared and he regarded me with a frown. 'What boy?'

'The boy in the Sick Bay, who was ill…who had catching ill?'

'He was taken to the hospital in Pultanpur.'

'When he comes back, will his face be…' with my middle finger I dotted my face to show the pitted scars that remain after people recover from small pox. 'My *Daadi* had *mata*. She has…'

'Stop! And don't do that with your fingers.' Gupta bent forward and wagged his forefinger. 'Bad luck. That boy…' Gupta took a sharp breath. 'The boy is not coming back. Sadly he, the poor boy, died.'

I started, my heart pounding, and stared at Gupta. 'But when people die, everybody knows… when my mother died, the whole village know. Women coming to grandfather's house…all sit down, covered heads… made crying noises…' I pulled my shirt up over my head, rocked from side to side, beat my chest and mimicked the typically plangent, moaning sounds village women make at funeral gatherings.

'Stop! Stop! Enough. Put your shirt down. Don't make me angry. Like a good Buddhist I try hard not be angry. Listen. For Hindus dying is an end but also not *the* end. There is need to cry, but also need to rejoice. Hindus are sad and happy at the same time. But for Christians it is different. They bury their dead. That boy was taken to Pultanpur hospital the day before you came here. He died there that same day. The older boys were told.'

'Bury? In ground? Where? Here?'

Gupta shook his head. 'Pultanpur Church. Church is like big chapel. It has special garden at the back, where they bury. His body was put in wooden box and taken by bullock cart to that place. Padre sahib, Sister Agnes, even *Missybaba*, went in tonga to Pultanpur Church.'

'Esther also went?'

'Yes.'

'And you? Did you go?'

'Yes. It is my job, though I'm not a Christian. The boy, Mohan, I mean Jonathan, that was his Christian name, was a good boy. I, we all liked him very much.' He paused for a thoughtful moment, his bony forefinger across his lips. 'I think Christians show great respect for the dead. Prayers and singing songs to God... But enough, no more questions, I must get on... Now what is it? Is something more troubling you?'

'That funny woman...we saw. My first day... that woman sitting under a tree, singing English songs...Esther's ayah, you said. Rose...'

'Rosie Almeida? Esther's old ayah? Yes.'

'She...has she got a son?'

'Are you saying you have seen her with some boy?'

I nodded vigorously.

'How, I mean, when did you see that boy?'

'When I was sitting with Esther.'

'Did you not ask Miss Esther?'

I shook my head. 'I wanted to ask you. You say all boys, here, are Christian. But this boy, I don't see him in Chapel. Don't see him in School.'

'*Bus, bus*! Enough! You don't have to know about that boy. When it is not their business to know it is good for people not to know.'

'He wears nice clothes and shiny shoes.'

'Forget him. And you must not talk about him to anyone. Don't even ask James...'

We were interrupted by Walid Khan, who came in carrying a small parcel. '*Darzee* gave me this,' he said. 'New school uniform he make for *Missybaba*. For her to take school, tomorrow.'

At the mention of Esther's departure, an echo of my earlier pangs of despair returned.

'Leave it with me,' Das Gupta said.

Walid Khan rolled his head. 'I could take it to Sister Agnes, now.'

'No, no. No need for that. I will hand it over to the Sahib when he returns from Rambagh. Also, you must not leave your post by the Gates. In fact, I will take it now to Sister Agnes. Right now Miss Esther is with her in the classroom. Michael, stay here. I will be back.'

With Gupta and Walid Khan gone, I found myself alone in the office and in a flash saw the opportunity of putting into action my earlier thought of escaping to Pali. I tiptoed to the open doorway and stared at the bars of the Main Gates. At first the sight of Walid Khan's huge frame discouraged me, but his back was turned away from me and the turnstile. I crept out, tested the gap in the turnstile and squeezed through it to find myself, unchallenged, on the broad dust road outside the Mission Compound. My heart beat wildly and a rush of blood induced a paralysis, till a swift glance over my shoulder assured me that Walid Khan was still looking straight ahead. Without another moment's hesitation I ran, turned the corner and almost crashed into a tonga coming straight at me.

'Michael! What on earth...' The voice was unmistakably that of Dr Rivers. He sprang off the tonga, gripped me by the shoulders and shook me. 'What on earth are you doing here?'

I burst out crying. 'Please Father don't be angry!'

'Angry, I'm furious.'

Just then, Walid Khan, stirred into action by the commotion, ran up towards us.

'Walid!' Dr Rivers took a deep breath and then with deliberate calm spoke in Hindi. 'How did this boy get out? Where were you?'

'Sahibji, I...'

'*Chuprao*! Enough! Go back! Let the tonga in, then see me in the office. No! Stay at your post! Where's the Munshi? Ah, there...'

Dr Rivers spotted Das Gupta leisurely coming towards us and marched me through the gates to meet him. Confronted by the sight of us, Gupta was visibly shaken.

'Oh, Padre sahib,' he said hoarsely, 'what indeed is the matter?'

'The matter? I find this boy outside the gates on the open road and almost under the wheels of my tonga!'

'The boy was not well this morning,' stammered Gupta, 'and I... Oh Michael, what have you done! Sahib, after taking the boy to the Sick Bay to see Miss Tolly, I trusted the boy, told him to stay in the office for a moment, while... But forgive me Sahib, there can be no excuse for my irresponsibility. It will not happen again. I deserve to be reprimanded. I must...in truth I must forgo pay of one month's salary. I am deserving of penalty for my shortcoming. I...'

'Enough, Das Gupta, please! Don't go on. You're being melodramatic. Let us all get inside the office and tell me your side of the story, calmly.' As we went in, Gupta looked at me sadly, and shook his head. I wanted to rush to him and take his hand, but Dr Rivers's vice-like grip on my collar prevented me making the slightest move. In the office they sat at their usual places.

'Michael, stand here next to me. Now Gupta, and remember there is every good reason for us to be calm, since, fortunately, thank the Lord, nothing serious has happened.'

Das Gupta related the morning events in meticulous detail, ending with why he had left me in the office unattended. 'I am so at a loss to understand the boy's conduct. He has until now been most trustworthy.'

'I agree with you there, Gupta. In the circumstances I would have done exactly as you did.'

'Still, Padre sahib there has been dereliction of duty, for which I have no excuse.'

'Don't bring that up again. Excuses can be valid and, like you, I can't understand Michael's behaviour. But, how on earth did Walid miss him?' Dr Rivers stood up, walked to the open door and looked out. Thoughtfully, he stroked his trim beard. 'Gupta, we'll have to adjust the turnstile and realign it. I suppose the boy squeezed through it when the chowkidar's back was turned. Is that what you did, Michael? Squeezed through the gate?'

I nodded and turned to look at Gupta. Throughout his narration Gupta avoided looking at me, and now, when I tried to get his attention he looked away. By my unthinking, childish act I had destroyed a beautiful friendship and we were never to be quite wholly reconciled. But to his lasting credit, Gupta showed neither impatience nor anger. He continued to maintain a distant and professional attitude towards me.

Dr Rivers noted Gupta's hurt and assured him he would see to it that I fully apologised for letting him down. But Gupta raised his hands and shook his head sadly. 'No, sahib, please!' He bowed and hid his face in his hands. 'Please no! No apology needed. I have failed in my duty and my responsibility. An apology will only increase my present misery. In fact, may I now beg your indulgence to leave the office and go over to the school to assist your worthy wife.'

'Very well, Gupta. I'll respect your feelings.'

The Munshi got up to leave, stopped at the door and turned to say: 'I was to escort the boy to the dining hall for his *bhojan*.'

'Leave that to me. It's not important. The boy deserves to miss a meal. You could on your way question Walid. I'll leave you to handle that matter. I'm sure this would not have occurred if I hadn't gone to Rambagh, because the tonga driver always sits by the turnstile. Michael could not have slipped past him even if Walid had missed him. Also, tell my wife I'm back.'

'How was sahib's trip to Rambagh?'

'Not now Gupta. Later I'll make a report for you to record. I'll say this much, the epidemic is serious enough for you to consider not going back to Rambagh, till it is well under control.'

'My diet is simple and prepared by me, in accordance to all the rules of good hygiene. And I only drink boiled water.'

Dr Rivers smiled and spread his hands. 'Still, think about it. You could stay at the Sick Bay till things are back to normal.'

'I am indeed most grateful. But the fact I've never had to absent myself in all the time I have been with the Mission is proof that you may rely on the adequate precautions I take.'

'You're a good man. But we need to take Miss Tolly's advice and act accordingly. Till then I want you to forget about this unfortunate incident.'

Gupta bowed and shut the door behind him.

'Now, Michael!' The stern tone in Dr Rivers's voice made me gasp. I stared anxiously at his penetrating, unsmiling, brown eyes. 'I want an explanation,' he added.

'I wanted to see my *Daadi*. I was going to come back. Truly, I promise.'

'And do you know where your *Daadi* lives?'

'Yes, in my village. In Pali.'

'Pali is at least twelve miles away and, even if you know how to get there, it would have been dark long before you reached it. Also, it is not safe for anyone, let alone a wandering small boy, even a clever boy, to be alone outside the Mission Compound. Even grown-up people, strong, brave folk, won't travel alone if they don't have to. There are many bad people in the world.'

A dreadful picture flashed through my mind as I recalled hearing grandfather tell my father of a robber band, who stealthily followed strangers by cover of darkness, sprang on them when they were asleep and strangled them. In utter panic I burst into tears. 'Father, sir,' I cried, 'sorry, but I felt lonely and I was sad.'

'That is when you talk to your elders. James or Gupta or ask to see me. Michael, this is not a prison. Boys are free to go, as long as they ask if they can and if they have a good reason. But there has to be good, safe reasons, like if your family wants you back or if there is a good home to go to, with good people prepared to take care of you. Or if you're old enough and there is a job for you to do. Till then we protect you. We can't let you wander around, get lost, starve or come to harm. Do you understand? Say yes, or nod your head,'

I did both and Dr Rivers sighed and sat back in his chair. He looked unhappy.

'I wouldn't have got lost,' I whispered. 'Sir, I know the way to Pali. I am good walker.'

Dr Rivers leaned forward. 'In the dark you could have lost your way. And what if you were kidnapped?' After he explained what kidnapping meant, I trembled and wiped my face on my shirt sleeve.

'Come here, stand next to me.'

'What must I do? Can you forget today?'

'Michael, let this be a lesson you won't forget. You must learn there are things we may think we are free to do or can do but, if it is wrong or know it will hurt someone we don't wish to hurt, then we must not do it. Then there are things that will hurt no one but ourselves, because we're too young to do them or just not able to do them.' He paused for a moment. 'Michael is there any thing I'm saying that you do not understand/'

I shook my head.

'You've been here for some time. During that time, things have changed. Your family is no longer in Pali. Michael, your *dada* and *Daadi* left Pali some time ago. They are now living with your uncle Ganesh. His farm was sold and they have moved to a new village called Mandi. Do you know Mandi?'

I shook my head and started to cry again.

'Stop crying. That won't help. Crying makes you feel defeated. Tell yourself, I am going to be strong and sensible. You are ten, now. Until now, you have been a good lad and made good progress.' He paused again. 'Esther would've been disappointed if you had gone away.'

'But...' I began and in a flash of regret, realised I had foolishly forgotten about Esther. 'But, sir, I was coming back. I would have come back, I promise!'

'Suppose you were not able to? Suppose something terrible happened to you and you were prevented from getting back. Things often never go the way we plan.'

'Have I committed a mortal sin?'

'No. Where did you hear the word mortal?

'I can't remember. But, sir, is it not a wrong and bad thing to disobey elders?'

'There, now you are being sensible. Yes, it is also wrong to break the rules of the Mission.'

'I won't, sir. Never again.'

'Now, when we do wrong, we ask God to forgive us. We say a prayer. Ask for God's help to make a new start. Michael, think of a prayer you use to say sorry.'

'In English? I know one. "Now the day is over, night is drawing nigh, shadows of…'

'Stop! God does not want something you've learned by heart. You have been a naughty boy. You have to say sorry. Ask God to help you to be good. There is a very special word, which all good Christians remember.'

I thought hard and asked tentatively: 'A Christian word, sir?'

'Yes, but it…'

'Is it love! Because God is love?'

Dr Rivers repressed a smile. 'Yes, a good start. Now, think of another word. It comes with love, or from love and kindness. Something I told you on Sunday, in the Chapel.'

I loved answering questions and, in my eagerness to show off what I had learned I forgot my sadness and tears. 'Is it charity?'

'That is love. Think of a word for something you feel, inside you. It is something that makes you want to say thank you to people for their love and charity and kindness to you. What is that something we feel which makes us want to say thank you?'

'Sir, sir! Gratitude!'

'Well done! And you pronounced it correctly, as you did last Sunday evening. Gratitude is why we worship God. Thank God for the gift of life and the world in which we live. There are many people who are not Christians, who fear their gods. They are afraid their gods will punish them. We, Christians do not worship God because we fear Him.'

'Gratitude,' I said slowly, mulling over the word. 'We also say thank you to people.'

'Yes. We must be grateful to all who care for us. I am grateful to Sister Agnes and to Esther and Gupta and Walid and yes, to you…everyone I meet and live with. You must do the same. There, now run along. Have your *bhojan*. You don't need me to take you there. Wait, just a minute, did Esther teach you the words of that prayer "Now the day is over"?'

'Yes, sir.'

'Right, off you go. And let what happened today be a lesson you will never forget.'

Next morning, as we filed out of the Chapel, I saw the dark profile of a box-shaped carriage, drawn by two sturdy bays, outside the Rivers' bungalow. It had four wheels, four windows and a projecting shelf-like ledge at the back. As I looked on, I saw two men lift and strap down a steel trunk on the roof of the carriage. One of them was Namdeo, our syce and tonga driver. Esther was watching them closely, till with a sudden movement she turned round to join the two ladies, who were standing behind her wrapped in earnest conversation. One was Sister Agnes; but the other, a tall, elegantly dressed woman in a long blue skirt and white blouse, was a stranger to me. Her face was hidden behind her open, light blue parasol. I felt a firm tap on my shoulder. It was James. 'Don't stare,' he said. 'Look away, it's rude to stare.'

'Who's the tall lady,' I asked, making a mental note to learn more about James. It was not the first time I was intrigued by him and by the respect the Mission elders seemed to give him.

'That is Mrs Mackay, cousin of Dr Rivers. She's come to take Esther back to her school.'

'Tara House.'

'Yes. How did you know?'

'Esther told me. It is about fifty-two miles from here.'

'Yes. Up in the hills near Panchmarhi. They will get there this evening.'

'But there are robbers in the hills. It is dangerous for them.'

James smiled. 'They are well guarded. Two soldiers on horseback. *Sowars*, they are called. They will join them and ride out with the carriage. They are from Pultanpur. They have guns. Here, keep this. It is from Esther. She gave it to Gupta yesterday, who gave it to me. No, not now, read it later.'

Reminded once again of Gupta's coolness towards me, I nodded, tucked the envelope in my shirt pocket and, glancing back, saw Dr Rivers come out of the bungalow. Esther ran up to him with a loud squeak. As we moved out of sight, that tender picture of filial love lingered, stirring a peculiar thrill within me, so that on entering the classroom I felt a strong desire to sit quietly in a corner, looking without seeing, the boys wander around and chatter till James called for silence.

Increasingly I had begun to feel distant from the boys of the Mission and clearly their feelings were the same towards me. I had thought Luke might wish to continue our short friendship but, apart from meal times in the dining hall, he avoided me. My own attitude left no reason to find fault with his, but I did wonder why the civil conduct of the boys towards me did not lead to one of warmer friendship, till James told me it was because I was the only Brahmin there. I had no urgent wish to remedy this. It was different with James. He had such a sweet temperament and I was no longer repelled by his dark and ugly presence. With him I felt the compelling need to find companionship.

I opened Esther's envelope. Inside was a card with The Lord's Prayer printed in red on one side while on the other side Esther had written:

Dear Michael, we can't write to each other, but I will copy my favourite poem and send it to you when I write to Mum and Dad. Learn it by heart. Recite it to me when we have our next first lesson. The poem is Tiger, Tiger by William Blake. Be good! Esther

I put the card away in my shirt pocket with the intention of later showing it to James to read, explain and make doubly sure I understood its message. Esther would be back in November. I counted on my fingertips-- eight months from now--stole another glance at her card and recalled from her Alphabet book what a tiger looked like. The tiger's yellow eyes got confused with the light golden brown of Esther's and a shiver ran through me. I couldn't think why. I looked up and watched James chalk 28 March 1883 on the blackboard as Gupta entered the classroom. We stood up and greeted him: "Good Morning, Sir" and sat down for our Maths lesson. He nodded and James left the room.

After the lesson we filed out for morning breakfast. Gupta stopped me. 'Young Michael,' he said. 'You wanted to know about that well-dressed boy you saw when you were at Padre sahib's bungalow? Well, that boy wants to meet you. I will only say this. You won't see him in Chapel because he is Muslim. His name is Sorab Ali Baig. His father is a very rich merchant who owns cloth mills in Bombay and, for padre sahib's kindness towards Sorab, he, now and then, makes generous donations that are a great help to the Mission.'

'But Guptaji...' I began.

'Padre sahib will tell you more.' Gupta raised his hand and with a cold nod left me to gaze at his retreating figure with regret. But I was hungry and immediately ran to join the queue for the spiced chickpeas breakfast. As I waited my turn I saw James in earnest conversation with Gupta outside the Gate Office and I wondered if James knew of my abortive attempt to run away to see my grandmother in Pali. If he did, he never mentioned it.

The English lessons in basic grammar and sentence composition, till now, were little more than simply learning words and useful sentences by rote. These were mostly from Bible stories told by Sister Agnes or Dr Rivers. But today both were present in the classroom and the session took an unusual turn. The twenty-four of us were asked to sit on the floor in a big circle. James came in carrying the harmonium, which he placed on the desk in front of Sister Agnes. Then he went out and immediately returned with a small sack, which he laid on the floor. Dr Rivers had a word with James and then he entered the middle of our circle. 'Now boys,' he said, 'you must wonder why, this year, we did not have our Christmas Nativity Play. Well, as some of you know, our plays always include some older children from St Peter's. That is the High School in Pultanpur. Sadly, this year there has been many serious cases of cholera in Rambagh and a few also in Pultanpur. So, to make certain nobody here got sick, Nurse Tolly decided to close our Mission to anyone from outside. That is also why all of us had injections and why Mr Gupta had to stay in the Sick Bay for two weeks. Now the Mission is open and though it's too late to have a Christmas Play, it is never too late to hear the Christmas Story, especially for the benefit of our two new boys, Michael and Silas, and also because his Marathi is so much better than mine, I have asked James to tell all of us the Christmas Story.'

In fact I did know the Christmas Story, because Esther had told it to me and said she hoped to play Mary, the Mother of Jesus. When she was told it was not to be, she was quite tearful. As I do have an excellent memory, I expected to be bored by James's retelling of it. But James was magnificent. He did not just tell the story, he also presented each character with a distinct voice and demeanour and began by astonishing us with a tremendous athletic leap into the centre of our circle. Holding the corners of a white sheet behind his back with raised hands outstretched, he announced he was the Archangel Gabriel sent by God with a special message to Mary, who is to be the Mother of God. Then, speaking for her, James astounded us with the softest, gentlest of voices. His brilliant acting knew no bounds. With the skill of a juggler he threw three gold circlets in the air and, as they landed neatly on his head, proclaimed himself, in turn, to be each of the Three Kings from the East, bearing gifts of Gold, Frankincense and Myrrh.

We were transported by the exuberance of his telling and, as I watched, he changed before my very eyes. Gone was the dark, ugly, wild young man, in his place stood a mischievous satyr full of joy and religious fervour. I looked about me. There was delight on every face.

James ended his narration with another athletic leap to depict the angel directing the Magi to return to their countries by another route without reporting to Herod. A delighted Dr Rivers rose and led the applause. When it died down, Sister Agnes struck a chord on her harmonium. 'We will now all sing,' she said, 'the Christmas Carol we know best: "Away in a Manger"; after that Father Jacob will lead us down to the river, where there will be a special picnic lunch for all of us to feast together.'

By the river bank we formed a queue and collected our picnic lunches, which was a sandwich of two large *puris* with a spicy potato filling, each wrapped in a banana leaf. These we took and sat down amid rocks and dry sandy mounds and waited for Father Jacob to say Grace before we could start eating. He stood, eyes shut and hands folded under the bright, warm afternoon sky. 'For what we are about to receive, may the Lord make us truly thankful.' Then James and the cook came round serving sweet lime juice in earthen cups. Later Luke and another boy, whose name I always forget, came round pushing a wheelbarrow to collect the waste and rubbish. We ended our picnic by gathering around Sister Agnes, who said a prayer, after which we thanked James with a triple "hip, hip, hurrah".

THREE

The next day, at the end of the breakfast break, Dr Rivers took me back to his bungalow, where, on the rush carpeted floor, we sat down facing each other.

'You know, Michael', he said, 'your father and I were friends for nine years. And, when he was working in Pultanpur, we met at least once a week. I miss him.' Dr Rivers turned away with a sigh and after a short pause added: 'There's much I'd like to tell you about your father, but you are too young and what he and I talked about was very grown up.'

'What was he like?'

Dr Rivers smiled. 'Yes, Michael, you remind me of your father,' he said intuitively.

'I can't remember him…Was he tall, like me? Was he like my uncles Ganesh, Ramoo, or was he like my grandfather?'

'I've never met your uncles or your *Daada*. I did see your uncle Ganesh on that day at Baroli Station. He was quite far away. But, I feel sure your father was not like him.'

'Guptaji said my father was handsome, like an actor who could play a god.'

'Yes, he was, and a wonderful man, in every way…good-looking, wise, thoughtful, kind… and why your mother could not live without him. He could have played Jesus. People quite forget that Jesus was an Asian.'

'Jesus was born in Bethlehem in Judea.'

'Yes, and Judea is in Asia, the continent of Asia. Your father was a good friend and he was a great help to me. I hoped one day he would work with me, here in this Mission. Wouldn't that have been wonderful?'

'I will help you. I can work for you,' I said fervently.

Dr Rivers looked at me with a strange, joyless smile; and in that look of sadness lay revealed an element of clairvoyance; for in times ahead, despite all my good intentions, I would fail him.

'Well,' he said, 'begin by making friends with the boys. They keep away…I mean, they don't mix with you. I know it's not your fault, they're more to blame. But they are from poor peasant families and they know you're a Brahmin. That you had a privileged childhood.'

'What does that mean?'

'Well, that you had a nicer childhood; less painful, less hardships… Some of those boys had little to eat. But, I'm glad you seem to get on well with James.'

'I like James.'

'Good. Try to make new friends. Luke's a nice boy. There's also his brother, Noel. It may be easier to start with Noel.'

'Father why, why Noel?'

'Noel and Luke are from Goa and don't know about caste. Noel's older than Luke. Luke looks up to him. But there's no rush. It must be something you want to do. Friendship should come naturally.'

'I want to help. Sir, I would like to help you.'

'That, Michael, is why you are here, why I am talking to you. Your father greatly helped the Mission by getting Nawab Ali Baig to be my friend. Do you know what a Nawab is?'

I nodded. 'A rich man?'

Dr Rivers gave a short laugh. 'Yes, indeed. Nawab Ali Baig lives in a big house in Pultanpur, with his only son Sorab.'

'Sorab? That's the boy I saw here. Guptaji told me his name.'

'Yes, I know. Sorab is about your age.'

'Why does he live alone? The Nawab. *Daada* told me that Nawabs have lots of servants.'

'Of course, Mr Ali Baig has a lot of servants. He also has a house in Bombay. And when he goes there, sometimes he stays there. Stays for two or three weeks; and he can't always take his son Sorab with him. He does not like leaving Sorab alone in the house. Sorab's mother died soon after he was born. So your father told the Nawab that Sorab could spend time here at the Mission. And spend time usefully, learning English and that a servant could bring Sorab here and take him back. But the Nawab is a good Muslim. He wants Sorab to be a good Muslim and plans to send him to the best Muslim School, which is in Aligarh, when Sorab is twelve, two years from now.' Dr Rivers then went on to explain that my father told Nawab Baig of the good work done by the Mission for orphans and the poor; and that Allah—Muslims call God Allah—that God will bless him if he helped to support the Mission in its good works. And in return Sorab will get an education. 'Your father also knew the Nawab was afraid we may try to make Sorab a Christian and…yes, Michael?'

'Sir, why do…Sir, does everyone have to be Christian?'

'It is what I pray for. That is the only answer I can give. It is why I am here. I'm a Christian missionary. Not a good one, but it is my job. I believe I have found the one true religion. So I must tell the world about it. One day, I hope, everyone will find Christ. It may take a long time for that day to come… Michael, why are you frowning like that? Michael?'

'Why you say you are no good? Sir, everyone say you are too, too good.'

'Some people, the people I work for, think I am not good enough.'

'I know why.'

'You know why? How can you know why?'

'I know why some people say that. Gupta, James…they say because you believe many people are good, even if not Christian.'

'Good Lord! Hush…no more of this. We are here to talk about you. How you are going to help.' Dr Rivers caught the leg of the chair he was leaning against and stood up. 'I can't sit like this for long. Come, walk with me to the bench outside.'

It was the bench where Esther was sitting when she first spoke to me. Thinking of her, as I sat down next to Dr Rivers, once again that peculiar and inexplicable thrill stirred within me.

'Now, Michael, where was I? Yes! Your father also knew the Nawab would worry about his son mixing with the boys… You know, Michael, what is sad about this wonderful country? That people, even those who don't believe in "caste", also keep away from low caste people. So, lower castes remain poor and uneducated. Any hope of helping them to live happier, healthier lives has to come from good and kind people. People who want to help them.'

'But Sorab comes here. I have seen him.'

'Yes, but not with the boys… I am not happy to give Sorab special treatment, but the Nawab's been good to us. He's been a great help. The plates in the dining hall were given by him. The cloth for the boys' uniforms comes from his Bombay Cotton Mill. Sister Agnes and Rosie…'

'Rosie? Esther's ayah?'

'Goodness! Michael, Gupta is right when he said you are all eyes, ears and nose.' Dr Rivers pinched my nose and I laughed.

'Sir, what does that mean?'

'Well, for eyes it means someone who does not miss anything; for ears, someone who listens with great curiosity; and nose… no, that's not Gupta, that's me. In English we say "nosey", which is not a good thing for grown-ups to be. It's all right as a child…"nosey" children learn fast. But now, we must get on. Sorab has seen you and told his father he would like you to be his friend. I too would like you to be his friend, because I think, that way you could help the Mission. His father knows about you and has agreed. I know you wouldn't mind being Sorab's friend.'

'I'll be his friend, yes sir, I will, if you want.'

'Thank you, Michael. You will be going to Sorab's house in Pultanpur. I will have to trust you to be a good boy.'

'I promise, I will be good.'

'And promise you won't ever think of running away.'

'I promise.'

'Good. One of the Nawab's servants will take you there and bring you back in Mr Baig's very grand tonga. You see, you are a lucky boy.'

Dr Rivers stood up; a little dazed, I did too. 'There is one other promise I want you to make. A promise not to do something.' Dr Rivers paused to study me closely. 'This will be a hard test for you. I know the sort of man the Nawab is. He and Sorab may give you things, things that as a boy you may like to keep. You may even wonder why you should refuse to take them. But I want you to say "no", or rather "no thank you". They may insist and leave you no choice but to take their gifts. That's when I want you to be good and hand them over to Walid Khan or to Mr Gupta. They will keep them in the office storeroom. The Mission will find a good use for them and I have to say this, because Michael, the boys here have accepted your good luck, but I don't want them to see you with nice things that they cannot have.'

And so began my friendship with Sorab Ali Baig. But our first meeting was not as I expected at Rosie Almeida's quarters. Instead, one morning, exactly a week after our talk, Dr Rivers led me to the Mission gates where Walid Khan took me by the hand to a waiting, brightly painted tonga drawn by a well-groomed horse with a green and red feathered pompom on its halter and little brass bells fixed along its reins. The tonga driver, a tall, thin man, pointed to a space next to him on the driver's seat. I climbed up and noted his white skull cap with its fine lace border. He had no moustache, but the ginger of his crinkly, henna-dyed beard contrasted sharply against his dark, polished brown skin and large, very black eyes. He did not speak, took me in with a brief glance, turned away, cracked the reins and the horse lunged forward.

It took thirty minutes at a good trotting pace before our hard-packed, earth road, went past a cluster of grass-roofed, mud brick huts, sheltering amid a grove of *neem* and *banyan* trees. As we turned a corner, I saw a small, plain domed mosque encircled by neat brick-built houses. The tonga driver pointed with his leather crop beyond the mosque. There within a large walled enclosure was a grand sprawling mansion. Architecturally the mansion and the mosque had the identical features common with seventeenth century Islamic pillars and arches. We drove past the mosque and drew alongside a flight of stone steps that led up to a long veranda of scalloped arches. From each of these hung light-green bamboo blinds, half drawn up to let in the air while giving some shelter from the hot, dry afternoon sun; and waiting at the bottom of the steps was a tall, black-bearded man wearing a fez. He lifted me off the tonga and led me by the hand up the steps. Inside the veranda I had to remove my shoes and wear a pair of loose canvas slippers he gave me. They were hard to keep on but I did not draw attention to that fact. I shuffled along behind him through a large, dark room and into a smaller one. Here, from an open window, daylight streamed on to a multi-coloured, Persian carpet and a rich brocade covered divan. On that divan, sitting with legs crossed, I recognised the boy Sorab. He was wearing a pillbox cap of green velvet with gold sequined designs. He sprang off the divan as I entered the room.

'My name is Sorab. You are Mike. Rosie told me your name.' He waved a hand to dismiss the fez wearing retainer, who escorted me, saying: *'Doh Rus Malai lao.'* Then he put his hand out. 'It is how, Rosie says, English people, welcome friends. Handshaking.' He spoke with a slight lisp, in a slow sing-song way, but his English was more fluent than mine.

I looked down at his hand and hesitated. If he was my age he was much smaller than me. I smiled. He grasped my hand with both his and shook it warmly. 'Come,' he said, 'sit on divan with me. Then we will have *Rus Malai.*'

'What is that?'

'You don't know, *Rus Malai.* Arrey, you will like it, milky, sweet *Rus Malai* with *badam.* You know *badam.* Yes? Almonds.' He turned away and raising his voice called out: 'Yusuf!'

A shuffling sound came from a dark corner of the room as a young man with oily black hair, combed flat over his forehead appeared. He had a shaven upper lip and a neat black beard.

'Yusuf, *woh buksa lao.'* And I wondered what was in the box Yusuf was told to bring.

Yusuf left and I asked, immediately regretting asking, if Yusuf was a member of the family.

'What! No, no!' Sorab burst into giggles. 'Yusuf, my servant, he is getting my box of toys. *Buksa* means box. We will play game, building houses, here on floor. Come sit, sit.'

We had barely sat down on the diwan when another servant entered carrying a tray with two silver bowls. He went up to the rosewood table next to us. Sorab waited for the bowls to be placed on the table, then sprang up and stood behind a green-cushioned chair. He pointed to the chair opposite him. 'Come, first we eating *Rus Malai*. Sit, sit.'

I sat down and glanced back at the retreating servant. He was a stout, elderly man with a full white beard and skin of light olive complexion. Sorab watched me. 'He is *khitmutgar*.'

'Khit...What's that?'

'That means...' After a pause Sorab shrugged, 'oh, another servant. He serves food.'

'You have many servants?'

'Six. No, Seven. *Tonga-wallah* makes seven.'

'And all have beards.'

'Yes. My father has beard. I will have beard. One day. Now eat.'

I picked up the silver teaspoon and copied the way Sorab ate the *Rus Malai*. It was delicious. 'It is like cold, juicy *burf-ee*,' I said excitedly.

'Yes. *Burfi*. Do you want *burfi* or *gulab jamon*?'

I shook my head vigorously. 'No, thank you,' I said, remembering Father Jacob's caution.

While we ate Yusuf brought a large leather box and placed it on the carpet. With an excited squeak Sorab left the table and dashed to it leaving much of his *Rus Malai* behind. As I finished mine, I stared at his bowl wistfully, before joining him. 'Come, come,' he called out impatiently. 'Hurry, in one hour you must go back.'

Together we fished out of the box, another box, with its collection of small wooden pieces of various shapes and sizes. Some had pictures of bricks and windows stuck on them, others were shaped like pillars and semi-circular arches. A set of flat, thin rectangular pieces with tiles carved on them and painted red, Sorab put to one side. 'Those are for roof,' he said, 'they go on last.'

I nodded and picked up the printed leaflet, which had four house-design illustrations. Sorab waved it aside. 'No need for that,' he said impatiently.

He had a clear idea of what he wanted to do, and turning very proprietorial, snatched at any piece I picked up. So I let him play solo and I watched, as he, unaware of his selfish behaviour, busied himself with intense concentration. But he soon tired and sat back disappointed.

'There Michael,' he said, as with a careless hand he knocked down what he had made. 'One day I will build real houses; grand houses.'

When it was time to leave, he came down the steps with me. The tonga driver helped me on to the driving seat. 'Why you sit there?' Sorab said. 'Sit inside tonga, sit in the back.' He then spoke in Hindustani to the driver, who appeared to ignore him. Sorab threw his hands up in a fit of pique.

'You know Michael, Gulab,' he pointed to the driver, 'that is Gulab. You can't talk to Gulab. He is deaf and dumb.'

I thought I heard Gulab growl angrily.

'But he does what papaji says.' Sorab stared at Gulab, arms akimbo. 'Oh, Michael, wait, you don't have hat. Take mine.' Sorab threw his velvet hat at me, which Gulab caught and passed on to me. Again I was put in the embarrassing position of having to decline keeping the hat. By happy chance I was able to demonstrate it was too small for me. A disappointed Sorab took it back. 'I tell papaji to get you one, new one.'

We started to move. I looked back to see a rather downcast look on Sorab's face. I waved, but he appeared not to have seen it as he sullenly walked up the steps. We turned the corner and the mansion disappeared, as if by magic. A moment later Gulab reined in the horse to stop the tonga. I looked at him. He pointed to a dust-devil, which came from behind the Mosque, whirring rapidly across the road in a cloud of dust and flying leaves. Somewhere in the distance I heard a dog bark.

Subsequent visits to Sorab's house, which he kept reminding me was called a *haveli*, followed much the same pattern. During the third visit I asked if he would be coming sometime again to the Mission to be with Rosie Almeida. He shook his head. 'No. I am tired of Rosie.' That left me speechless, but when Dr Rivers asked how the day went, I mentioned it to him.

'That's not strictly the case,' Rivers said. 'It is more to do with his father. Rosie is a sweet old lady but, despite my warnings, some of the stories she told Sorab worried his father. Well, there you are. Rosie is Rosie. She is a Christian. She can only be what she is...'

FOUR

*A*ll the boys in the Mission, without exception, were convinced that good etiquette and polite speech was Dr Rivers's chief concern. There was, he stressed, no occasion simply to say "Yes" and "No". Always, it had to be "yes, please" or "no, thank you!" And his own politeness was an example to us all. He never talked down to us and his free, open manner made it easy for us to approach him. His answers were open and honest, even to questions that were challenging or a trifle awkward. And so, when he questioned us it never occurred to any of us to hold back on anything. He always asked about my time spent with Sorab and it never occurred to me to hold back anything…well, not till the time of my fourth visit to the *Haveli*.

The afternoons spent with Sorab routinely began with some sweet snack we ate together, but on this fourth visit, the dish before me needed explaining, and by chance this explanation gave me an insight into Sorab's religious background. The dish was a bowl of saffron vermicelli, red and yellow in colour, with generous sprinklings of desiccated coconut, almonds and raisins. It was exquisite and, Sorab told me, the traditional dish for the Muslim festival of Id. There were, he said two Id festivals. This was the less important one. When I asked why, he stared at me blankly, then, waved his hands brusquely. 'Don't ask why,' he said, 'just eat.' I later discovered that his impatience was because the Id festival was celebrated the day before and for the first time that he could remember, in his father's absence.

After the snack we sat on the carpet with a square box between us. The cardboard box had a pretty picture, which Sorab said was of a lake in Scotland. On hearing that, my heart beat wildly. I recalled Scotland was where my father was last before he died. Unconsciously I reached out to touch the box.

'No, Michael, wait!' Sorab shouted. 'Sit and watch. This is jigsaw puzzle. Papaji got for me, from special English bookshop, in Bombay. This is new. Don't touch. You watch.'

I sat back, took a deep breath to keep calm, reminding myself that for the delicious snacks alone, it was worth eschewing his irritating, selfish conduct. It also struck me that Dr Rivers must have guessed that at Sorab's house such treats would helpfully boost my diet. So I folded my arms, looked on, as he opened the box and stared at its contents. Then he looked up. I did too. We were startled by the unexpected and silent appearance of Yusuf. With a brief nod and a cold look at Sorab, Yusuf picked the box up and took it to the rosewood table.

'Oh, yes!' Sorab leapt up. 'Papaji wants to see the jigsaw on that table. He is coming here tomorrow. Come, Michael, come to table. Sorry I shout. You I like. You my *dost*, my friend.'

We were back where a moment ago we had had our snack. The table had been cleared and wiped clean. Sorab spread the contents of the box and held up the cover. 'Look, see this, this lake picture. Let me make first. Make by fitting pieces together.'

The lake picture included a steamboat with a yellow and black funnel. I had never seen a jigsaw puzzle, let alone done one, but while Sorab struggled to make sense of it, I almost at once began to see where many of the pieces could easily slot in. There were not many pieces, about a hundred, not more, and I found it hard to resist telling Sorab what to do.

'*Bus, bus*, Michael, no talking.'

I sighed with sheer frustration, slid back in my chair and looked away. Yusuf caught my eye and made a deprecating gesture with his hands. Some minutes later, with a cry of despair, Sorab pushed the pieces away from him, got up and left the room, closely followed by Yusuf.

I waited awhile. The house was silent. I studied the pieces in front of me. Slowly, without much difficulty I completed the puzzle. The silence now made me uneasy. I got up and tiptoed nearer in the direction Sorab had gone. I heard voices. At first it was hard to make out what was being said, though clearly Yusuf was drawing attention to Sorab's misconduct, for a moment later I clearly heard Yusuf say, in Hindustani, that he would make a report to the Nawab *sa'ab* if Sorab did not return at once to attend to his guest. There followed a reluctant grunt and sounds of footsteps coming towards me. Fearing that the completed puzzle would annoy Sorab, I moved towards the table but, before I could get to it, Sorab had caught up with me and I felt his hand squeeze mine. Then, seeing the completed puzzle, he dropped my hand sharply and his eyes widened. Just when I thought he was about to break into a tantrum, his face broke into a wide, happy smile.

'Ah, Michael, you so clever! I told papaji, I knew you be clever. But I wanted to do it.'

'We could start again,' I said quickly. 'We could do it together.'

'No, leave it,' he said in Marathi, to my surprise. Then in English, 'what we do now? Come, I show house. Many rooms. See also my toys and books. Some books I gave Rosie.'

We went into that large dark room, which had intrigued me on my first visit to the *Haveli*. It still intrigued me. I asked about it and why was it empty except for that throne-like chair? Sorab shrugged but, speaking in Marathi, Yusuf said it was the Durbar Room, where the elders of the community and the Mullah of the Mosque meet with the Nawab Sahib. 'They come twice every year to discuss problems.'

It was a pleasant sensation to walk barefoot across the cool marble floor, and as I got used to the dim light, I saw that the grand chair had a silver frame and its plush cushion upholstery was a dark red velvet. Some distance behind this chair was a door, which Yusuf led us to and opened. We entered a small bright room with net curtains and an open dome-shaped window, bordered with three rows of little gold and blue mosaic tiles. The room was unfurnished apart from a red and green Persian rug in the centre of the floor. 'Prayer mat,' Yusuf said as he guided us away from it.

'Yes,' said Sorab, 'this is where papaji say prayers.'

'That window facing Mecca,' Yusuf said, adding in English, 'Muslims pray five times a day.'

I was surprised not by what Yusuf said but by the fact he spoke in English. I nudged Sorab and whispered my surprise to him.

'Only little. His father is that old man. Our *khitmutgar*. Before, they work in Agra school.'

Yusuf rolled his head with pride and stroked his trim black beard. We then turned right into another room with a big four-poster bed. At the foot of the bed was a small rope-strung cot with a soft mattress and white sheets. 'This where I sleep,' said Sorab. 'And look,' he pointed up to the ceiling. Overhead, hanging from the ceiling, was a long wooden beam with brass rings along its whole length. Hooked to the rings was a heavy brown fabric which, Yusuf said, was the fan or *punkah*.

When we left the room we were out on the veranda again. Some distance away by a well and behind a tamarind tree was another building. It was a smaller version of the *Haveli* but though the arches were similar in look and style, they had heavy green screens reaching right down to the floor and the whole building was cube-shaped. A movement caught my attention. Standing by the well was a woman robed all in black. She studied us briefly then quickly covered her face and rushed indoors. Soon after, a rustle of secret movements behind the blinds, accompanied by feminine laughter could be heard.

With a firm gesture and a calm 'now going inside" Yusuf ushered us back into the bedroom.

'Whose house...?' I began and checked myself as I caught sight of Yusuf directing at Sorab a warning shake of his head.

'Come Michael,' Sorab took my hand, 'one more room to see, my books and toys.' And he led me behind the large four-poster bed to a small door, which I had failed to notice when we first entered the room. He stood and waited outside the door; looked at me and asked. 'You want *pani*? *Gulab sherbet* drink?' I nodded and he turned to Yusuf. Yusuf bowed, left us and immediately I wondered about the strange relationship between boy and servant. It was one which seemed to switch from abject respect to gentle reprimand.

We entered a little room with a low ceiling. The daylight from the square window was just enough to look around. I recognised the leather box that contained the building blocks that we, or rather Sorab, played with on my first visit. Opposite the window was a small three-tiered shelf with enough books for a classroom to share. Next to it was a table with a pile of flat cardboard boxes. Sorab went to it, chose a box and opened it. 'Michael,' he said, 'we can play a game of snakes and ladders? Nice game. Just luck. Anyone can win. You know, lucky winning?'

'Yes. And I know that game. I played with my *Daada*. Why you say... you said Snakes? We called it *saap aur seedhi*.'

'Same thing. In English...snakes and ladders. So, you know? Show me, how you play,'

I opened the box. Of course, it was different. This had bright, colourful pictures of snakes and ladders printed on a board that folded in half, while my grandfather's game was on a printed cloth; and we played with large cowrie shells for tokens and a white, marble cube dice with black spots. I searched the box and found four different colour disks but no dice. 'Sorab, we can't play without dice.'

We searched again, in vain. He shrugged, stared at me; and in the way he looked I detected fear. Then without warning he put his arms round me and gave me a tight hug. My immediate reaction was to free myself, but he clung on. 'Oh, my friend, Michael,' he said. And I knew he was about to say something that had nothing to do with the board game. 'You my friend? Yes? Say no, *aur* yes?'

'Yes,' I said, a little alarmed.

'Michael, I worry. You telling papaji what you saw. Keep secret, the woman you saw.'

'But I never see your father.'

'You will, next time. He wants to meet you.'

I freed myself and held him by the shoulders. 'I won't tell anyone. But will Yusuf?'

'Yusuf say many things to me. But never telling father. Yusuf and I have many secrets.'

'Sorab, who was that woman?'

'No one. My aunty.'

'But there were more women in that house.'

'I don't know. I am not to go to there, that house. My father, he go, when here, alone.'

Before I left the *Haveli* that afternoon, Yusuf traced my feet on two separate pieces of white paper. When I asked what he was doing and why, he said, 'Nawab sahib orders'.

Dr Rivers guessed I was holding back something from him, but not for long. After a splutter I blurted out the incident of the woman at the well and about Sorab's fears.

'I listen to a lot of stories, Michael. I don't talk about them.'

'But you said Sorab has no mother. That she died when Sorab born?'

'That's the truth. But he could have an aunt. There must be other members of the Nawab's family. And Michael, Nawab Ali Baig is a Mussalman. Mussalmans can have more than one wife. Some Nawabs, even Hindu ones, can have two, three or more. So, now, forget about the whole thing. Gossip never helps.'

'Gossip?'

'Telling stories about the lives of other people.'

Next week I was disappointed when the tonga did not arrive to collect me. It came the week after and on this occasion Gulab, the mute tonga driver, was not driving it. Instead, I saw Sorab sitting next to a handsome, well-dressed man with a neat grey beard and moustache. He greeted me with a broad smile. 'Hello, young man. Come on up, sit next to Sorab.'

Dr Rivers dropped my hand and bent forward to touch his forehead in a Mughal salutation; and from that gesture I guessed that the distinguished man sitting next to Sorab could be none other than his father the Nawab. Also, this was no tonga. It was a carriage with four wheels and they were sitting on a low leather upholstered bench with steps that made it easy for me to climb up by myself. As I did so, the Nawab sprang down and gave Dr Rivers a double embrace.

'What is your father doing?' I asked Sorab.

'I tell later,' he giggled. 'I gave you handshake English way. This Muslim way.'

'But Father Rivers is not Muslim, he is...'

'I respect him like a friend and brother,' interrupted the Nawab, having overheard me, and climbed back on to his seat. Then he took up the reins, waved farewell to Dr Rivers and set off towards Pultanpur.

'This is not like tonga,' I whispered to Sorab, looking up and admiring the oblong umbrella that protected us from the sun. 'It is nice. Not so bumpy.'

The Nawab laughed. 'So, you're Michael, the good-looking, clever lad I hear much about.' He reached across and offered his hand. I took it after a slight hesitation and remembering the respect I was taught to give elders, by my mother and Father Rivers, I bowed deeply. But I was quite awed by the Nawab, not only because he was smartly dressed in a fawn-coloured, English suit, which I was seeing for the first time, but also because I did not expect him to sound so very unlike an Indian. Later I was to discover that he had spent five years of his boyhood in England and was educated in an English College for Indian princes in Lahore.

'I hope, Michael, Sorab has been treating you well.'

'Yes, sir,' I said, at last gaining confidence and finding my voice.

'Good,' he said and then spoke rapidly, making it hard for me to follow him. I did not know what to say but, fortunately, the Nawab appeared not to expect an answer, for when I looked up at him he was gazing straight ahead. I turned to Sorab and whispered. 'Where is Gulab?'

'Gulab is tonga driver. This is buggy. Big buggy. Papaji only drive it.'

I glanced back at the Nawab and saw him looking at my feet. 'Ah, yes!' he said, stopping the buggy. 'I almost forgot.' He reached under his seat and took out a large cardboard box. 'Now, Michael, this is for you. Two pairs of shoes...no, don't worry. Last week Dr Rivers and I talked about it. It's all right by him. These will fit you. Yusuf measured your feet. Try them on.'

I opened the box and saw a pair of brown, canvas shoes and a black pair of leather sandals. At a glance I knew the canvas pair would fit perfectly. But the sandals fascinated me. I studied them carefully. They had two broad strips of shiny, black leather, which overlapped at the front and then tapered to a pair of narrow straps, each with a fastening brass buckle.

'Those are called *pathani chuppals*,' said the Nawab. 'Put them on. Sorab, show him how.' Then, a little impatient with Sorab's fumbling, he looped the reins round the metal bar in front of him, dismounted, came round to my side, drew the narrow back straps behind my heels and buckled them at the ankles. 'There you are! Wear these when you are at the *Haveli*. Dr Rivers is right. They won't do at the Mission. But the canvas ones, plimsolls we call them, take those back with you. Or you can put them on now and get rid of your old ones. No, not here! Put them in the box for now.'

Then it dawned on me, as to why, early this morning, Father Rivers rehearsed me to speak up and say thank you in Urdu. '*Shukri...*,' I began, but seeing the puzzled expression on the Nawab's face, I changed to: 'Thank you, sir, thank you very much.'

'Don't mention it, my boy, don't mention it.'

I was about to add something complimentary about the shoes when my attention was drawn by Sorab's disgruntled moan as he sank his head on his chest. To my astonishment, the Nawab pulled him up roughly and smacked him swiftly and hard on the back of his head. 'Stop this at once, stupid boy!'

I was appalled, although I was used to seeing parents scolding and hitting children, but my time at the Mission had set all that behind me. Of course, as Gupta had assured me, the fact that we boys of St Thomas's are not corporally punished was entirely due to the kind of people Dr Jacob Rivers and his wife Agnes were.

We were on the move again. Now the atmosphere was tense and the silence, broken only by suppressed whimpers of the terrified Sorab, was awkward. Fortunately it was not long before we arrived at the steps of the *Haveli*, to be greeted by pandemonium. People running around in all directions, while, coming down the steps were Yusuf, his portly father and Gulab, *salaaming* and gesturing with great ceremony and deference... and then, a most moving scene of father and son in a tender, reconciling embrace.

'There, there! My son! I'm sorry, dear boy,' the Nawab said and signed me to stay seated.

I watched him bend down to kiss Sorab and hand him over to Yusuf. Then he raised both hands above his shoulders to acknowledge the greetings of the small gathering of folk seemingly arriving from nowhere. Then he turned, climbed up on to the carriage and sat next me.

'Don't get me wrong,' he said. 'I love that boy dearly, but at times he can be difficult.' He must have realised I found it hard to keep up with his rapid-fire English for now he spoke with deliberate clarity and a mix of some Marathi and Hindi words. 'Sorab has been spoiled,' he went on. 'He gets far too much attention. But I'm more to blame for that.' He looked at me long and hard and I noted his eyes were a peculiar kind of grey, almost wolf-like. 'That is why I asked Dr Rivers to find me a sensible boy of Sorab's age to be his friend...so, young Michael, I want you to do a good job for me. I want you to help Sorab. You don't have to do much. Just be your sober, sensible self. Will you do that for me?'

I nodded. 'But I...'

'Go on, don't be afraid.' He jiggled the reins and the horse ambled on at a steady pace.

'But, I am Michael, a Christian. I thought you don't...'

'Yes, but it's all right. You are not going to talk about Christianity to Sorab, are you?'

'I can't.'

'Well, there you are, a truly sensible young man who knows his limits.'

While I tried to work out what he meant, I had nothing to say. So I smiled and gazed at his handsome, patrician profile.

'And,' he added, 'that is why I expect you to be a good example to Sorab. You come from a good Brahmin family.' He turned to look at me and caught my look of admiration briefly and looked away.

I tried hard to say something and with an illogical leap asked: 'Do you know Gupta?'

'Yes,' he answered with a slight frown, 'like you, a Hindu but, of course, no longer.'

I nodded. 'He believes in Buddha.'

'I know Gupta well. A good man, interested in all religions...' he looked at me. 'And what about you, are you interested in religion; and in what people believe?'

I shook my head.

'But you don't mind being a Christian; and having an English name like Michael?'

I shrugged my shoulders.

He smiled. 'A natural philosopher... Tell me, what do you like about Christianity?'

'I like the stories. Sister Agnes... James and Father Jacob too, they tell good stories. And, also, I like face of Jesus. Like my mother's.'

The Nawab chuckled and stared ahead.

'And Father Rivers is good teacher,' I continued in full flow, 'and Sister Agnes also. She says good prayers.'

'Well, my boy, you should be thinking about toys and books and learning. All that is much more important than prayers.'

'Sir, but you pray lots...five times. Yusuf say.'

The Nawab threw his head back and laughed. 'Yusuf is right. We are Muslim. Our life and our world is our religion. Our religion is called Islam. Islam means "submission to God". So, like slaves we must be obedient to God.'

'Where are we going?' I suddenly asked.

'Have you seen Pultanpur?'

'No. But my father worked there. He also was like Gupta, a Munshi.'

'I know. I knew your father.' He stopped the buggy under a banyan tree. 'Well, here we are. That is Pultanpur.' He used the handle of his horse whip to point. 'Look! There!'

I gaped. In front of me was a wide open gateway with a large, white pole resting across two low pillars. Standing next to each pillar were men in khaki uniform. They stood rock still, legs apart and holding what I imagine soldiers would hold, some kind of gun. But what caught and held my attention was the hard, compacted, smooth, grey, road that ran through an avenue of evenly spaced, lush *neem* trees. The bottom half of every tree trunk was painted white, which defined the road and contrasted it from the green swathes of trimmed lawns on either side of the road. Behind these green lawns were neat, brick bungalows with tiled roofs. Each bungalow had a small fenced-in, neat garden with a variety of flowers. My eyes followed the road through the heat haze, where some distance away was the entrance to a palatial building, two stories high, with a terraced roof, at the centre of which was a green dome. Flying high in front of the dome was some sort of flag of many colours, fluttering in the breeze.

'What is that?' I asked. 'That flag. Or is it a kite.'

'No, not a kite. You were right the first time. It's a flag. It is called the Union Jack' which is the great flag of the British. Do you see those two white soldiers in khaki, standing nearest to us, in front of that gate? They are Englishmen.'

'Yes! And,' I asked, to confirm what I had already half guessed, 'what are those pointy things the soldiers are holding?'

'They are holding rifles, guns. And those sharp pointy things are called bayonets.'

'Guns for shooting, for killing?'

'Yes. They don't shoot if they know you; and not, unless you do something bad or foolish. Even then they will warn you first. That is, before they shoot. Anyway, see how neat and swept clean the place is? Now, look at the road behind you.'

I looked and made a face.

'We have a lot to learn from the British, Michael.'

'My *Daada*, he does not like British…'

'Some Hindus and Muslims talk like that. But many more are glad the British are here.'

'Do you like…?'

'Yes. Your father also liked the British. It is the English I like. That is my honest answer.'

'British, English, same?'

'People mixed them up. English is a language but also people. And more British people are English. English come from England. You must like them too? Dr Rivers and Sister Agnes, they are English.'

'I only know them. They are kind...more kind than my *Daada*.'

'People with romantic ideas...do you know romantic? Never mind. But, having the British here has been good for us. They have given us roads, railways, schools, hospitals, clean water; and taught us how to keep clean and healthy. See for yourself; Pultanpur looks neat and clean.'

We started to move towards the soldiers. As we drew near, they stamped their feet together and raised their rifles. I looked at the Nawab a little alarmed. 'Will they shoot?'

He laughed as the soldiers struck their rifles and presented them in a salute. A third soldier came out from the sentry box and raised the pole, smartly saluting as we went past.

'They know me, Michael,' the Nawab said, as he acknowledged the salute by raising his whip handle against his forehead. 'Give them a wave.'

I did and turned round to see the pole go down again. The Nawab tapped my knee. 'I have to see the Station Commander. Jack Lockhart, Colonel Jack Lockhart, that's his name. You stay seated here, I'll be back soon. Bill is coming over to the *haveli*.'

'Will he sit here? Next to you?'

'Not enough room. He will come, as he always does, riding on *Chameli*, his chestnut horse. Now, when we get back, you play with Sorab. Yusuf will take you to the veranda at the back of the *Haveli* where there is enough room for Sorab to ride his tricycle.'

'Nurse Tolly has a tricycle.'

'That is a big one for a lady. This is for boys. Yusuf will make sure you get a turn to ride it. You will enjoy that.'

'Will I see Bill Lo...this commander?'

'Not today. This is a meeting for important men... making important plans for the future.'

'Gupta said, there are schools and churches...and, and a hospital at Pultanpur.'

'This part is where the military barracks are. This is where the soldiers live. But when I get back I will take you round Pultanpur and show you all the places Gupta told you and more.'

FIVE

*I*n the four weeks following that trip to Pultanpur, the frequency of my visits to the *Haveli* more than doubled and always the Nawab was there. Having sought my help in Sorab's reformation, Yusuf told me he had decided to forgo his business trips to Bombay till our combined efforts towards the education of Sorab proved fruitful.

'Michael,' the Nawab said, 'don't for one moment tolerate any selfish display or tantrum from Sorab. Say something about how such behaviour will make people dislike him. Don't be harsh, as I know you won't be. I know in time and with patience you will succeed. You will make him see what fun it is to have a friend and also to be friendly. After all, when I pressed him to choose a friend, he picked you. That is half the battle won.'

When the Nawab told me this at our second meeting, I was astonished and wondered how he could expect me, a year or so older than his son, to take on such a responsibility. Surely he was in a position to employ elders and more professional help. But he read my thoughts.

'You see, Michael, I am surrounded by people who fear me and afraid that a complaint from Sorab would anger me. Well, I am happy to keep it that way because in my position it's useful for people to fear me. One day you'll understand there are good reasons to keep it that way. As for servants! No, I can't allow any servant of mine to have power over Sorab. Yesterday Yusuf tried and I immediately threatened to dismiss him. You see, one day Sorab will succeed me as Nawab. Servants must know their place. Must know who is his master and his better.'

'Because they are poor,' I asked with slight tremor. 'I am a poor.'

'This has nothing to do with money. You are high-caste Brahmin. And though as a Muslim and believer in the one God, Allah, I cannot respect the Hindu way of thinking, you are now a Christian. The God of Christians and Muslims is from the One Book. Do you know of the Book I mean? Have you heard of the Koran?'

I vaguely remembered hearing that word. But I could not think from whom. Was it *Daada,* or Gupta, or Dr Rivers? I shook my head.

'The Koran is our Holy Book. The Bible and our Koran have the same beginnings.'

And so, with his encouragement and taking a prompt from Esther's manual I took my role of tutor seriously and, indeed, found Sorab a willing student, a change I set down to the fact that he noted the way his father regarded me.

…And then, as I began to believe there was in me a maturity beyond my years and hope in a new promise of contentment, my world crashed and fell about me in ruins…

It began with a peculiar series of events following the sudden disappearance of James on the morning of the day Bishop Robinson was due to visit the Mission. Early that morning I woke to the agitated cries of boys grouped by my bed. I recognised the brothers Luke and Noel, behind them three other boys, sullen in the shadows of the dormitory. Luke, unable to contain himself, shook me and pointed to where James ought to have been. 'He's gone! Gone! James is gone. I've looked! He's nowhere to be found.'

I sprang out of bed. 'Quiet! Luke, stop shouting.' I spoke firmly.

'But I tell you James has gone! And he is not coming back!'

'He can't leave the Mission! The chowkidar would have stopped him. Is that not so?'

Noel shook his head. 'No Michael, he does not have to go through the Gates. James will follow the river and cross it beyond the farm. He would have left in the middle of the night.'

I was sitting on the edge of my cot looking up at Noel. He intrigued me. Three years older, taller and lighter in complexion than Luke, the boys were proof of what James told me, that they were half-brothers. Their mother, a Rajput woman, served in a British household and Noel's father, an Englishman, stayed as a guest of that family. Sadly, the pregnancy when discovered resulted in her dismissal and she returned to her village, where some years later she died giving birth to her second child, Luke. No one knows or will ever know who Luke's father was. And now Noel intrigued me for another reason. Always a quiet boy, I was hearing his voice for the first time. It was deep and peculiarly musical.

'James will be back,' I said. 'Where can he go?'

The pale rays of morning light streamed through the windows casting monstrous shadows into which I peered only to realise all twenty-four boys were up, huddled together, their stunned wide-eyed faces directed at

Noel. 'Where can he go?' I repeated to no one in particular, as fear like a contagion stalked the air.

'Who will look after us?' whined a high pitched voice.

'Is that little Simon?' asked Noel. He thought for a moment. 'I suppose it will be me. Go, now, all of you, go wash and get dressed. Then we will go out and stand outside.'

'Outside?' The boys chorused. 'Where outside?'

'Outside the bungalow, the house of Dr Rivers.'

'It is raining,' I said. 'It has been raining for some time.' Then before any remark or move could be made there was a loud and urgent knocking on the dormitory door.

'It's too early to be the cook with tea and biscuits,' said Noel. 'Michael, see who it is.'

I did. It was Father Jacob and Sister Agnes standing under a large dripping umbrella. They entered carrying between them a large clothes basket containing the white robes for the brothers Noel and Luke and the two other Confirmation postulants. At noon, every Tuesday and Friday, these past six weeks, Sister Agnes had been preparing them for confirmation. But now she had bad news. The Service of Confirmation, she told them, had been postponed.

'But why?' cried Luke on the verge of tears.

'The Bishop has his reasons,' sighed Father Jacob. His face looked strained. 'Luke, it is not something to cry about. And boys, we know about James. We won't talk about him now. You will be told about James at the right time.' He took a deep breath and looked at us sadly. 'I am sorry. There is one other thing to say. The Bishop won't be staying with us in our bungalow, as some of you know he did in the past few years.'

'Nevertheless, Noel,' said Sister Agnes, 'the Bishop will be visiting the Mission, so I would still want all four of you to be ready in your white robes, in case the Bishop changes his mind.'

'Where will the Bishop Robinson stay?' I asked.

'He will stay in Pultanpur with his old friend Major Forbes,' said Dr Rivers.

'I saw him,' piped Little Simon, 'from that window. He was in a big tonga.'

'And when was that?'

'This morning.'

'And what were you doing, up so early?'

'Sorry sir, but I couldn't sleep.'

'Anyway, Simon, that won't be the Bishop. The Bishop is a good horseman. He goes about riding a horse. The gentleman you saw in the tonga is a priest. All of you will see more of him'

'Sir, I think I also saw a horse,' said a voice that no one recognised or cared to inquire about.

'Good,' said Sister Agnes. 'Now boys, I want you to wash, dress and since James is not here, Noel, take them to the dining hall, where you'll get your tea and biscuits. The rain has stopped.'

'After that, Michael,' Father Rivers said, 'I'd like you to take a note to Mr Gupta.'

During the English lesson Dr Rivers gave me the note, and as he did so he held my hand and detained me for a moment. 'Michael,' he said, looking searchingly into my eyes, 'don't miss this opportunity to make your peace with Mr Gupta. You hurt that good man's feelings. You may never again get another chance to do it.'

I found Gupta in his office almost invisible behind a heap of ledgers, the scratching of pen on paper being the only sound audible in the room. I coughed. The startled Gupta sat back.

'Goodness!' he cried, 'what a shock you gave me, Michael. Now, what is it?'

'I have this note for you.'

He opened the envelope and removed the note, read it, put it back in the envelope, took it out and read it again. Then he took a deep sigh and solemnly shook his head. 'I suppose Dr Rivers wants my answer?'

I nodded.

'There's almost nothing to say. So, no point writing note... I have one simple answer. I think you will be able to convey it to Padre sahib. I want you to say: "It is too late. Gupta has sent his resignation letter two days ago." Just that. Will you remember?'

I repeated his answer verbatim.

He looked at me and gave a wry smile. 'Always the bright lad. I knew you can do it.'

I turned to go, stopped and drew closer to him.

He looked at me. 'Is there something more to say?'

I knelt beside his chair, took his skeletal hand in mine, and begged him to forgive me.

He chuckled. 'I already have done so,' he said, 'but was too proud to tell you; and for my sin of "Pride" I ask your forgiveness. Come, now, stand up. We Brahmins are a proud lot. You'll know what I mean when I say we find it hard to climb down. However, by being the first, you've put me to shame.'

'No Guptaji, I waited too long. And Guptaji, what do you mean by resigna...?'

'I am giving up my job. I won't be Munshi, here, anymore.'

'I thought that was what you meant. But why, I know Dr Rivers needs you...he likes you.'

He looked at me steadily for some time before speaking. 'Michael, I have always been very open and honest with you. From the first day you came here. So now I'll confide in you again, but you must make no mention of what I say to anyone. I have resigned because Padre Rivers and Sister Agnes have been transferred. They have been told to go by the end of this month. Less than four weeks from today. They go, then also I must go. I cannot, won't work, for any other Christian sahib.'

'Why are they leaving? Why must they go?'

'I fear for the future, for the school and the boys. Life won't be the same for...why are they leaving, you ask? Is that what you ask... because their bosses do not like the way they have been managing the Mission.'

'Is it the bishop who... Is that why there is no Confirmation Service?'

'No. He is only messenger, bringing the bad news. It is Mission bosses who decide. Did I not tell you that other Mission Schools are not like this one? They want Indians to be Christian but also to respect their rulers. Did I not say what a good man Padre sahib is? He respects all Indians. He wants them to be as good as white man, and one day rule their own country. And why he, Sister, yes and even little Esther...slowly, surely, teach boys English and how to be like gentlemen...eating at table...all sort of things that make them as good as... but the bosses say that is not their job... oh, and that Padre sahib is not doing his job of making more Christians. They say this Mission has room for more boys... forty, fifty. That boys should sleep on floor, sit on floor, eat simple food, wear cheap uniform and... no picnics, no treats or teaching to be... *Arrey*, why you shaking?'

'If you and Father Jacob go, what will happen to me? Will going to *the Haveli* stop?'

'Many good things stop for the boys. But you are lucky. The gods are kind to you. Rivers sahib and Memsahib and Esther will go by train to Calcutta. And Rosie Almeida and you will also go with them. He told his bosses, told Bishop Robinson that you are son of his friend.'

I could not hide my excitement. 'But Esther!' I exclaimed. 'She is not here!'

'She will come. Next four, five days.'

'And you?'

'I have to work for another month.'

'Why?'

'That is called giving notice time. I have to hand over all books and show *hissab*, that means all accounts. Money matters. Go now, I have work to do.'

I turned to hide my face.

'What is this? No reason for sadness. No cause for tears. Lord Ganesh, sorry, I should say Lord Jesus, has been kind to you. Have I not said you are lucky?'

'I am sad for you.'

'No need for that. In any case I had just a few years left. I am getting old. I have money and only myself to care for. I shall leave here and travel to Gaya and live with the monks of my Lord Buddha. It will be the perfect way to end my days.'

'What about Father Jacob and Sister Agnes...and...'

'I don't yet know where they'll go after Calcutta, but I know they will put you into a Christian College in Calcutta.' He looked at me with a bemused smile. 'So, what a strange state of affairs! You, a Brahmin boy, of the highest Hindu priestly caste! You will be in the biggest, most British of cities; Capital of the Raj.' He sighed. 'If the fates are kind to us, we may meet again. Gaya is not far from Calcutta. But most difficult to get to.'

'Yes, Guptaji, someday we will meet again. I promise.'

He shook his head solemnly. 'Michael, it will be many years before you are able to travel on your own, and although I know the College address, I shall not trouble you by writing letters.'

'But, why not?'

'The young forget.'

'I promise I won't forget. Why will I forget?'

'The fates have willed it so. And life is as life will be.'

'But, Guptaji, Dr Rivers says we are masters of our fate. It is up to us.'

'Bravely spoken...but the gods gamble, play games with our lives. Life itself is a game, and as you will be on the threshold of building a new life, the past will get left behind. Hindus accept Fate, but the Christian lives his life with faith and hope.'

'What is threshold?'

'Never mind. Now run along and give my message to Padre sahib.'

'I will look into the dictionary. I have learnt how to. The Nawab gave me the book. It has a picture of Queen Victoria. Yes, on the first page.'

'Do that, but first give Padre sahib my message. And, on leaving this office, you will cross the threshold of that door.' He giggled. 'Yes, look in the dictionary. Good exercise. Seldom a day goes by without me opening my dictionary. Moreover, it teaches you how to pronounce words.'

I left the office, resolved to look up the words "seldom" and "moreover" and "threshold".

SIX

*B*ishop Cyril Robinson did not take the Confirmation service but after celebrating Evensong he agreed to have supper with us. He was a big man and his round, florid face sharply contrasted with his full head of white hair. His bushy dark brows and deep set grey-blue eyes, gave him a forbidding aspect, which was immediately contradicted by the good-humoured, curved corners of his mouth. Over his purple cassock rested a gold chain and cross, which he frequently toyed with as he spoke in a suitably loud voice. Normally, its droning, sacerdotal quality would have sorely tested the gigglers among us, but they managed to contain themselves, as all of us resolved to be at our best behaviour and were determined not to let Dr Rivers down.

It was a special supper of goat pilau, vegetable curry and *Rus Malai* pudding. Noel told me that our cook, Husain, normally starved from showing off his skills, begged Dr Rivers to let him create this menu, assuring him it was the Nawab's idea, and as the supper was not in honour of the Bishop but a farewell feast for the Rivers family, the Nawab was bearing its full expense.

Talk of this feast leaked out while we sipped our mugs of afternoon tea and the fact of it was confirmed by the delicious aromas wafted from the kitchen during Evensong service. The effect was magical. The boys sang the hymns with inspired gusto. I was by now along with the rest of them, a fully-fledged non-vegetarian, the last to give in. But for me, the evening's excitement began with a sight of Esther, sitting with to her father, behind Sister Agnes and her harmonium. Once, during the Service, she gave me a brief wave of her hand and for her pains got a stern look from the Bishop, followed by a nod and a smile.

Before entering the dining-hall, Noel lined us up outside to greet the Bishop and reminded us that if offered his right hand, we will be expected to kiss his large amethyst ring. Fortunately, that did not happen. The Bishop seemed preoccupied with his thoughts and simply blessed us.

Dr Rivers arranged for me to sit next to him at his table leaving the grand, throne-like chair, on the other side of him, for the bishop. I looked for Esther. She was, with her mother, sitting at the other table with their backs towards me. But we had exchanged glances as they entered the hall. I thought she looked pretty, though a little sad.

Having been told not to queue for supper, we sat patiently to be served. For that Husain had recruited Yusuf and three other of the Nawab's retainers to serve at the tables. They stood alert in their smart green and gold tunics and red turbans. At a sign from Dr Rivers, we stood up for grace, which the Bishop boomed across the hall. He then turned to bless the food at the serving tables and came down to join Dr Rivers. Leaning forward from his chair he looked at me. 'Is that the son of your Brahmin friend?' Dr Rivers nodded. 'Well,' continued the Bishop, 'there's no mistaking high caste.'

'Oh dear,' said Dr Rivers under his breath, but there was no stopping the loquacious bishop. His clear voice carried even when he meant to confide and, because of his habit of repeating what Dr Rivers whispered to him before answering, I was able to follow their conversation.

'Did you say Gupta? Your man Gupta, has resigned? No matter. In fact, jolly convenient. I have this Maratha chappie, jolly good accountant, lined up for the job. Saves me some bother; and as for Jungle Jim, that Bhil James, that, dear Jacob, is particularly most convenient. Mission HQ have been unhappy about him for quite some time.' He sighed and began to eat. 'This is great stuff,' he mumbled, paused and studied his fork. 'I say, good cutlery this... far better than what we've got in Brotherhood House.' I quickly gathered he was talking about the cutlery, but I stumbled at the mention of "brotherhood", till I remembered being told that the Bishop was a monk. I also began to sense Dr Rivers's discomfort over the fact that the Bishop could be heard so I looked away and pretended not to be listening.

There followed one of those peculiar silences, which occur with an inexplicable abruptness at such gatherings, when all talk vanishes into thin air and only sounds of intense activity is heard.

'You know, Jacob,' said the Bishop breaking the spell and making everyone start and look at him. 'You know, Jacob,' he repeated, lowering his voice, 'though you did well to cultivate the generosity of your friend, the Nawab, it would have been better to have insisted on cash rather than kind.'

'It wasn't for me to dictate,' whispered Dr Rivers. 'Gifts are best left to the giver's discretion.'

'Gifts best left to the giver?' The Bishop threw his head back and laughed. 'There *are* such things as broad hints. Besides, you don't need tables, forks and plates, here. I see the boys are conducting themselves well, but they should be on the floor. I grant you, it's wise for the Head and his staff to be at a table separated from them. Some distancing is a good thing. Friendly but not familiar is a golden rule. Your concern, here is more for their souls.'

Dr Rivers forced a laugh. '*Mens sana in corpore sano*, Your Grace.'

'A sound mind in a sound body, I grant you that. But you're over doing it. You're teaching them to be brown Englishmen. Giving them the language and thinking...' The Bishop paused. 'Don't you see the dangers of such education?'

'With respect, Your Grace, no! By taking their rightful place alongside us, they will, in time, make useful contributions to the Empire and its Judeo-Christian culture.'

'You are missing out on the dangers. Take that chap, forget his name or where he is, stirring up trouble—a young Indian, and an increasing number of others like him, nearly all educated in Britain. They'll put all that to use against us... why give it to them on a plate.'

'Once, in our own country, we were afraid of universal education. But it's given us the gift of democracy. Soon women will rightly demand universal suffrage. It's progress.'

'Absolutely, I can't argue against that. But good things can be rushed. Things before their time produce disastrous results. Evolution not revolution... one day we'll get kicked out of here. In the longer term that is inevitable. But we don't have to bend over and ask for it. Till then, till that time comes there are benefits to be gained. The Government's right to see it that way. The labourer is worthy of his hire. Christ said that.'

'The British Government's aim for trade and economic recompense are understandable; and I'm full of praise for social reform, but surely the role of a Christian Mission alongside politics is both spiritual and altruistic, towards a building of character, good character, the good life.'

'Nevertheless, my point, of rushing in where angels should fear to tread, holds good. It took a thousand years of our history to achieve any semblance of parliamentary democracy... sorry, I know you'll say, we don't have to rediscover the wheel. That, now we know better. Well, let's leave it there. Thank goodness I was not directly involved in their decision to move you on. I washed my... abstained. I was asked for advice and help on staff and personnel matters, that was all. It's every Bishop's pastoral remit. By the way, I'm glad Miss Tolly is staying on.'

'I'd no problem coaxing her to stay. Her garden, more than anything else, was her incentive. And I also did my best to persuade Gupta to stay on.'

'You're a good man, Jacob. I am truly sorry to see you go…Agnes too.
  rreplaceable.'

 Ir Rivers gave a wry smile and looked straight ahead of him.

'I grant you,' continued the Bishop, 'one of the conundrums our Missionaries face is how to spread Christianity without also spreading Western culture.'

'Indeed!' Dr Rivers answered, 'and why we may as well do a good job of it? There are some practices in India that Christians cannot, must not, tolerate; suttee, the plight of women, and the harsh treatment of widows, especially young widows.'

The Bishop gave a long sigh. 'I suppose, we must, all of us, bow to the inevitable. Though I will say this, apropos nothing, I don't envy your sojourn in the wilds of Assam. God bless you.'

Much of this went over my head. I record here what I was able to piece together from my close, personal knowledge of Dr Rivers's character, and in the light of subsequent events.

Yusuf came up to ask if the Bishop wanted a second helping. Robinson rubbed his ample stomach and threw his hands up. '*Bus, shukria, bahut achcha khana.*'

Yusuf stared at him blankly then retreated.

'Was that not good Hindustani I spoke?'

'Indeed, Your Grace, and I believe he finally got the message. I have the same trouble too. We learn the vocabulary but fall short on the phonetics and intonation.'

'Quite. But don't belittle yourself. I've heard you. You sound like a native. What's this, ah the rice pudding. I see it's served in an earthen bowl. I'm quite full. May I pass?'

'No, Your Grace, make room for this. It's *Rus Malai*. Not our ordinary rice pudding. This has cream, almonds and pistachios, with a touch of saffron. Absolutely delicious!'

At my last visit to the Haveli, Sorab took the news badly. 'You're my best friend, Mike! Stay here with me. Don't go!' We were standing in the front veranda. Sorab had his arms wrapped round me and I could feel their tightening pressure as he spoke. 'Papaji, tell him he must stay.'

'No, *beta*, he can't. Michael has to go to his school. Soon you will go too, but your school is in Aligarh, a Muslim school. Michael's a Christian. His school is in Calcutta, very far from here and also far from Aligarh. But we'll meet again. He will know where to find us.' The Nawab cleared his throat to hide his emotion. 'He is always welcome. You won't forget us, Michael?'

I shook my head and we looked long and hard at each other. I knew he was fond of me and I enjoyed his attentions. And on my part my affection for him brought a lump to my throat, but yet again the world was opening up to me and the thought of new adventure stirred within me an excitement I felt tactful to hide. As the Nawab drew near, Sorab released me and turning away he began to sob. The Nawab gripped my shoulders. 'See, Sorab my boy, how calm Michael is, and sensible? He is not crying.' Then he stood up and gave Sorab a handkerchief. 'Here wipe your face, be like him. Come, it is time. Doctor Rivers is waiting.' He put an arm around each of us and led us down the steps to the waiting tonga and the tall figure of Dr Rivers standing next to it. Before we reached the bottom step Sorab broke into another bout of sobbing forcing the Nawab to call Yusuf to take him indoors. Yusuf's uncanny ability of somehow appearing from nowhere always intrigued me.

The Nawab greeted Dr Rivers and embraced him. I climbed into the tonga, sat down next to Namdeo and watched them. They looked the same height, Dr Rivers possibly an inch taller.

'They're bastards the lot of them,' roared the Nawab, then realising to whom he was speaking slapped his mouth. 'Sorry, Jake, pardon my French. But, what they've done is unforgiveable.'

'Well, whatever I may feel, I couldn't put it so strongly.'

The Nawab laughed. 'You should try, Jake. And I'm sure the Lord will understand and also forgive. Hypocrites, they've betrayed the trust and genius of one of their best men.'

Dr Rivers led him to one side, hopefully, but fortunately for me, still within earshot.

'I'm livid, Jake. Let me say it again. Swearing makes me feel good. Bastards!'

'Look at it from their point of view. Remember, it's hard for some, especially the older Brits to forget the Mutiny. Nawab sahib, you know...'

'Stop there, Jake, its time I insist you called me Hesky. All my friends in England do. There ought to be no formalities between us.'

'I will, when I write, not now. There are people around. But, why Hesky?'

'From Hasan, one of my names on the school register.'

'I see. Is it after one of the Prophet's descendants? But why Hesky?'

'I don't know,' the Nawab grinned. 'Schoolboy parlance, catchy, easy to remember.'

'Anyway, back to what I was saying. You admire the English. You're an Anglophile!'

'Yes, but Jake I'm condemning this stupid lot... I suppose even the English can be stupid.'

'Human, you mean.'

'Inhuman. They've bungled, messed things up, failed to appreciate the good work you and Agnes have done. And there's my own axe to grind. They've ruined my plans, just when things were looking up for Sorab, with young Michael there, a model of exemplary conduct.'

'Never mind. Aligarh will be the making of Sorab.'

'Inshallah. We Nawabs have to be on our toes. We need to ensure our heirs are worthy.'

'Get Sorab to write to Michael. I'll post you the College address.'

'Yes, do that. Although I don't suppose he will, out of sight out of mind, that's my Sorab. He is fortunate to be a rich man's son. By the way, fifty-seven, the Mutiny, you know, some of my forbears were ready to take up arms against the Brits. But for the brilliant Lawrence of Punjab... he won them over, or so I was told... I mustn't keep you. Everything will be ready for tomorrow morning. I'll see you then. I've got a reliable chap to escort you, till you get to Calcutta.'

'You have been kind and generous when you needn't have. We would've managed with the Pultanpur bullock-cart. There is no furniture to carry, just ourselves, our clothes and a bed-roll each. As I've said, it has been extremely thoughtful of you.'

'No question, I had to do this. Bullock-carts are slow, uncomfortable and there's no cover. You would've fried in the heat. Also, I've seen that cart, there's barely room for three, let alone the five of you.'

'Four, Rosie's bowed out. The prospect of a three-day long train journey, after an exhausting bullock-cart one, discouraged her.'

'You're not telling me she is staying on?'

'No, the new management has no place for her. She's decided to go back to Goa. You must have known she's part Portuguese.'

'East Indian, I thought, whatever that is. Calcutta would've suited her. It's also the Eurasian capital. Anyway, let me do this...I want to do this. The covered wagon's there, lying idle, and Gulab has got it ready. Let me at least make sure you've got to Cal.'

'Have I seen this contraption you are talking about?'

'No, haven't used it for ages. It's a box-wagon, a large four-wheeler, the wheels keep it flat, so a little more comfortable than two-wheelers. It's a sort of stagecoach with wooden top and sides. There'll be a cushion or two for the memsahib and Esther. Also it's horse–drawn, sadly just one horse, but you'll make good progress. Gulab, your driver will see that you're fed and have a room for the night, at Jalgaon, before you take the train to Allahabad, where you break journey and then go on to Calcutta.'

'I see you've done this journey…but, of course, your family is from Lucknow, that is…'

'Yes, Lucknow is not far from Allahabad. I have an uncle there, keeps the old palace going.'

'Well, I'm grateful. I don't know how to thank you.'

'Don't try, my pleasure. By the way,' the Nawab directed a slight nod at me, 'you may have a problem there. They may not let him travel in a compartment reserved for white passengers.'

'I'd planned for him to travel with Rosie in the servant's coupe linked with ours. But now I'll put Agnes and Esther in a "ladies only" coupe and personally accompany Michael.'

'You're a good man, Jake. May Allah bless you. Here wear this.' The Nawab held up what looked like a locket. 'This is a silver *tabez*, wear it as a talisman.'

'I have mine,' Dr Rivers held up his plain wooden cross. 'But I'll cherish this. Thank you.'

'Good. Silver to a Muslim is valued above gold in such matters. See, even our wedding rings are silver. Now, tell me. Who is taking over from you?'

'The Reverend Mark Hasting, the Bishop's man. He knows India better than I do. He's been in India longer than I have.'

'Jake, here's one way to thank me. I ask this one big favour of you. Whatever charities I've given, till now, was for the sake of Michael's father and our friendship. No more. Please avoid, if you can, mentioning my name to this new chap. I have decided to draw the line on any future support to a Christian Mission.'

'I can do that with a clear conscience. I don't know the man. I may know something of him but that is all. In any case our paths are unlikely to cross. He arrives a week after tomorrow and we won't be around. But I'll warn Gupta. The poor man's holding fort for another month, by which time the school will see radical changes. I also gather Hastings is arriving with a new batch of nine boys.'

'I see. Good man, Gupta. I'm sure he's doing it for your sakes. He knows, you and Agnes would hate to prolong the agony of departure. Actually, Jake, if this Hastings Johnny arrives a week after you've gone there's no reason for either of us to worry about him contacting me. By the end of next week I will have handed management of the Bombay Mills to my cousin. I am moving to Lahore. I'll give you my Lahore address, when we make our good-byes, tomorrow.'

'Lahore? This is sudden?'

'I've been toying with this idea for quite some time. Eventually Aslam, that's my cousin, will take over this Haveli. He has a family, two boys and three girls. It'll be good for this Haveli to be a family home again.'

'How will you get to Lahore?'

'As in an Arabian romance,' the Nawab laughed, 'a caravan of camels. There's a lot of stuff to take and, of course, palanquins for the women.' The Nawab looked at me. 'I say, do you think the boy heard me?'

'He's all ears, but surprisingly discreet. Gupta treats him like an adult.'

'I can believe that. Now tell me, after you've got him settled at this school or College, what of the future? Your future, I mean.'

'Back to where we first started, in the wilds of Assam's tribal areas.'

'Good Lord, Jake! You're a stickler for punishment. You will take care. Tribal folk can be unpredictable.' The Nawab studied Dr Rivers for a while before he spoke again. 'No, Jake, I'm not thinking about James. I believe he confided in you before he disappeared.'

Dr Rivers nodded.

'Well, it's none of my business to know. But I was wondering about your sister and Esther.'

'Cousin-sister, as Indians say. I was an only child.'

'What about your cousin's school? Is it also linked with your Mission?'

'No. Margaret's school is doing fine. But we couldn't leave Esther there. Assam is too far for comfort. And sadly there's no school for her where we are going.'

'What about in Calcutta?'

'In a year I'm due a long leave. She'll have to miss schooling till we get to England. There's an excellent school for girls in Kent, and Agnes has family there.'

Once again the thought of Esther in England stirred in me a strange feeling of emptiness.

'Couldn't we take the train from Pultanpur,' I asked Dr Rivers on our way back.

He shook his head. 'The train from Pultanpur goes only to Baroli. That would be going in the opposite direction and the line does not link up with the railway to Calcutta, which starts in Bombay. And as we are far from Bombay, we have to catch the train near Nagpur. Why are you frowning? Ah, I know, you are wondering about your father? He was going beyond Baroli to Poona.'

There was much I wanted to ask but reluctant to admit I had been eavesdropping on his and the Nawab's conversation. Also he appeared preoccupied with his own thoughts. A sideways glance from me caught Namdeo's enigmatic smile, which from past knowledge I knew was for no one but his mare, *Chameli*; and as if to confirm that, he clicked his tongue, tossed the reins, leaned forward and patted the animal's bobbing rump affectionately. Namdeo approached all his tasks with single-mindedness. I cannot remember ever having exchanged a word with him.

It was getting dark and a strong, humid wind blew across our path, causing the oilcloth of the tonga-hood to flutter wildly. I looked back to find Father Jacob in tears. He turned away, waved his hands to stem any comment and mumbled almost inaudibly: 'It's the boys I am thinking of, the poor lads, I'll miss them.' He coughed to clear his throat; and taking a deep breath spoke to Namdeo in Hindi: 'Looks like the monsoon will be early this year.' Namdeo grunted.

We alighted by the main gates. Walid Khan came up to say the boys were having afternoon tea and biscuits. Dr Rivers reminded Namdeo not to forget to collect Mr Das Gupta before six tomorrow morning. He then put an arm round my shoulder and we walked together down the kapok avenue towards his bungalow.

'Do you want me to join the boys for tea?' I asked tentatively.

'No, Michael, now that they know you are leaving with us tomorrow, it is wiser for you not to have to face them. We'll join Sister Agnes for tea and whatever she has to go with it. I'm afraid we've run out of biscuits.' As we entered the bungalow compound, Father Rivers led me to the bench under the jujube tree. 'Now, Michael,' he said as he sat down with me, 'a word before we go in. I've arranged with Rosie for you to sleep at her place tonight, after chapel, when we will have said farewell...' He leaned forward and covered his face with his hands. 'Dear, Lord, this is hard to bear!' He broke down, groaned, shivered and wept. I stared for a helpless moment, then wrapped my arms round his waist but could think of nothing to say. He freed himself and stood up. 'I wish I could take all of them and not just you...but this is how it has to be.'

'Thank you Sir,' I said breathlessly.

'It is the only way I can repay your father's love and friendship. I made a solemn promise to take good care of you.'

'Sir, I know. Mr Gupta said he will do his best to get Noel and Luke into St Peter's.'

'St Peter's Pultanpur? He told you that? I hope he succeeds. But don't talk about it.'

I shook my head and placed my forefinger against my lips. Dr Rivers laughed. 'Come,' he said, 'let's go in. You must be hungry. Ah, there's Rosie with a mug of tea for you and a plate of something. Ah, I remember now,

I had forgotten, she promised to produce some *oppers* for all of us... you're in luck. The *oppers*, as she calls them, are rice and coconut pancakes. I've had them before. Quite delicious. Hello Rosie, this is kind of you. And Michael, Rosie has found you bedding for tonight.'

'Thank you, Miss Rosie,' I said.

'Bless you darling.' Rosie said, pinched my cheeks and laughed, making her large soft body ripple. She handed me the mug and plate. 'Here, sit down on these steps.' Then turning to Dr Rivers, she added: 'You know Father, I've also managed to find a canvas hold-all. Michael can pack the bedding and his clothes in it. I'll help him.'

'Thank you Rosie. Now, tell me, have you had news from your nephew in Goa?'

'Yes, thank you. But it will take him a month or more to get to Pultanpur.'

'Pultanpur? Why Pultanpur?'

'It's easier for him to get to Pultanpur from Goa. In the meantime I'll be helping Miss Tolly at the Military Hospital there. She has arranged a job there for me and a small payment.'

'That will be useful. I've always said, behind Miss Tolly's grim exterior is a heart of gold.'

Rosie raised her arms and slapped her thighs. 'Oh, Father,' she said, choking to control another fit of laughter. 'If only you knew how much she scared me the first time I met her.'

Dr Rivers turned to greet his wife.

'Dearest,' she said, 'Rosie would like to come with us in the morning. We could drop her at Pultanpur before we move on.'

'But we won't be going into Pultanpur. At least not all the way there. Never mind, Namdeo can take her in the tonga.'

'Thank you Agnes and Doctor sahib,' said Rosie, 'I'm all packed and ready. And thank you both for all the years we have been together. I will miss Esther.'

'I know she'll miss you,' said Sister Agnes, 'as we will too. Jacob dear, there's a pot of tea in the kitchen, help yourself. And Rosie, tell Esther to get back here, she's at your place.'

'I will when we get there. Come Michael.'

Rosie and I went through the kitchen, where I left my empty mug and plate, and out into the herbal garden, past the Mission godown, but before we could enter Rosie's hutment, Esther came rushing out and almost crashed into me. 'Oh, Michael, isn't it wonderful!' She squeaked. 'Tomorrow we set out. It's exciting. My aunt Maggie gave me a book, which I will read to you during the long journey. It's *David Copperfield.*'

'But Esther dear,' wheezed Rosie, 'that is much too hard for Michael.'
'No, Rosie, this is the school version, it's shorter and...and Michael is
a clever boy.'

That evening, before the atmosphere in the chapel promised to be
funereal, Dr Rivers broke the tension by jovially announcing there will be
jelabies served after dinner and, as they are best eaten hot, the evening's
Service would be a short one. 'No hymns or prayers,' he added, 'just a
brief Bible reading and a few words of advice.' Then, with the help of
Sister Agnes, he drew the low wooden bench to face the boys and sitting
between her and Esther read, in Marathi, slowly, the opening verses from
Chapter Fourteen of St John's Gospel. 'Now,' he handed the Bible to Esther
to hold, 'I want you to listen to a story I was told, when I was a boy like
you, a story from my country, England. England is an island surrounded
by seas. But there can be storms at sea, and though the English are good
sailors, a storm can put their lives in danger. Those lives need to be rescued.
So we have Lifeguards. Brave people, who go out in special boats to save
people from drowning. One day, a boy asked his Lifeguard father if next
time he could go with him in his boat. His father agreed. Well, one dark,
stormy day, a boat was in trouble and sailors cried for help, but when the
boy heard the storm and saw the huge waves crashing against the shore
and making the boat pitch and toss dangerously, he was afraid. "Do we
have go?" he asked his father. "Yes", his father answered, "we have to go."
"But,' said his son, 'if we go, we may not be able to come back!" "We don't
have to come back," replied his father, "but we have to go." So, my friends,
we have to go. Good-byes are painful but they are very much a part of life.
Life is a journey and we, you and I must face that journey through all the
changing scenes of life.
'I was not born here. This is not my country. I was born in England.
But here I am. As a child I loved my mother and believed we would be
together forever. That was not to be. We, all of us, know parents and friends
who are no longer with us...Time brings changes. You won't be the same.
You will grow into men with jobs to do and duties to perform and work for
the sake of others. We cannot look back. We must gather strength to face
the world. So be strong and make your lives beautiful...There is no good
reason to waste time in sadness or regret. Jesus tells us to have courage
because He is always with us.'
Dr Rivers stood up. As he did so, starting from the back of the chapel,
there arose a stir and an uproar that took all of us by surprise. Secretly,
Das Gupta, Walid Khan, Namdeo, Husain, Rosie and even Miss Tolly
had gathered outside the Chapel quietly waiting for Dr Rivers to end his

talk. When he did they entered, cheering and clapping and telling all of us to stand up and join in. Then Rosie, raising her strong voice sang: 'For he's a Jolly Good Fellow, For he's a Jolly Good Fellow... For He's a jolly good fellelooo... And so say all of us.' Gupta joined in, as did Husain. I was astonished that both of them knew the words.

At eleven the next morning, we set out. Dr Rivers was the last to leave the bungalow wearing his clerical collar, khaki bush shirt and shorts, knee length woollen grey socks, strong brown shoes and a solar topi. Waiting outside for him was Esther and Sister Agnes, both in white, full-length, loose fitting dresses, and wide brimmed straw hats. The Mission staff and some of their family gathered at the Main Gate, many holding garlands of marigolds. Conscious of their caste status, the sweeper, Biku, his wife and ten-year-old daughter, stood some distance, apart from the rest. The girl held a bouquet of red roses. After a brief hesitation, Esther ran up to collect it. More garlands were presented by people I had never seen before and by the time we got to the gates Dr Rivers and Sister Agnes were almost smothered by them.

Outside the gates, with its driver Gulab, patiently standing by two Afghani horses, was a large covered, four-wheeled wagon. Earlier Walid Khan, Namdeo and Husain had loaded our bed–rolls and suitcases in the hold immediately below the driver's high bench. Behind this hold was the larger compartment for passengers. It had a thick Persian rug and four fat cushions. Gulab tactfully signalled me to climb up and sit next to him while Sister Agnes and Esther got in at the back. Before joining them, Dr Rivers folded his hands in farewell amid hand clapping and loud cheers as we set off at a dignified pace towards Pultanpur. Moments later Namdeo's tonga came alongside and then overtook us. His chestnut mare Chameli looked a good deal livelier than it did yesterday. As it went past I saw Rosie sitting regally between her tin-trunk and bulging bed-roll. I waved but her eyes were shut.

When we arrived at the steps of the *Haveli*, we were told to wait for the Nawab to join us. Dr Rivers got out to stretch his legs and inspected the wagon. 'You know, Michael,' he said looking up at me, 'you won't find another like this in India. It's a copy of an American post carrier and possibly the result of the Nawab's short stay in California.'

'Indeed,' interrupted the Nawab as he joined us. 'I sketched a wagon I saw in Sacramento, some years ago, and got my team of carpenters to build one of teakwood and iron. And now that a rail network is criss-crossing India, I have also applied for the privilege of having my own railway carriage. Pity, it's not ready, or you could have had the use of it.'

Dr Rivers laughed. 'You have more money than you know what to do with.'

'That's what happens when there's an accumulation of wealth over generations. We began with land and property and the brassware trade. Now we have cloth mills in Bombay, Calcutta and soon a new one in Lahore. I don't feel too guilty about it. We do employ grateful workers.'

'And you have done much charitable good work. Your generosity has won you the gratitude, prayers and blessings of strangers.'

'Yes, well, say no more. But now dear friend, kindly introduce me to the only member of your family I've not had the privilege of meeting. This must be Esther.'

'Yes,' said Esther with a wide smile as she walked up to hold her father's hand.

'How charming,' said the Nawab, 'pretty and I gather wise beyond her years. But time is of the essence. If you have to get to Jalgaon before dark I mustn't hold you back. So, before I say Godspeed on your journey, meet your guardian.' He turned round and called: 'Sher Ali!'

A towering figure in black shirt and trousers and carrying a huge brass-banded musket, came forward from behind the wagon. He wore a grey turban, Afghan style, with its long tail resting on his right shoulder. His beard was wild, as were the unruly locks of hair that stuck out from under his turban, giving him, true to his name, a leonine look. '*Huzoor!*' he said, as he gave the Nawab a smart military salute and struck the butt of his weapon.

'There's really no need for all this,' protested Dr Rivers.

'Wrong, Jake. Part of your journey is through dacoit country. This man and his *jezail* gun will protect you from them. Mind you I'm not sure that works, but just the look of it would deter anyone. Besides, I'm not happy with your plan to travel with Michael and leave Esther and Agnes by themselves. It's dangerous to leave women without male escort. Sher Ali will travel with Michael in the servants' coupe and make sure that your compartment is next or as near to theirs as possible. He has orders to see you get to Calcutta safe and sound.'

'That is all we will need. Thank you. I won't pretend it takes a weight off my mind. What will Sher Ali do after we get to Calcutta?'

'He takes up his post as chowkidar at the Rashid Cotton Mills. That's his reward for taking care of you. He's a good man, loyal and reliable.'

'Thank you. I also note you have provided us a pair of horses.'

'Yes, Jake, I'm glad I've been able to do that. A brace is less exhausting for the single horse, and it would also be speedier. By the way, Farouk will drive you instead of Gulab. Gulab is a deaf mute. Farouk speaks and understands English and Hindustani too. That's him, up there, in the driver's seat.'

I had witnessed the exchange. And now Farouk greeted us with a wide smile and a roll of his large, fez-covered head. '*Salaam, memsahiba,*' he said, and I turned to see Sister Agnes standing next to Esther and her husband. She acknowledged Farouk's salutation with a friendly wave of her hand, then turned to thank the Nawab profusely for all his generosity over the years.

The embarrassed Nawab spread his hands and shook his head. 'Well, now dear friends,' he said, his voice a little hoarse, 'there's nothing left but to bid you Godspeed. May Allah protect you... I hate farewells...' He swung round to hide his face and rushed up the steps of the *Haveli.*

Dr Rivers watched him with compressed lips, while Esther walked back with her mother to the rear of the wagon. Then he turned to me. 'It's a pity Sorab was not here. No doubt there was a good reason for his absence. He can be a difficult child. I do hope Aligarh will make all the difference and that he will eventually be a blessing and a worthy heir to his father.'

I said nothing. With a slight nod I climbed up to sit next to Farouk. At close quarters, his dark, aquiline face, reminded me of Sister Agnes's illustration of "Egyptian" for the letter 'E'. At that moment Sher Ali joined us and sat on the other side of Farouk, his brass-banded jezail held upright between his knees. 'Now,' sighed Dr Rivers, 'we can be certain of reaching Calcutta.'

About an hour later, we heard a knock on the roof of the wagon and Dr Rivers asked Farouk to stop. He alighted and told him this was where he was meeting a friend. 'Please wait here, I won't be long.' Then he asked me to join him. Together we walked up a steep goat track till we reached the top of a low grassy mound. There we waited. I looked back. Sher Ali had followed us, keeping watch from a distance. 'What are we doing?' I asked.

'You'll see,' Doctor Rivers pointed to three thatched covered mud huts in a hollow. Then he took out a silver whistle and blew on it three times. A man in a strange flame-red tunic, armed with a long bow across his chest and a dagger in his black waist band, came out from one of the huts. He waved with both hands and ran towards us, shedding his bow on the way. Dr Rivers opened his arms in welcome and stepped forward. But the man stopped short and knelt down to touch the Doctor's feet.

'No, James, no,' said Dr Rivers, 'we are friends.' They embraced.

'Forgive me Father, but I had to.'

'James, there is nothing to say and nothing to forgive. I'm sorry we can't stay long. We are, as you know, on a journey and I have come to say goodbye. Esther and Sister send their prayers and blessings. Michael here is with us. He will be at Christian College in Calcutta. Yes, the very same College where we, Sister and I, first saw you sitting by the College Gates.'

'And Father, you! Where will you and Sister go?'

'Back where I started, in the hills of Assam. Next year we will take Esther back to England, to a school in England. Michael is here to bid you farewell.'

James turned to me. I could not move. I froze, astonished by his appearance. His face and hair were covered with some sort of ash and there were red marks on his forehead and *kohl* on his eyelids. But he approached me with the friendliest of smiles. I took both his hands in mine. 'Hello Mike,' he said, and I simply stared, taking in his strange costume.

'James, this is for you,' said Dr Rivers, handing him a pocket-size *Book of Common Prayer.* 'Goodbye my friend, God bless you and keep you! When once again you wish to turn to Christ, He will welcome you. His arms are ever open. Till then he understands why you left. Come, now Michael. We must not keep Farouk waiting.'

As we walked back, Dr Rivers said: 'You see, Michael, how easy it is for people to get hurt.'

I did not quite understand what he meant by that. 'James looked different,' I said, 'I couldn't recognise him.'

'He has gone back to his people.'

'Sir, why did he have to leave?'

'Because he knew I was leaving and... well, he felt he would be unhappy.'

'But, he knew the story of Jesus.'

'That, I hope, will stay with him forever.'

'Gupta said he was a Bhil from here. But you met him in Calcutta.'

'That's right. James was an orphan with Pastor Erikson, a missionary from Sweden--that's another Christian country. Erikson worked with the Bhils in Sholapur—not far from here. He took care of James and when he left India, he got James a job in the College, in Calcutta. That is where we, Sister and I saw him...Hush now, no more questions.'

We were back at the wagon and I started to climb up to join Farouk. 'No, Michael,' said Dr Rivers, 'you sit at the back with us. Esther wants to read to you.'

The covered wagon had four square openings, two on each side, with canvas flaps fixed on the outside to protect the inside of the coach from dust and flying debris. By lifting the flap one could glimpse the landscape, as Esther often did, greeting the changing scenes with squeaks of delight. 'Esther,' her father said, 'soon you'll see a stark change in the scenery.'

'Why, daddy? Have you and mummy been here before?'

'No,' said Sister Agnes, 'but we've been in the Nagpur area, and as we get near to it this rocky countryside will get more lush.'

'Esther,' said her father, 'now, why don't you sit back and read to yourself so as not to disturb mummy. She's resting. Your mother didn't get much sleep last night.'

'She can read to Michael. That won't disturb me.' And turning away Agnes shut her eyes.

It was late evening and almost dark when we arrived in Jalgaon, exhausted. Farouk drove up a gravel-packed, laburnum drive and stopped in front of a grey building. It was a large bungalow with a veranda of Mughal arches. Farouk sprang off his driver's seat, lost his fez to a strong gust of wind and chased to retrieve it. He signalled us to wait and rang the brass hand bell, which was on a stool in front of the main door. A moment later three young men ran out of the building and carried our luggage inside. He then left Sher Ali to keep guard by the horses and took us through a room, which had furniture under dust covers, and on to a bedroom containing a large double-bed. Farouk said he would arrange to have an extra cot next to the bed for Esther and that bedding and mosquito nets would also be provided. He then opened a side door, pointed to a large bathroom with a water tap and a brass bucket beneath it and said: 'Wait sahib, young man bringing towels.'

The Rivers were left to freshen up after being told that dinner would be served within the hour, while Farouk led me to the back of the house where there were two widely separated outhouses. One was the kitchen, because framed within its doorway was, I assumed, the cook. He was all in white and smiling smugly, till he saw Dr Rivers, who had followed us, and salaamed politely. The other outhouse was the lavatory with four cubicles and doors assuring privacy. In front of the kitchen, against the back wall of the house, a stone stairway led up to its flat-roof terrace.

Farouk, obviously familiar with the geography of the house, invited us up to the terrace and pointed to a charpoy on which my bed-roll rested. I glanced from Dr Rivers to Farouk with trepidation. 'Alone?' I asked. He shook his head. He had been speaking to us in Hindustani but switching to English said: 'I also sleeping there, but no charpoy for me.' Flashing a proud smile at Dr Rivers he added: 'I sleep hard floor and only one blanket.'

Dr Rivers asked about shelter from the elements, this being the season of monsoon. Farouk, astounded by Father Jacob's fluent Urdu, was speechless for a moment. Then he pointed to the far end of the terrace.

In the failing light we had missed the tent-like structure. '*Shamiana* tent is there,' he said. 'We go there if raining.' He picked up a hurricane lantern, lit it and placed it at the top of the stairs.

'It is cooler, more refreshing, to sleep under the stars,' Dr Rivers said with a nod. 'You'll get a good night's sleep, Michael.'

Dinner was laid out on a long table in the room adjacent to the Rivers bedroom. Farouk said I could eat in the kitchen but Father Jacob would not hear of it. 'Michael is my friend's son. He will eat with us.' I sat next to Esther opposite her parents and noted she was less bubbly in front of them. It didn't matter as I was myself a little depressed. During our three-hour journey to get here, Esther read to me, two rather dramatic instalments, from *David Copperfield,* and had got to the sad part in the book where David's mother dies in the arms of Peggotty. It evoked tragic memories of my own mother's sad death and a sense of being alone in my bereavement.

Two of the young men, who had earlier carried our luggage, entered with white china plates and cutlery, followed on by the cook bearing a steaming tureen of lamb *biryani* and a bowl of plain yoghurt and placed them on the table. A moment later he was back with a plate of sliced onions and tomatoes in a fresh lime and green coriander dressing.

'Oh, Jake!' Sister Agnes exclaimed excitedly. 'This is a feast!'

'Indeed, it is. Thank you…what shall I call you?'

'Ronny, all people call me Ronny. I cook for many English. My name Rumi, so they call me Ronny. But Madam, this nothing… you come to Nawab sahib's dinner parties. So many dishes preparing…taking three days… twenty, thirty people come…two kinds *biryani*, roast chickens, hot naans, pickles, two three pudding… sorry no pudding today, I no…' he stopped midsentence as Dr Rivers waved his hands.

Agnes stood up, collected the four plates and began to serve. Ronny briefly stayed to watch. 'This hotel food,' he said. 'I, Ronny cook better.' Shaking his head ruefully, he left the room.

Sister Agnes came round the table and put my dinner before me. 'Michael, it'll be all right to eat with your fingers.' I looked up at her, then at Dr Rivers. 'No,' I said, and picking up a fork waited till they did the same. Esther giggled and started to eat. I copied her actions to a chorus of praise, and there and then resolved never again to let my unhappy past affect my emotions.

SEVEN

The train journey from Jalgaon took a whole day and a night. We arrived at Allahabad early in the morning to be told by the stationmaster that our train to Calcutta wouldn't be ready to leave till after eleven that night. Sher Ali told him that we were friends of Nawab Hasan Ali Baig and that he was our escort. This news had a remarkable effect on the stationmaster.

'I am Denis Hay, Stationmaster. It is an honour to be of service to friends of the Nawab.'

Dr Rivers introduced each of us and asked how a stationmaster in Allahabad happened to know Nawab Ali Baig.

'Gawd, mun,' said the stationmaster, betraying the fact he was Eurasian, 'the Nawab is from Lucknow, an ancient family known all over the United Provinces. His family goes back to the days of Clive and the Battle of Plassey. His ancestors fought the British, yeah mun. But Brits gave them a good thrashing, mun.' He paused as he regarded the implacable face of Dr Rivers. He could see that Dr Rivers was not impressed and changed tack. 'But I must now see to your comfort. Please follow me to the First Class Rest Room. This way, please.'

'Just one moment, Mr Hay,' said Dr Rivers. 'Agnes, since we have many hours to kill, why don't we visit the town centre.'

'Yes, let's do that. And find a light breakfast. If we stick together it should be safe.'

'Safe, Madam! Allahabad is safe. Big town with many English people. Some famous ones.'

'Yes, Mr Hay, and I assume some famous Indian ones, too.'

'Indeed, Madam, but you must visit Holy Trinity Church and go to the *sangam*, that is where the two rivers meet… pardon me but I cannot help noting the coincidence. The Rivers, to see the rivers meet.'

'Indeed,' said Sister Agnes and Dr Rivers laughed helpfully.

'Don't miss it mun. The Jumuna flowing into the Ganges before your very eyes. The waters looking different in colour. Then there is the Old

Fort... Excuse me, but is the young man well? He is a very quiet fellow. What is he, sixteen seventeen?'

Dr Rivers laughed aloud. 'No, Michael is thirteen. Don't worry about Michael. One day he will outshine us all. But now I'm concerned about our luggage. The porter, I mean coolie, he has left it on the platform. There it is, you can see Sher Ali keeping guard over it.'

'Have no fear, sir. It will all be taken care of. I will personally supervise its safe-keeping and transfer it to your train compartment tonight. Sher Ali tells me that the boy will be travelling with him. Well, I'll see that they will be in a carriage next to you.'

'Thank you Mr Hay, I'm grateful for your help.'

'Don't mention. Glad to be of help. See that sign over the big green door, that's First Class Waiting Room. All your stuff will be there. And that door at the end of the platform, that's my office. I'll be there till your train leaves tonight. Any problems, any arrangement for meals etc... please don't hesitate. We have Station Restaurant serving English style meals, but now too early for proper breakfast. But if you will kindly relax in that Waiting Room, I will arrange for waiter to bring you a tray of potted tea and slices of toast, butter and jam. Food in town is dangerous. I mean for health. You know what I mean, tummy upset.'

Mr Hay swung round and marched briskly away. Esther came up to her father. 'He has a funny way of talking,' she said with a nod in the direction of the departing stationmaster.

'India is full of people speaking in strange accents. You should be used to all that by now. You've heard so many... Gupta, Farouk, Sher Ali... Michael.'

'But Michael talks like me, daddy. And sometimes like you.'

Dr Rivers laughed. 'That's because you taught him well. He probably mimics us. Michael is a good mimic. Ah, but here's Sher Ali. I know he will insist on following us to town'

'Sahib, what is programme?'

'Daddy, wait!' Esther cried and running up to her mother, whispered in her ear.

'Joseph,' said Sister Agnes, 'Esther is not well. We'll stay here in the waiting-room.'

'Not well? Oh, that girly business.'

'Daddy!' cried Esther. 'I'm seventeen!'

'Oh, Joseph,' mumbled Sister Agnes. 'You're so dreamy at times. That's way past. Esther, in school, in Tara Hall, your cousin, Maggie, I thought she mentioned it.'

'I'm sorry Esther, I had forgotten.'

'Love you, daddy,' said Esther and blew a kiss.

'But this poses a problem, Agnes. I mean, Sher Ali can't be in two places, unless... Michael you and I can manage without Sher Ali. If we go to town by ourselves, can't we, yes?'

I nodded. 'Yes sir, we can.'

'Then Agnes, it's settled. Incidentally, Michael, I'm intrigued by that cloth satchel you have across your shoulders. What's in it?'

'A shirt, a vest and two books... a dictionary and...'

'It looks familiar, the satchel I mean.'

'Mr Gupta gave it to me and also the other book.'

'What other book?'

'*Tom Brown's School Days.*'

'Goodness! Where on earth did Gupta find that? Anyway, are you enjoying it?'

'Yes,' I said a little doubtfully. 'It is a good story. I don't know some words. The dictionary helps, but some words are not in it. But it is good story.'

'It is a very English book. Ask my help, Michael, don't hesitate.' He smiled and turned to Sher Ali. 'Will you stay here with the ladies? Michael and I, we will go into town.'

'But sahib, my duty also protecting you... that being Nawab sahib's *hokum*... sahib's orders.'

'Don't worry, you are doing your duty. The Stationmaster also will say that. We'll be back for lunch. I would like an Indian vegetarian meal. Tell him, I will settle expenses with him.'

'Sahib, I will see you get good, clean food. And, sahib, in town, don't go to market area.'

'Sher Ali, for your sake I will be careful. Just Allahabad Fort, and the Church.'

Outside the railway station were a few horse-drawn carriages, but a lot more tongas and even rickshaws drawn by barefoot men in loin cloths. They were naked to the waist, their oily, sweaty bodies glistening in the sun. On seeing us, these men called out in a chorus begging to be hired. Speaking flawless Hindi Dr Rivers politely declined but asked if they would be kind enough to give him directions to Allahabad's ancient fort, which one of them rather reluctantly did, and we set out through a crowded, broad street with shops and low brick-built houses on either side.

For the first time in my life I was in a big city, gaping in astonishment at its teeming life and commerce. Nor had I seen such bustling crowds of men and women weaving among the shops displaying such a variety of goods.

Many were draperies, decked out with colourful saris of the finest silk. But the ones that caught my attention were the stalls that sold pots and pans of shiny brass and copper, because next to their wares were artisans, with the tools of their trade, making or repairing them. Spicy aromas of freshly cooked foods drifted in from the myriads of narrow lanes that led from this main street. When we finally reached the fort, it was to be disappointed. The fort was closed to visitors.

'Never mind,' said Dr Rivers, 'we'll walk around it and get to that promontory, that's where the two rivers meet. Do you know what a promontory is?'

'No, sir, but I can guess. 'Is it that bit of land that sticks out?'

'Yes,' said Father Rivers and ruffled my hair. 'By the by, you're not hungry, are you? There was no toast, but good sweet tea, excellent *chapattis* and jam. Did you have a good breakfast?"

I nodded. 'What jam was that?'

'I can't decide whether it was apricot or mango. Anyway, we'll have a good lunch when we get back. A good vegetarian, Indian meal... I've told Sher Ali to tell the Stationmaster he could get it from outside... we are used to it... and we like *puris*, don't we.'

'Yes,' I said and looked up. Dr Rivers seemed to be talking to himself.

When we got to the promontory, it was as the stationmaster said. Where the rivers met, the colour of the waters of one was different from the other. The Jumuna, I thought, was muddier.

'You know, Michael, a third river also meets here, the Saraswati. It is what Hindus believe.'

'I should know that. Grandfather told me about the sacred Ganges and holy Banares... and, and about this place too. Every ten or twelve years Hindus gather here for a big, big, festival.'

'Yes. Come, I would like to see the Church. Then we must get back to the railway station. I can see people staring at us; and they don't look too friendly.'

We walked briskly and half an hour later entered the Church and sat in a pew at the back. Father Jacob put his arms around me. 'From now on, Michael, you must stop calling me "Sir". You are with us, a family member. I want you to be free from feeling you are of any less... how can I put it. I've never been happy with people looking up to me as if I was someone special and they are not. Soon we'll be parted; you in Calcutta, we in the hills of Nagaland, in Assam.' He paused and studied me. 'One day, you will understand why I lost my job at the Mission.' Again he paused but looked away. 'Soon you'll be fourteen and getting wiser. Did you hear Mr Hay? He thought you were much older and...'

'And, then you said something about me. "He will outshine us all". What does that mean?'

'Well here's a word you must look up in your dictionary. Genius, you are a genius, clever... what most people find hard, you'll find easy. Genius is a natural ability to work things out by yourself. But you mustn't let that make you proud.' Again he studied me with a slight quizzical look and when I stared back he burst into laughter.

'What is it, sir? Why are you laughing?'

'Esther told me. Yesterday you said, if we, her parents, are Rivers, then she's a rivulet.'

'She told you that? Sorry, I was only joking. Not being rude. Sorry.'

'No, no, don't be sorry. It made me, laugh... Sister Agnes too. I think it was clever of you.'

Late that night, our party, with coolies carrying our luggage, followed Mr Hay to an isolated part of the station, where a freshly painted, brown wooden compartment stood on a siding.

'Here, padre sahib,' Mr Hay announced, proudly pointing to it. 'Here, see, I've arranged for you a four berth bogie, for you and ladies, and a two berth compartment for Sher Ali and young lad. Only a partition separates. If you knock on it, Sher Ali will hear.' He unlocked the door using a heavy T-shaped bolt key and told the coolies to put the luggage in. 'The coolies will open your bed-rolls and prepare your beds. The engine for the Calcutta Express has not yet arrived so the train to Cal is now scheduled to leave almost an hour late, near midnight. But you can rest in this boogie, anytime from now. It will be shunted on to the train. Yes, not to worry.'

'Thank you, Mr Hay.'

'Don't mention. But I hope you have been comfortable and enjoyed your dinner; also I do hope the chicken curry was not too hot.'

'No, Mr Hay,' said Sister Agnes, 'we are used to Indian meals. It was all very good.'

'Then Madam, write and make mention of it to the Nawab sahib.'

'Certainly we will,' said Dr Rivers. 'Now tell me, when do we get to Calcutta?'

'Two nights. Tonight and tomorrow night, reaching Cal at ten next morning. Train speed is twelve, fifteen miles an hour. So just make yourselves comfortable. I've signalled the stations en route, so your meals will be brought to you.'

'Many thanks again, Mr Hay. Oh, that reminds me, I have noticed that Sher Ali did not eat with us.'

'No worry, sahib,' Sher Ali interjected. 'I know Allahabad well, I like station food.'

'Station food?'

'You know, Dr Rivers,' explained the stationmaster, 'it's what hawkers on the station sell with *chai garum*, that is hot hot tea.'

'It very good, sahib.' Sher Ali rolled his head. 'Most tasty food, but not for you.'

Dr Rivers smiled. 'Well in that case, all that remains, Mr Hay is to settle your expenses.'

'Not one penny, I mean paisa. Not one paisa. I have been paid by Sher Ali.'

'Sher Ali? What does this mean?'

'Sahib, the Nawab Sahibji giving me one hundred rupees for food for whole journey.'

'Good gracious!' cried Sister Agnes. 'The Nawab's generosity knows no bounds.'

'Indeed, my love, had I known I would've protested. Not that it would have made any difference.'

If the city of Allahabad came as a shock to me, the first sight of Calcutta staggered my senses. Dr Rivers hired a Victoria to Bishop Heber's College and, as the Rashid Cotton Mills was in the opposite direction, we bid goodbye to Sher Ali. He sprang to attention, raised his musket to his shoulder and struck the butt in a military salute. I had forgotten about the *jezail*, it had been so much part of him, but now once again I wondered where and how he obtained it.

'That weapon is lethal,' said Sister Agnes. 'I'm surprised no one's questioned him.'

'Wonders never cease,' chuckled her husband. 'They probably know him, the authorities, I mean. But I believe that musket doesn't function, serving more as a deterrent than... now, what is the matter. As the Nawab sahib assured me.'

Sher Ali came rushing back, musket raised in one hand, while the other hand thrusting out in urgent ecstasy. 'Dr Sahib,' he called, 'take it sahib, twenty-six rupees left.'

'Why, Sher Ali, what is this about?'

'Left money, from hundred rupees, left.'

'But, why are you giving it to me.'

'So, my Nawab sahib know all money for you, I gave all. I not keep any money.'

'In that case, thank you. I will write letter, *chitty*, to Nawab Sahib, saying thank you. But you also must tell him, when you see him... when do you see him next?'

'Not too soon. First he going Lahore.'

'Then promise, when you do meet, you won't forget. Give him our most grateful thanks.'

In the coach I sat next to Dr Rivers. Opposite us was Esther with her head resting on Sister Agnes' shoulder. Her eyes were shut. 'I hope Esther gets over this,' said her father.

'I'm all right, daddy. I just didn't sleep well. Did you sleep well, Michael?'

'I always sleep well.'

Esther giggled, and with a determined effort sat up and at once shed her tired look. 'Michael I'm sorry about not reading more of *David Copperfield*, but dad will post the book to you when I've finish reading it.'

'That won't be necessary,' said her father, 'Michael will find a copy in his College library.'

'I suppose so,' Esther sighed and looked away. I thought she looked beautiful.

We started to move through the City and immediately I was struck by its vast streets and the grandeur of its buildings. But I controlled my excitement and curiosity. The sedate indifference of my company inspired me to control my feelings. I wanted to be like them.

'Dad,' cried Esther, 'isn't that the Writers' Building?'

'Well remembered. You were six when we were last in Calcutta.'

'Tell Michael about it.'

'Your mother and I are tired and, now that Michael will be living here, he'll have all the time in the world to get to know all about the Writers' Building and all about Calcutta.' Dr Rivers looked at Sister Agnes and in a measured, rather ironic tone added: 'This is the Capital of the British Empire.' The look they exchanged stayed in my mind. In time its riddle unravelled. There was much about British Imperialism of which Dr Rivers disapproved.

EIGHT

For a week after Dr Rivers enrolled me at The Christian College for Boys, I heard nothing from him. The silence was uncharacteristic. Uneasy at first, I soon relaxed into the day to day timetable of the College, till one dull, rainy afternoon I was told to go to the Dean's office. I arrived to find Sister Agnes seated there all by herself.

'Hello Michael,' she said simply. 'I've come to say goodbye.'

I stared at her a little confused. 'Where is Father Jacob...and, and Esther?'

'Esther and I leave for England tomorrow, by boat. The Mission have arranged for Father to go by railway to Dhaka, then by palanquin to Shillong. From there he'll complete his journey to Dubri on horseback or by bullock-cart.'

I said nothing, simply because it meant nothing to me and mainly because my thoughts were on Esther. She had been unusually subdued since we set out from Pultanpur on the start of our long journey to Calcutta. Years later I learnt she was in fact unhappy. Unhappy at the prospect of going to England, unhappy at having to live with Aunt Holly, her mother's elder sister. 'Give Father my salaams,' I said mechanically.

'I will. You know Shillong is in Assam. Did he not point it out to you on a map?'

I nodded. 'Oh, yes, I remember now. And Hoznibagh, which he said was near Dubri.'

'Then you know it is in the Hills of Assam. Far from here.'

I had nothing to say. I looked at her and waited.

'Oh, I mustn't forget, this is from Esther.' She dipped into her large handbag and took out a parcel. 'Esther wrapped it herself.'

I took the parcel and mumbled my thanks.

'Open it later. I must be off, now.' She walked to the door, stopped, turned, and after a split moment's hesitation rushed back to me, gathered me in her arms and hugged me. 'God bless you and may Christ be the light of your life!' She whispered.

I stared in astonishment at the retreating figure of this remarkably self-contained woman. In all the time I knew her, this was her first instance of emotional betrayal.

She paused at the door. 'You'll be fine,' she said and turned to face me. 'Your Scholarship will see that you get text books and stationery and a little pocket money, which the Dean will give you every Friday. Did you get it this week?'

'Yes,' I said, 'sixteen annas.'

'Sixteen annas is one whole rupee. You don't have to spend it. I hear the food is good?'

I nodded. It was bright and dry as she stepped out and faded into the haze.

Slowly I made my way back to my classroom. It was empty. The boys had gone out into the playground. I opened my locker, studied Esther's parcel and recognised the ribbon. It was the navy blue hair band she was wearing when she sat next to me reading aloud the opening pages of *David Copperfield*. I felt a strange thrill as I rolled the ribbon neatly and placed it in the locker. Then I looked at the book. It was Goldsmith's *The Vicar of Wakefield*. On the inside cover she had written in her round hand, "Goodbye and Good Luck, Much Love, Esther." I shut the book, put it to one side, covered my face with my hands and wept.

The Christian College for Religious Studies, to give it its full name and purpose, was a private institution, independent of any educational board. At the end of its four year course students sat for a written examination, papers were assessed and certificates of graded qualifications issued. These held no value outside the College but it was expected that students who completed the course would volunteer to join a Christian Missionary Society or apply for training into the priesthood, when those Certificates would be of preparatory significance. Being a small College unable to maintain no more than forty students, the annual intake was strictly controlled. Only five scholarships were awarded to sponsored orphans, the rest paid fees with concessions made in proportion to family incomes. Founded twelve years ago, the College was also funded by the London based St Paul's Missionary Society and occasional donations from associated charities. It was run by a voluntary staff of four retired, academically qualified Englishmen, of whom the eldest was Bill Foster. Before joining, Bill had spent time in the administration department of a hospital in Bath and was, therefore, the ideal person to take charge of student accommodation and welfare. His short rather plump figure combined with his bluff, jovial manner earned him our affection and the nickname of Friar Tuck.

Heading the staff team was Dr David Hollins, a gaunt, solemn looking man with an attractive smile that softened and lit up his heavily lined face. He was the second Dean of the College and as our Principal Tutor revered and referred by all of us as "The Don". Apart from Biblical and Christian Studies with him, we studied History and English Literature under Dr Arthur Collins, while the odd juxtaposition of Philosophy and Mathematics was the subject of Professor Derek Wilks. For their services, this dedicated team took no salary, being content to accept free board and lodging. They dined with us in the College refectory and, except for Derek Wilks, lodged in a refurbished bungalow that was built to be the cricket pavilion. Derek Wilks, the youngest and only married staff member, lived in town. His wife, Mrs Enid Wilks visited the College on Monday mornings to supervise the two *dhobis* and to check the previous week's laundry list.

After my first year at the College the Don took a particular interest in me and suggested I join his extra-mural tutorial group. I did. And my next two years were serenely happy ones. Sadly, at the end of the second year one of our group contracted typhoid. Rushed to the Old Swedish Missionary Hospital he died a few days later, bringing our number down to four. Then, early in my third year, Philip Mazumdar joined the College and the Don's special tutorial group. A year older than me and at first aloof, I was drawn to his peculiar charming manner, and soon we were good friends. Before coming to us he had spent four years at The Government School of Arts.

Close as our friendship grew, we met only at lectures, tutorials and when we managed to sit together at meal times, because Philip was one of the privileged eight "parlour boarders". They were higher fee-paying students from well-to-do families and, (unlike the rest of us, who slept in the long, first floor dormitory above the lecture rooms) were separated and paired off to lodge in furnished bedrooms--rooms in the new, purpose-built two-storeyed cottage across the cricket ground and opposite the pavilion. Literally knowing which side our bread is buttered, we did not regard these privileged boarders with envy or resentment. We knew our good quality meals owed much to their financial contribution.

Gradually, Philip and I did manage to spend more time together without breaking College rules. One rule, under the peculiar heading of "Liberty Day", did not apply to the "parlour boarders" but prevented the rest of us from going into "town" during week days. Sunday was "liberty day", when all were free to spend the day in town after compulsory morning Matins or Mass at the College Chapel. These services were taken by visiting clergy. Compline was said by the Don or Bill Foster at a quarter past seven every evening before dinner at eight. It was a way of checking we were all in.

Lunch was not served on Sundays, but the Tuck Shop provided free tea and snacks for those who chose not to go into town. I was one of them, as I saw no good reason to take advantage of this freedom and invariably spent Sundays in the College Library. It was quite some time before Philip discovered this and insisted, henceforth, we spend Sundays in town together. After some persuasion, I reluctantly agreed.

'Michael, good as you find the food here, surely you'd want a break from it. There's always something in town to spend your pocket money on. How much do you get each week?'

'Sixteen annas.'

'Sixteen annas! Good Lord! Sixteen annas is nothing.'

'It is sixteen annas more than I need.'

'Poppycock! Anyway you're coming out with me from now on.'

'But what is there in town. Don't you get bored?'

'No, and you'll soon change your mind and regret what you've been missing. I promise you.'

We began going out together. But it took some getting used to as it introduced a new strain on my autonomy. On our third outing Philip suggested we ventured beyond the local precincts of the town. 'I know a place where they serve an excellent lunch,' he said, 'about two miles out. I also know where we can get hold of two bicycles and cycle there.'

'No, we can't,' I said. 'I've heard of bicycles, but I've never seen or learnt to ride one.'

'You're joking. Seriously? Well, then we'll take a rickshaw. My invitation, so it's all on me, rickshaw and lunch.'

'Why don't we walk? I enjoy walking.'

'That will be four miles, there and back. No thank you.'

'Oh, come on. Four miles is nothing.'

'You may have been a good walker, but when did you last do a long walk. You'd be out of practice. I tell you what. I know a place much nearer, in Howrah. We'll cross the river Hoogli, using the pontoon bridge. I say, we can have a drink with our lunch at that place.'

I looked at him suspiciously. 'What do you mean by a drink?'

'A drink, don't you know. Not tea, sherbets or water. Something stronger, you'll see.'

I shook my head doubtfully.

'Don't tell me you haven't tried…Well there's a first time for everything.'

Phil ordered beer with our lunch, but I could not drink it and gave up after a few sips. 'It's bitter,' I said. 'Phil, how could you... I mean, what do like about it?'

'Famous last sentiments,' he laughed, lighting a cigarette. 'Soon there'll come a time when you'll ask for more.'

I shook my head doubtfully. But the lunch was good. I suggested we walk back. He agreed. 'That was a waste of good beer,' he said, as we set out. 'Sorry for not offering you a cigarette but after the beer fiasco it felt wrong to tempt you with one. I'll wait till you get to my age.'

'Next year!' It was my turn to laugh. 'You're just a year older than me. Anyway, I was five when I tried to smoke one of my *Daada's bidis*.'

'Good Lord! That's strong stuff. I bet it made you sick.'

'Yes. Violently sick.'

'Then that would have betrayed you. I'm sure you got a good thrashing.'

'Not for long. My *Daadi* intervened. She shouted at grandfather for not hiding the *bidis*.'

Phil did not speak.

'Anyway it put me off smoking.'

It was as if he had not heard me. We walked in silence on the pontoon bridge and stopped in the middle to look at the river. Philip was lost in thought. This habit of abruptly withdrawing into himself I found increasingly characteristic of him. I studied his profile, his thick, dark curly hair, prominent nostrils and heavy lower lip. He turned and faced me squarely. 'Mike, you've got something on your mind.'

'Yes,' I said. 'I don't mean to be inquisitive... but I've been wondering about your English... I mean it is good, very good... fluent. How did that come about?'

'It's the only language I know. I'm a Bengali but I can barely understand the lingo, let alone speak it. You see, dad's Bengali but mother is from northernmost Punjab. Different languages, I mean, he spoke Bengali, she Urdu. English was the only way they could communicate. So my sisters and I were brought up speaking English. Mind you, they, mum and dad speak English as or like most Indians do, in a strong sing-song way.' He laughed briefly. 'It rubs off. The Don says I sound like a Welshman.'

'I wouldn't know.'

'But you, your English always sounds pukka. Don't explain. I know why. By the way, have you heard from him? You've said it's been over a month since you last heard from Dr Rivers.'

'He doesn't write often. I've had just seven letters since I've been here. But I have waited longer. His first letter came after six weeks. But after receiving it I realised there's good reason. He's out in the wilds and recently he's had to get to Kersilang, in the hills beyond Shillong and at a mule's pace. It's the only way he's been travelling, on a mule.'

'And with a train of coolies carrying his luggage… that would even further delay him.'

'Just two, he said. Two coolies, he doesn't have much. Most of the stuff was Sister Agnes's, and that went ahead by bullock-cart. Now he's in the middle of nowhere. According to his last letter, he's has had to move on.'

'Where to?'

'I expect to find that out in his next letter.'

Phil drew from his jacket pocket a hob watch and glanced at it.

'Hey! What was that?' I asked.

'A watch dad gave for my birthday, last month. Do you want to see it?'

I would have liked to but decided to choose some other time to satisfy my curiosity. I shook my head. More importantly I was pleased he did not probe further into Dr Rivers' letters to me, as I feared he might. Few as those letters were, they were movingly personal. Discussing them would force me to bare sentiments I was not ready to share. But by his asking, Philip reminded me of the impact the first letter had on me. It was little more than an apology, but having waited so anxiously long for it, to salve the ache in my soul, I read it again and again, till now I am able to recall it, word for word:

"Michael, my dear boy, I know this letter will take some time to reach you. When you read it please find it in your heart to forgive me for not meeting you to say goodbye. But in my heart and through Sister Agnes I embraced you with every good wish for a happy and fulfilling future. I was sorry to learn from her that you looked unhappy. I'm not very good at goodbyes, but tell yourself that our love and prayers are with you always.

"I'll write as often as I can and not expect replies. Your pocket money is meagre, save it. Dr Hollins will give me news of you and any personal message you have for me. Remember me! With love and God bless you. Jacob Rivers"

Philip coughed discreetly. 'A penny for your thoughts?'

'Not worth the penny.' I smiled defensively and started to walk on, stopped and turned to face him: 'Except to say, having an excellent memory can be a curse. It increases pain.'

He laughed. 'The advantages outweigh the disadvantages, old chap,' then he slapped me on the back and we moved on. As we approached within sight of the College, he placed a hand on my shoulder. 'Michael, one moment…' We stood facing at each other. 'I say, Michael, you won't tell my dad you saw me having a drink and a smoke.'

'Your dad! Why, I mean, when am I ever likely to see our dad?' I waited for a laugh or an explanation. I got neither.

'Well, I've been thinking about…' he began and then checked himself. 'Sorry, forget it.'

For the next two Sundays Philip and I seemed mutually to have decided to avoid each other and inexplicably neither made any attempt to confront each other to discover why.

The third Sunday was the Sunday before Advent. In a fortnight the College would break up for the Christmas and New Year vacation, when students and Staff vanish all over Calcutta and further afield, to spend the holidays in ways they had planned. As in the past, this did not affect me apart from making up new excuses for avoiding the other three scholars, who also stayed on at College during the holidays. This was not hard as they mostly kept to themselves and none were in the Don's tutorial group. Two of them were Bengalis, the third was an Armenian with a difficult name, which no one could pronounce, and consequently he begged to be simply called Ivan. Ivan was always to be seen with a pack of cards and occasionally he showed me a few tricks, which were beyond my ability to learn. Sadly, he had a terrible stammer.

On Advent Sunday, after service in the Chapel, Philip came up to me. 'Michael,' he said, 'what's the matter, why have you been avoiding me?'

'Because I thought you were avoiding me.'

'Don't be ridiculous,' he said using one of his familiar chides.

'I could say the same.'

'You mean it's all been a silly misunderstanding? All right, let us say no more about it.'

I nodded. 'As if it never happened?'

'Yes, forget it. Now tell me, what do you do at Christmas or any holiday for that matter?'

I frowned. 'Why do you ask?'

'More than mere curiosity, as you'll see.'

'You know, I've told you before, I have no home to go to.' It did sound rather pathetic so I quickly added, 'and my dearest friends are beyond reach.'

'Of course, the Rivers. But, you must feel terribly alone, almost by yourself at College.'

'I like my own company.' I chuckled. 'Rather enjoy it.'

Phil raised his brows and rolled his eyes.

'And I keep myself busy. I've a lot to do, a lot of reading to catch up with…sorry, with which to catch up. So much good stuff is coming out of

England these days. Dickens may have gone but there's Hardy and this new man, Kipling. The Don tells me Kipling was or is in Allahabad.'

'I know you do a lot of writing—those diaries of yours. Still, you could do with a break—all work and no play...'

'Makes Jack a dull boy.' I forced another laugh, less convincingly. 'Not true. That has never passed a test.'

'Then let's say, you'll end up a hermit, locked in an ivory tower or on some column like one of those Desert fathers of old.' Philip grinned. 'The first agony column, as the Don put it.'

'No chance of that... the ivory tower, I mean, and the column even less. The Don and I are planning to bring out a new College Journal or House Organ, as he calls it, which I'll be editing. We have already given it a name, "The Pentecost".'

'Forget all that for the moment. I'm talking about fun and friendship. I've heard about "The Pentecost", by the way, it will die at birth.'

'What makes you say that?'

'Don't you know, the Don's going back to England?'

'Yes, but he'll be back, won't he?'

'Unlikely... He's due retirement. I say, doesn't he remind you of Gladstone, whiskers and all. Like the Gladstone portrait in the College Hall? Anyway, this Christmas you're coming home with me. I'm inviting you. I'll be disappointed if you don't come. You'll enjoy yourself, I promise you.'

'I don't know. I don't like being a guest and a trouble to others.'

'No trouble. As you know, my dad is in business and rich, so there's no reason to hesitate.'

'All right I'll come. Sorry to appear as if I'm conferring a favour by...'

'By accepting one. Forget it.'

'Thank you, Phil, thanks indeed, but I won't be hurt if you change your mind.'

'Not my style. Glencoe, that's the name of our house. It's a big house, in Motiganj, a village not far from here. Life's easy. Plenty servants around... friends and relations come and go and nobody takes a blind bit of notice.'

'Why Glencoe?'

'My father had spent some time in Scotland.'

'My father was there, too. He died there. Someday I'll tell you the little I know about it.'

'Tell me.'

'In truth, I saw very little of my father and know nothing more than that he went to Scotland to become a priest. Why was your father in Scotland?'

'He was there on a short holiday... and fell in love with the Highlands.'

'Did he go there from Calcutta?'

'No, he went there from England. This is many years ago. I would have been five years old. He was in Coventry and Leicester, learning the business of the company he wanted to run.'

Coventry, Leicester, Mazumdar, those names, they had a familiar ring.

'Phil! Good heavens, Phil!' I exclaimed, unable to hide my excitement, 'is your father first name Air...something?'

'Aaron Mazumdar.'

'Yes! That's it! Yes.'

'I find this hard to believe! How in the name of all things impossible do you know that?'

'Does your father know an English businessman named Bill Tolly?'

'Yes, of course! Twelve or thirteen years ago, Bill stayed with us, helping dad to establish his new business. Dad put him up in one of our guest-houses. How on earth did you hear of Bill... and, and, my dad?'

'Bill's sister is or was, in my time, our Mission nurse or Matron, from Pultanpur.'

'Well now, Michael, you've got to come. It's a must. Surprise dad with this story, all you can remember... not on the first day, later, choose your time.'

'Okay, I'll do that. Motiganj did you say? I've seen it on a map.'

'Yes, it's marked, north from here, up the Chitpore road and past the Black Pagoda.'

'The Black Pagoda, what's that?'

'You astound me. Four years you've been here and you've seen nothing of Cal. You don't know what you're missing. It's a beautiful town, city. Anyway, you won't see the Pagoda in all its splendour. Dad says, it was the tallest building in Cal but most of it collapsed sometime around ... I think dad said 1805, which means he wouldn't have seen it either.'

'I did see something of the city, in the first four or five days after I arrived.'

'You mean, with the Rivers family?'

'Yes, and I did see Fort William, from a distance... the Writers' and other grand buildings... Churches too, and wide roads, all very crowded. I've never seen so many people.'

'Then, the Rivers showed you around?'

'No, not really... they did not appear to be proud about Calcutta as an Imperial Capital, and I didn't press. I suppose I'm a country boy. But we did go through Lal Bazaar to get here. They liked that. There were huts with thatched roofs…some very like those in the villages near where I came from, except that the main road was dusty, crowded and busy.'

'It's a bazaar, a marketplace, that's only to be expected. If you've had a look around the Fort William that's the Esplanade area and you couldn't have missed some of the grand bits around Chowringhee. What about St John's Church, Government House with the statue of Bentinck, a past Governor General in front of it. And how could you have missed the new Cathedral?'

'You mean St Paul's? Yes, I remember Esther pointing it out to me. I also remember, at one time having to stop our carriage and told to wait till the grand procession of the present GG, as the Don refers to Lord Lansdowne, went past.'

'Still there's a lot more of Cal to see. And even the bits you've seen need a longer and closer look. Years ago, when I was with dad, visiting the Asiatic Society, I saw boys from this College at the Old Mission Church and Mission Row. They were on some sort of outing, and I could've sworn Friar Tuck was with them.'

'Just our bad luck. The Don told me he, Friar Tuck is too old for those excursions, oh, and actually, you were wrong. It's not the Don who is going back to England, it's Tuck. He will be retiring and he, that is the Don, hopes the College will get a younger volunteer to take over. But I suppose these things take time.'

'Don't you think the days of this College are numbered? It can't go on like this. After all it won't be easy to find staff who'll do it for nothing. Anyway, it's a pity to lose out on outings.'

'It's only us scholars who are losing out. You have all the freedom you need.'

'No, there is a rule against inviting you to visit my room, for instance. Actually I'm surprised how the boys here are so well behaved.'

'That's because they're hand-picked; anyone not prepared to conform has to leave. Don and his team may be a kind lot but they won't tolerate any rebellion or misbehaviour.'

'Yes, all that was made clear from the start.'

'And our chowkidar at the gate is an ex-sepoy. He told me he was in the Bengal Army.'

'If he's to be believed… but we want to be here because it's a privilege to be here. According to dad, the Don's staff, as a teaching team, is matchless, the best teaching team in Calcutta. But in case you're worried, there'll be no objection to your coming home with me for the Christmas Hols. Dad's a prominent citizen of Calcutta.'

'How far is Motiganj?'

'Twelve, thirteen miles, dad always sends a carriage. I say, when did you start shaving?'

Motiganj was local enough to be a suburb of Calcutta and Glencoe turned out to be not one house but a colony of well-appointed brick houses within the privacy of a walled compound—a rather grand statement in a surround of mud and thatched huts. The main unit, where Philip's parents and immediate family lived, was the large, central bungalow, flanked on either side by four single bedroom chalets. It had an open veranda, a large sitting room, four bedrooms and two bathrooms. Kitchens and lavatories were outhouses behind the bungalow and connected to it by sheltered pathways. The sitting room, referred by all as the "drawing room" was, I was later to learn, in tasteful Victorian decor. A false fireplace had on its mantelpiece a clutter of framed photographs of family members, while a highly polished grand piano, which seemed not in use, took pride of place. A rich, floral patterned wallpaper, imported at a great expense, covered the entire length of one wall and on the other three, pink distempered walls, hung prints of popular paintings, all in expensive, heavy gilt frames. Prominent among these was a Gainsborough lady in large bonnet and feathers, entitled "Sweet and Twenty" and a print of Joshua Reynold's "The Age of Innocence".

Philip and I had arrived at teatime. He asked me to wait in the drawing room while he went in to inform the family of my arrival and soon returned with, I correctly guessed, his mother. Her presence was announced by the jangle of the silver chatelaine round her waist. A moment later she was joined by two other richly dressed ladies. 'This is mater,' he said, 'and sisters Muni and Lily.' I bowed. We shook hands. Muni, clearly the eldest of the siblings, had a serene but deeply pockmarked face, which caught me unprepared. My startled expression was inescapably noted by her mother.

'Poor Muni,' she said, 'was born when there was a small-pox epidemic in Motiganj. Many, so many people died. We are grateful Jesus spared her life.' She pointed to a picture above the mantelpiece, which I had missed. It showed Jesus with outstretched arms, identical to the one in Gupta's office. I struggled to say something positive, but before I could speak, Mr Mazumdar entered the room. On this occasion I managed to hide my second startled reaction by greeting him with a wide smile. For, Aaron Ramchander Mazumdar was extremely dark in complexion and his three children bore little resemblance to him. They had taken after their olive-skinned mother. But he had a commanding presence. His easy manner immediately established that obvious charm one meets in the style and doubtless ability of a successful businessman.

'So,' he said, 'this is Michael. Delighted to meet you! Phil speaks very highly of you. I can see at once, you are, unmistakably, a Brahmin.' He reached to shake my hand and as he did so he glanced at his daughter Lily. 'Has Phil introduced you to my wife Monica, and my daughters Muni and Lily. Yes?'

I nodded.

'Good. Michael, you're most welcome. Treat this place like home.' He glanced at his wife.

'Please, everybody,' said Mrs Mazumdar, 'please sit down. Let's all have tea and hot *jelabies*. Phil, *beta,* go, go. Tell servants *jaldi, jaldi.* Quick, quick. No, no. You stay here. I'll go.'

Mrs Monica Mazumdar left the room and before Mr Mazumdar turned from me, I had had the opportunity to study his neat dapper appearance. He was my height, taller than Phil and tall for a Bengali. His straight black hair was sleekly parted in the middle and the greying temples placed him to be a little over fifty. From his still fine features I assumed he would have been an attractive young man, whom the regal Monica would have found irresistible and, as he had married outside his community, theirs would have been a love marriage; rare for that time.

Mrs Mazumdar returned closely followed by servants carrying trays of teapots, teacups and plates of golden, steaming hot, saffron rich *jelabies*.

'Come on, Lily look after our guest,' said her father.

It was then that Lily caught my attention. I was struck by her obvious good looks. Her large doe-like eyes were very black and strikingly beautiful; and as they looked at me with frank regard I fell hopelessly in love with her.

'I say Monica, it will be good to get those two together,' Mr Mazumdar whispered to his wife.

I overheard him and in the split-second hiatus of revelling in its joyous promise, I missed the grimace on Lily's face, though, even had I seen it then I would have read nothing negative from it. Such was my blinkered infatuation and destined failure to save myself from years of pain and soul-searing anguish. It is a regret I record now with hindsight, for at the time I was defenceless and so smitten that when Lily's early indifference towards me later changed to warm attention, it never occurred to me to question or suspect the sudden switch in her attitude.

That fortnight's holiday with the Mazumdars was my initiation into unimagined pleasures. I was feted with good food, experienced homely comforts I had never known, and enjoyed family outings that were occasions of fun and learning. We played cards, word games and sang Carols by the piano—I was mistaken to assume the piano was just for show, because it was then that the quiet, unassuming Muni came into her element as an adept pianist and lead singer.

And then, halfway through the vacation I asked Phil if now was a good time to tell his father the story of how I heard of Mr Mazumdar some years ago.

'Yes, I was wondering when you'd get down to it, but save it till dinner time, when we are all sitting down together.'

I did. The effect on the family, apart from Phil, was astounding. Mr Mazumdar jumped up from his chair and gaped at me speechless; and the women squeaked with delight.

The first to speak was Mrs Mazumdar. 'So, Michael,' she said, 'fate has brought us together.'

'Then papaji,' said Muni, 'you must take Michael to the factory. It will bring good luck.'

'Why don't we all go to the factory tomorrow morning and have a picnic lunch by the river. Monica you haven't been there for some time. It is looking good. Yes? Then that's settled.'

'Dad has been producing some of the best hand pulling rickshaws used in Cal,' said Phil.

'But what about the bicycles,' I asked. 'Isn't that what Bill Tolly...'

'You see, Michael,' interrupted Mr Mazumdar, 'I've only been able to assemble less than a dozen bikes and four trikes. I want to make a lot more before putting them in the open market. I have got frames for twenty more, but some parts are missing and due to arrive by boat. Bill's promised to ship supplies from England. Right now England is bike crazy. Sales have shot up and his Company can't meet the demand. I've no choice but to wait for those shipments. But hopefully, one day we'll make them here; frames, wheels and all, here in India, to the English design, and even improve on it.'

'But, dad, first we need to produce the steel,' said Phil. 'Bikes need good steel frames. Isn't that what we... steel is what we lack, da.'

'Yes, and we also lack someone prepared to take over from me in the near future.'

Mr Mazumdar regarded his son with an enigmatic smile then he turned to me. 'Michael, talk to Phil, get him to take an interest in "Ajax Rickshaw & Cycle Company", that's its new name.'

'Oh, dad! You promised not to bring that up again. We've agreed uncle Joyti is the best person to take over. He, Michael, is dad's younger brother, besides dad's already agreed to get me into Oxford. There, see, dad's a great one for teasing.'

'Yes, Satya, don't embarrass the poor boy,' said Mrs Mazumdar, 'really you must stop that.'

'Monica, you know I'm not serious, much as I would like Phil to change his mind.'

'You know, Michael,' Mrs Mazumdar said, 'Phil wants to be a priest. In the Oxford Mission, a monk, one of the Cowley Fathers… but that's where I put my foot down. I've found a nice girl for Phil… look, look at the boy, my, my, look at him blushing.'

'Please, mother!' pleaded Phil.

'Enough, enough,' Mr Mazumdar coughed firmly. 'I'm sorry to have brought this up, Phil, but Michael, maybe you'd like to join my Company. There'll be no problem for an intelligent lad like you. It's mostly accounting, and Phil tells me you're good with numbers, arithmetic.'

'Dad, Michael is the Dean's blue-eyed boy. He'll have plans, the Dean I mean, already has plans for him. Normally, the boys, who have no homes to go to, stay on at the College and then take on jobs with the Mission.'

'But Michael must have ambitions of his own. What are your plans for the future, Michael?'

'Phil's right, sir.'

'But you must have ambitions, Michael. Some ideas of what you'd like to do and be?'

'I'd like to be a teacher and run a school, a free school; or something totally different, like joining the army and being a soldier.'

'No, no, laddie. Don't for a moment think of becoming a soldier. There's trouble brewing in Afghanistan. There are better things to live for.'

'An idle thought, sir, I haven't given it much thought. I'm in no position to choose.'

'Don't say that. For a bright youngster life is full of opportunities. I know Dean Hollins. He is a good man. He won't stand in your way if he knows I can offer you better prospects.'

Mr Mazumdar's words created an expectant hush. All eyes were on him. His wife broke the silence with: 'Satya, are you serious?'

'Yes. I like the young man. I want him to know he can have ambition. Michael, it is time to make your mind up. You and Phil are in your final year. Tomorrow you'll see my Workshop. You may like what you see. But whatever you decide to do, I'll help. You're no longer alone.'

'I don't know what to say, sir.' I stammered.

'You've got time to think it over. And when Phil brings you here again, at Easter, tell me. Right now, I can promise you, you won't have to stay on with the Mission. I'll get you out of that. That's my solemn promise, even if I have to buy you out.'

'Buy? But sir, that could mean four years fees. And your business is not yet er… paying.'

All except Lily burst into laughter and when that died down Phil spoke, still not quite able to suppress his laughter completely. 'Michael, the bicycle business is like a hobby for dad. Yes, an expensive hobby but still a hobby.'

'Stop, stop. Give the boy his due. He is showing great sense and maturity,' said his father. 'You see Michael, I come from a family that for many generations have been in business; and, what is more, one of the first Indian pioneers to exploit and promote the jute and indigo trade. I'm heir to all that and I can afford to branch out. So, give serious thought to what I've said and even if you are still undecided, after you come out of College, come here. You can stay in the very cottage that Bill Tolly stayed in when he was here.'

'Thank you, sir,' I said, a little overwhelmed, but Mr Mazumdar waved his hand.

'Right,' he said, 'that's settled. Now let's get down to the serious business. Monica's special treat for us,' Mr Mazumdar said, rubbing his hands gleefully, 'are her delicious *russogullas*.'

After dinner Mrs Mazumdar kept me back while the rest went into the drawing-room. 'You know, Michael, my husband is too modest. To be in the jute trade is something special. Nearly all that business is managed by Europeans, in fact, I won't be surprised if we are the only Indian family in jute and indigo. And, you know, Europeans, especially the English, keep themselves to themselves. They avoid mixing with Indians. But they invite my husband. Even to their clubs. I also go with him, but not so often. In some clubs women are not allowed to enter.'

When it was time to leave, Phil's parents pressed me to come again, not just for Christmas, but also for the shorter break at Easter and then... Lily's kiss, planted gently on my lips, woke a sleeping giant of libido within me...

Phil and I were back in College on the last day of the holiday, but before we parted I thanked him profusely. Phil waved his hand but stopped me parting by a quizzical look.

'I say, you know Michael, it's like as if I didn't know you. You've really shown me a side of you I didn't... I mean, I don't know how to put it... Hello stranger.'

'Stranger? What's this, I'm no stranger. What are you trying to say?'

'Who is the new Michael, the Mike I did not know, the Mike who oozed charm all about the place. I say, you've charmed the family, utterly. I couldn't believe my eyes and ears.'

'I don't know what to say. But there's something I'd like to know about you. You always, or often, begin with "I say". Why or rather where did you pick that habit up?'

'From dad. He picked it up from his American friends. But don't dodge my question. You seem particularly to have charmed Lily. What was all that about?'

I studied his face for a while and in that momentary pause sensed a certain delicacy in the air. 'Have I crossed some line? I mean, do you object to my paying attention to Lily?'

'Not any of my business, that's the parental department. It's just that I was taken by surprise. I thought you were, like me, a man's man and that you preferred the company of men. Where did this interest in women come from?'

'It was there, but no occasion till... I mean, we seemed not to have brought women into our conversations. Had we, I'd have mentioned my beautiful mother... my first love and... oh, yes, Esther too. But I'm not one for gossip sharing or chatting about something just for the fun and excitement of it.'

'Esther? Oh, the Rivers girl. Well, I... you might think who am I, not much older than you, to expect you to take advice from me, but may I say, about Lily... and if you didn't appear to be so taken up by her, I would not be saying this, but I would advise you to take care... tread with care, with eyes wide open.'

'Are you trying to discourage me?'

'I have no objection to you becoming my brother-in-law. In fact, I'd rather like the idea, but I wouldn't like you to be hurt. Just be watchful. She's a strange one, my sister.'

'Why are you telling me this? We are good friends, close enough for plain talking.'

'I'm confused. I didn't think she would, but she did respond to you.'

'Why does that confuse you?'

'Because I know she's got a young man in tow. Mum and dad don't know about this but, and keep this to yourself, because I promised Lil I wouldn't tell anyone, but sometime last year, quite by chance, I went one evening to collect her from her college and saw her in conversation with a young man.'

'Do you know him?'

'No, and she wouldn't introduce me.'

I had nothing to say except to ask, rather irrelevantly, 'how old is Lily? Your mother told me that Muni was five years older than Lily.'

'True. There's also quite a gap between Muni and me. I'm quite close to Lily, less than two years. So she'd be the same age as you, getting to be nineteen.' He studied me for a while. 'Oh forget everything I've said. The important thing is, you impressed dad and if you can work with him or help him in any way that will be wonderful.'

We parted. I was left a little uncomfortable, and found myself thinking of Esther.

The next day Dr Hollins saw me at his office. 'I have a letter for you,' he said, 'read it and if you have any message, tell me. Father Jacob would like to hear about your Motiganj trip. Write it down. I'll see it gets to him.'

'Thank you, sir. I'll do that.'

'That's not all, Michael. While you were away, you had a visitor, Nawab Ali Baig. He spoke very highly of you. I told him where you were, but he was only in Calcutta for two days, and on his way to Burma.'

'What a pity, I would have loved to see him. I thought I'd never see or hear from him again. He owns some Cotton Mills here, in North Calcutta, actually not far from Motiganj.'

'Yes, he knew Motiganj, but he had no free time. He was here to close down his Mill. Sadly, he seems to have suffered a loss. Some new project in Lahore went wrong.'

'Oh, no! I'm sorry to hear that.'

'Well, he didn't seem too worried about it. He's obviously a rich man.'

'Yes, and an extremely generous one.'

'Indeed. He's left you a beautiful leather suitcase and given me more than enough money to buy you a tailored suit. He assumes you would have outgrown your old measurements he had.'

'A grey suit?'

'Grey? Is that what you'd like? Fawn is the more usual colour here.'

'What is fawn? Oh, is it a light brown. But I'd like grey. Phil's father was wearing one.'

'If that's what you want. He gave me the name of some outfitters, tailors, on Esplanade Road and I promised to take you there. I told him the College *darzi* would produce a suit for less, but he insisted I took you there. They would also have a good pair of shoes. I'm sure his generous allowance will cover that as well. We shall see.' He smiled. 'Your face is your fortune. Now off you go. Come back, tomorrow, with your letter.' He stood up. 'And when you do, I'll fix a day when we'll go to the tailors. Leach and Webbourney, never heard of them, but then, I'm a man of simple tastes,' he laughed.

I lay back in bed to read Father Jacob's letter. It was short, written on a single page of an old exercise book. "Dear Michael, It's been some time since we've had news of each other. I have not been able till now to find the time to write. It is hard work running a Mission, small as it is, singlehanded, and to crown it all, I've suffered a nasty spell of malaria and even though I am a fortnight on my road to recovery, I feel weak and exhausted. The good news is, I'm no longer alone. Agnes has joined me, and what a blessing it is after another six months absence. She was shocked to see the state of affairs around me and, in her usual efficient way, has set about getting help and a promise of one more helper from the Mission Station in Shillong. I thank the Lord dear Agnes will be with me a long time, a whole year before we leave together for England. She has seen Esther settled at her old college at Oxford. So things are looking up.

I hear good tidings about you. Dr Hollins is full of praise. He says you have a natural ability to master the English Language. I am happy for you. You have achieved so much. I hope you will one day use your talents to be among those to free your country from the burden of foreign rule. I have nothing seriously against the Raj. They have done a lot that's good for India, but chains are chains even if they are golden. Blessings and prayers, Jacob Rivers."

NINE

*T*he Mazumdar Factory was ideally situated on the East bank of the
river Hooghli, an inland waterway navigable for small cargo boats
to chug up north from Calcutta's seaport. On this, my second visit, I was
surprised to see how much, in a matter of months, the Ajax Rickshaw &
Cycle Company had changed. In front of the now rather shabby looking
old building was a new shed, brightly painted in blue and yellow and in
front of it a raised, wide landing pier projecting over the waters-edge. Phil
and I arrived an hour after the rest of Mazumdars, because we had to wait
for the return of the Victoria carriage to pick us up.

'Michael, this is for you,' said Mr Mazumdar, directing a factory
worker to hand me a brand new Ajax Bicycle. 'As you can see, up there, I've
produced twenty-five. The consignment from England arrived last month.'

'Thank you,' I said, 'but, as Phil may have told you, I wouldn't know
how to...'

'A few hours practice with Phil and you'll be able to, and then I would
like you and Phil, sometime tomorrow, to ride around Esplanade Row and
Chowringhee. That should arouse interest. And by next month I plan to
put at least forty Ajax bikes in the market.'

'I'll do my best to show this off, even if I have to just wheel it around,
anywhere you wish.'

'Good man. Now, this afternoon, I'll take you round the city. You can
then advise me on the best place to have a showroom for the bikes.'

'Dad, why wait a month,' Phil said, taking hold of the second bike the
same factory worker wheeled up to him. 'Sell those you have now, there's
room for them at our Rickshaw Shop.'

'Which shop? I have two.'

'The one by the Customs House and Railway Station, but I'm sure
you've thought of that. Is that why you want me to go there while you and
Michael enjoy yourselves in town?'

Before his father could answer we were joined by Philip's mother and Lily. 'Oh, Satya,' said Mrs Mazumdar, 'you're not suggesting the boys cycle all the way back to College for...'

'Why not, we are only seven miles from the College, as the crow flies. An extra mile or two won't kill them. They're healthy young men.'

'Don't worry, mum. We can't in any case. Dad's forgotten we are not allowed to keep bikes at the College.'

'Why not? Explain. I have seen at least two bikes in the open shed next to the pavilion.'

'Those bikes belong to the Masters. And dad, it's a College with Christian rules. Any luxury which the other boys can't afford to have, we can't. That rule is there so that no one feels...'

'Yes, yes, I get it. The cardinal sin of envy...Those bikes, Michael, belonging to the Masters, those are English bikes, the Masters brought with them.'

'Anyway, mum, don't listen to dad,' said Phil, 'he's teasing you, as usual.'

Monica Mazumdar threw her hands up with an expression of despair. 'Come Lily, we'll sit in the office. Satya, get one of your men to bring us a pot of tea and biscuits.'

'Yes, and we'll be with you in a minute. By the way Lily can join us when I show Michael the grand parts of the city, after lunch.'

'Of course, she will, and if you're taking the Victoria, I'll come too.'

'But mum,' pleaded Lily, 'remember your embroidery class. And dad, I'm helping mum.'

I watched the two women cross the factory floor to the office, deeply disappointed at the thought of losing Lily's company.

Aaron Mazumdar asked me to wait for him by the stables. 'I won't keep you long,' he said. 'Just a quick change into my light suit and then we'll be away. By the way, Michael, I like your immaculately tailored grey suit. Looks brand new, tell me about it.'

I told Mr Mazumdar all about the Nawab and how I came by my new grey suit.

'Nawab Hasan Ali? I know of him, though I've never actually met him. A good man and it's sad he's had to close down his cotton mill. Well, you know the way to the stables.'

I nodded, having seen them and been briefly introduced to the two bays, Romeo and Juliet. I had also gathered from the syce that Juliet was the mare Aaron Mazumdar chose whenever he rode alone into the city because she was smaller and a lighter ride. And so I was not surprised to see

Romeo harnessed to the Victoria. I walked up to Manju, the coachman, who salaamed me smartly. The little old man, in his neat red and gold striped turban and long green coat with brass buttons, carried a curved dagger in a leather scabbard, tucked in his orange cummerbund. 'You know, sahib,' he said, 'we go in white city area. White people not like see Indians in white man's area. But okay for burra sahib. See, come look.' He beckoned me to follow him round the back of the Victoria. 'There, sahib. See this special number plate given by Gov'ment Raj. When white people see, they know Mazumdar sahib is big man. Then not asking why in white area.' Manju put his forefinger over his lips and shuffled back with unexpected alacrity to the front of the carriage, and I realised he had seen his master approaching.

I stayed and studied the large, highly polished brass plate Manju had pointed to. It depicted, in prominent relief, a passant lion and next to the initials VR, the number six.

'Get in, Michael,' Mazumdar said and climbed in after me. He was carrying an elegant silver knobbed cane with which he tapped the driver's seat. '*Challe challo*,' he said to the driver and then turned to me. 'Manju knows the route. It's one we always take when we tour the city sites. In fact, I wouldn't be surprised if Romeo knows it too.' He laughed briefly. 'But now, Michael, it is time you stop calling me mister and sir. How about… why not by one of my first names… Satya or even Aaron?'

'Please sir, I couldn't. I'd feel I'm being rude.'

'Then, how about Monty. It's what my English friends call me. Or, since you are now very much a member of the family, how about dad?'

'Uncle, can I call you uncle?'

'That will do nicely.' He acknowledged the two Gurkha sentries salute as we drove out of the factory gates and into Strand Road and then Clive Street. Soon we passed Lal Bazaar on our left and entered Esplanade Row. By the Treasury we turned right into a broad, rather sandy avenue that Mr Mazumdar said was a recently constructed road called The Course. Not far down this road we came to a stop. 'There, Michael, this is where Calcutta spreads out before us.'

'Yes', I agreed unable to hide my astonishment. 'It is very grand, I've seen nothing like it.'

'And every year Calcutta keeps changing, always for the better.'

In front, at a distance, I recognised Fort William and said so. Mr Mazumdar agreed and told me to look back and along in the direction of the River. He pointed to the Supreme Court and the Town Hall and regretted we could not get nearer because of road works being carried out in front of those imposing buildings. 'Michael, all that open space before you is the great Maidan.'

'And the statue in front of the Town Hall, that must be of Lord Bentinck.'

'Yes, how do you know that?'

'Phil mentioned him. He admires Bentinck for pursuing the Thugs and ending suttee.'

'True, true, Phil also admires Macaulay, who made English Education compulsory. But, you know Michael, both Macaulay and Bentinck succeeded because of a great Indian gentleman. It is forgotten that they and their policies had the support of Raja Ram Mohan Roy.'

'Uncle, I knew that. Ram Mohan Roy even travelled to England to protest against plans by the Government to establish a Sanskrit School. He insisted on English Education. Also he took up the cause for young widows to be allowed to re-marry. I'm a great admirer of Mohan Roy.'

'Did you tell that to Phil?'

I made a wry smile and shook my head.'

'You know Michael you must share your wisdom with Phil. He won't mind. He thinks very highly of you.'

I sighed, took a deep breath and gazed across the Maidan. Gangs of busy labourers filled the area. Stripped to the waist their brown bodies glistened in the hot bright sun. Behind them the wide ditch of muddy water shone like burnished gold and a camel, its forelegs splayed along its edge, drank from it. In fact there were quite a few animals about, oxen, mules and an elephant in the distance, with a mahout goading it to drag a raft of wooden planks. Still further beyond all this, I picked out an attractive area of greenery. 'What's there?'

'That'll be the Calcutta Cricket Ground and behind it, where you see palms and cyprus trees, that's where, you'll remember, we had a picnic during the Christmas holidays. Eden Gardens?'

'I remember, and you said the name has no connection with the Eden of the Bible and that it is named after two sisters of Governor General Lord Auckland?'

'Yes, Auckland, well remembered. He was GG, six years from 1836. In my father's time.'

'What did your father do?'

'Like me, a businessman. A boxwallah.' He laughed his characteristic brief laugh. 'But, of course, then the gardens were named the Auckland Circus Gardens. Later it changed to Eden in honour of the Auckland's sisters, Emily and Fanny Eden, who re-planned and improved it.'

'Auckland, 1836, that's twenty-one years before the Mutiny,' I mumbled thoughtfully.

'What made you think of the Mutiny?'

'I can't think why,' I lied, dismissing the memory of the argument between my grandfather and uncle Ramoo over the failure of Indians to be united in their revolt.'

'Of course, I wasn't around then, just seven when the Mutiny broke out. But my father told me about it and Emily Eden. He also told me about the Holwell Memorial to the Black Hole of Calcutta, which was at the corner of Tank Square, within sight of the Writers' Building, which I pointed out to you the last time you were here. It's no longer there, the Memorial I mean, it was demolished long before my time. My father could not have seen it either. I think he saw it on a Thomas Daniell's etching, which I now own.'

As we drove on past Garden Reach towards Fort William, the broad stretch of water behind it displayed all the evidence of the fact that Calcutta was a vast, busy trading seaport. Small ships and passenger transporting barges, colourful, with masts of all sizes flying international flags and pennons, plied skilfully through this melee. And along the banks, some right up to waters-edge, were grand villas, isolated in cradles of green lawns and manicured gardens. There, indeed, was proof of Calcutta being a City of Palaces. And I could see the pride with which Mr Mazumdar directed me to the scenes before us and shared in the enthusiasm of his descriptions of them.

'You know, uncle...'

'Stop, stop. Michael I've changed my mind about you calling me uncle. Let me treat you like a grown-up. Call me Aaron, so few people do. My father did. I'd like that. Yes? Good. Now, we'll turn round again, pass the Fort and then turn right into Chowringhee. I want you to see St Paul's, the new Cathedral. We won't go in, because we will, all of us, as a family, be there on Sunday.'

We stopped briefly to take in Fort William and saw a few soldiers in pith helmets. 'Aaron, I've been wondering why we haven't, till now, seen many more English people around?'

'Because Michael they're sheltering from the sun. It is the end of April,' he added, watching Manju, who had dismounted and was raising a canopy over us. 'It gets unbearably hot and May is the worst for heat. Soon a lot of the Brits will escape to the hills, Simla, Muree, Darjeeling... and those who stay on will be nursing their Prickly Heat. We Indians are made of sterner stuff.' Again he gave another of his brief chuckles. 'Mind you, Monica gets it. And that's because she's light skinned. It's awful, prickly heat. All that itching and scratching, leaves the skin sore. Your skin's quite light too. Have you suffered?'

I shook my head. 'But, Aaron, I'm hot, soaking wet under my shirt.'

'Then we'll give St Paul's a miss. You'll see it on Sunday.' He told Manju to turn round and race up Chowringhee. 'The breeze will cool us by the time we get to Old Court House Street and Lal Bazaar. Then we'll get back to the Factory.' Aaron tapped the side of the coach with his cane. 'Did you get that, Manju?' He asked in Bengali

'Huzoor!' Manju rolled his head. 'Yes, yes, I understand.'

Aaron smiled. 'We won't stop, but I'll point to Government House and St Andrew's on the way. Oh, by the way, Michael, had we set out early, say around eight in the morning, you would have seen quite a few Brits riding to exercise their horses on the race course.'

'I see. Aaron, I know how proud of your City you are, but some parts of it, especially near the Old Court House area, Lal Bazaar and places where there are open drains and rubbish lying about... the stench and sight of it, it can be quite awful. Sorry, that just slipped out.'

'Don't apologise. I'm aware how unhealthy Calcutta is... dangerously unhealthy. Life here is touch and go. Epidemics of cholera, typhoid, dysentery, even small pox, can mean one's here today, gone tomorrow. That's why I didn't take you down past the Fort, where sometimes the waters are deeply polluted. People behave so irresponsibly. Carcasses of dead animals and bodies of half cremated people are seen floating on it. It's why Monica watches the servants like a hawk. She takes no chances.'

'Aaron, the idea of servants is new to me.'

'Do you have any memories of life in your village?'

'It was open country. Not many people. Not crowded like here. In my grandfather's house food was prepared by my mother or grandmother.'

'I've watched you. You take great care about what you eat and how you eat. I suppose it's your Brahmin roots.'

'I wouldn't know. But I do know I'm not the same boy I was. I've certainly learned about good hygiene at the Mission and at the College; and I do like to eat using cutlery.'

'The Brits have introduced some good habits into India... clean living... good government... by the way, you reminded me about the Mutiny. My father said the Brits grew less friendly and more suspicious of us after the Mutiny. He also said, they had made a big mistake giving the last Mughal Emperor a pension and the title of King of Delhi, because the Emperor's Delhi palace became a hive of dangerous intrigue and activity.'

I made no comment. Aaron was looking away and as I studied his dark, handsome profile I wondered about the strange circumstances of history. Here was a man who clearly admired the British Raj, while in a village somewhere was my grandfather, dead or alive, regarding them with growing hatred; and somewhere in the hills of Assam, was an Englishman whose sole purpose in life was fired by his love for this country and its people.

TEN

A sumptuous lunch of lamb biryani, vegetable curry, green salad and mango pickles awaited our return from Sunday Service at St Paul's Cathedral. And while Monica and the girls busied themselves with the servants getting the meal together, Aaron, Phil and I were served cold beer in silver tankards. We sat round a large galvanised iron tub containing a sawdust covered block of ice on which we rested our tankards to keep our drinks cool. The ice, Aaron said was thanks to the ships from America.

'Dad, this is good, quite an experience,' said Phil as he eyed me with an anxious look.

I smiled and avoided glancing at Aaron, who leaned towards me and said above a whisper, 'Phil thinks I don't know what he gets up to. I'm sure he's taken you to that food bar across the bridge, the pontoon bridge. Or is it, I forget, the bridge across the *nullah* at Kidderpore?'

'Dad, I don't know what you are talking about,' Phil piped in saving me the embarrassment of making a noncommittal answer.

Aaron raised his brows with a mischievous grin. 'Don't pretend, Phil. Anyway, in a month you'll be twenty-one and free to decide on what you're going to do with your life.'

'I've been twenty-one for ages, daddy,' said Muni as she proffered a plate of fried aubergine slices spiced with turmeric, chilli, a squeeze of lemon and salt.

'Now Muni, don't start. You know, as your mother's made it clear, it is different for women and especially unmarried girls. But now you have nothing to complain about. All that is settled. Soon you'll be married and be in a world of your own. I see you haven't told Michael the good news and introduce him to Satish Basu. Michael, Satish, Muni's future husband, is a deacon at St Paul's. Mind you, Muni, I did not see him in Church.'

'Dad,' said Phil as he watched Muni blush, leave the plate of snacks on a side table and run out to join her mother and sister in the next room, 'that's because he wasn't there. He was at St John's. Michael, that's the Church at Fort William. He's assisting the new Dean.'

'I see,' I murmured, looking out of the window at a hive of activity being conducted outside. 'Aaron, what is going on out there?'

'Ah, that. Preparations for summer. Every year, at this time, windows, apart from these here in the drawing-room, are covered by panels of *khus-khus*, to shut out the heat. We spend much of the summer afternoons in cool dark bedrooms. Your chalet will get the full treatment. That reminds me, but you probably know this, when the rains come in June, open your window to let the cool air fill your room, but do make sure you close them when the rains stop or you'll be infested by hordes of insects.'

'Dad, you were going to get a thermantidote, this year.'

'What's that,' I asked.

'A huge, unwieldy contraption to keep the house cool in summer, not very successfully. I've got my chaps to produce a simpler version. We call it a desert-cooler. You will see one. They will set one up at your chalet. I won't say more. It's hard to describe.'

'What about this room?'

'We avoid using this room. If we have guests and we have to...' Aaron pointed to the ceiling, and the *punkhas* suspended from the beams. He stood up. 'I'll be back after checking on what the men outside are doing or know what they're supposed to be doing.' He left the room.

'I say, Michael, have you made up your mind?'

'About working with your father? No. Actually, he's not pressing me about anything.'

'I know. Mother tells me he's offered to use his contacts to get you into the Civil Service. If I were you, I'd forget about the Civil Service. You would need to know Latin and Greek. It's one of the requirements. Dad's forgotten that. But you really need to make some decision.'

'I'll think about it.'

'Really, Michael, for someone with a brilliant mind like yours, you're very indecisive.'

'Well, that's because all my life till now, I let things happen to me. One gets used to that.'

Phil stared at me hard and long. 'I don't know what to say. Father is fond of you, obviously more fond of you than he is of his own son.'

'Steady on. I think you're being unfair.'

'Don't misunderstand me. I don't mind. I'm happy not getting too much attention.'

'Are you suggesting I'm getting more of your share?'

'Yes, but for good reasons. You're a favoured guest and because of Lily. But I must say, the way you're going about this Lily business must frustrate my parents. Show some interest.'

'I thought it was rather obvious. I'm mad about your sis. I mean I'm in love with her.'

'Then show a little initiative. You barely pursue your... hardly show you care. I'm close to Lily and she must feel you're indifferent about the whole affair... and how it will turn out. But I suppose we are all prisoners of our own characters.'

'True, but that's no excuse. Falling in love takes us out of ourselves. But Phil, forgive me for saying this. I would be more... what's the word, demonstra... there I can't even say it, but I'd let my feelings be more on display if Lily also shows more than mere politeness.'

'There! Back to square one, back to my first warning about Lily. Keep your eyes open.'

'I've heeded that warning and treading lightly with care. If only you knew how painful it is.'

'I'm sorry. Michael, please don't suffer whatever happens. Don't let it defeat you. Look at me. Be like me. I don't mind if dad likes you more than me. Any future prospect is held back by attachments. My immediate concern is to get to Oxford. Dad will keep that promise.'

'What about this talk about a double wedding, Muni's and yours?'

'Just talk. My parents accept that will never happen. Women don't interest me. I'm what is termed "a confirmed bachelor". And the future has all the promise of my utmost desires.'

'That last sentence is pure poetry.'

'Yes, Mike, as Shelly would put it, a recapture of that fine "careless rapture". Hurrah!'

'What are you two chirping about,' asked Aaron as he entered the room. 'Michael? Phil?'

But before either of us could speak, Monica called: 'Come in, time for lunch.'

Next day, came a message that was to bring about an unexpected change in the direction of my life. I will not forget that Monday... the night before, for some inexplicable reason I was restless and, when sleep proved impossible, decided to give up trying and sit outside on my small veranda. It was early dawn, bright enough to read, so I thought of picking up where I left off in George Elliot's *Middlemarch*, but being in a reflective mood, chose instead James Frazer's *The Golden Bough*. It was the Don's parting gift to me. I wrapped a shawl round me, as there was a chill in the air, sat on a cushioned cane chair and opened the book. I had barely read a page, when I looked up to see the *bhisti* walking past, bowed with the weight of his bulging, goatskin *mussak*. He had not seen me but, fascinated by his movements, I watched him enter the main veranda of the Mazumdar bungalow. This was where the family kept large, round, earthen pots for storing drinking water. I saw him remove the wooden lids of the *chattis*, unlace his *mussack* and with a silver arc of streaming water replenish them without spilling a drop. I recalled Father Jacob telling me that the *bhisti*, water-carrier and bearer of life's reviving gift, is greatly respected. He is seen as an angel of mercy, and why the name *bhisti* is itself derived from the Persian word for Paradise. As I watched my eyes grew heavy, I turned the book, rested it against my chest and fell asleep. I must have been asleep for some time, because when I woke with a start, my face and neck were wet. The sun was high in the sky and shone hot on me. I looked up and blinked at the silhouetted head bending over me, giving me a start.

'Michael, Michael, wake up.' It was Phil. 'Derek Wilks was here with an urgent message for you. Why are you out here? Come, let's go in.' He took my arm and ushered me in.

'Wilks did you say? Is he here?'

'He couldn't stay. He had to be back in College.'

'And what?' I stared at Phil. 'What is the message?'

He shook his head and there was a strange look on his face.

'Why are you looking at me like that? Phil, what is the matter? Something's wrong. Phil?'

'Michael, the Don wants to see you urgently. He has an important message for you.'

'What is the message? Wilks must have told you. Surely you know.'

'Michael, get washed and changed. Then come over to the house. As quick as you can.'

'Why won't you tell me? You're really getting me all... all anxious.'

'Dad says he'll get Manju to take you to the College. It's the buggy this time, and Manju will wait to bring you back.'

Arriving at the College I ran straight to the Don's office. He was not in. I looked out of the window and, seeing him coming down the path, went out to meet him. 'Ah, Michael,' he spoke softly, 'come in.' I followed him back into the office. He pointed to the settle by the window. 'Do sit down.' I did. He went up to his desk, picked up an envelope and sat down beside me. 'Michael, dear boy, I've got sad news to give you. Father Jacob Rivers and his wife Agnes are dead. They were murdered.'

I was speechless for a while. 'Oh, my God! But why?'

He shook his head solemnly.

'I want to see them! Sir, I must get there.'

He nodded. 'Yes. Remember it's taken sometime for the news to get here. They will have been buried weeks ago. I am told that friends carried their bodies all the way to a Church near Shillong, where they lie side by side in the Churchyard.'

'Then I will go there. I have to.'

'I thought you would want to do that. Mr Das Gupta thought so too.'

'Gupta! Gupta!' I exclaimeed. 'Is he here?'

The Don nodded. 'It was Gupta who brought the news. The Assam Mission in Dubri had his address. They should have had mine too. He said you'd want to go but insists you shouldn't do it alone. So he's prepared to travel with you and meet all expenses. I've told him that if you decide to go I'll ensure you have some money too. Yes, Michael, I will loan you a part of what Mazumdar paid me for, well you know for what. Later, when you can, return it to the College.' He sighed. 'Getting there will be a long and hard journey.'

'Gupta? Are you thinking of Gupta, is he looking too old?'

'He looks his age, but wiry and alert. No, I meant long and hard for anyone. Now, although there's no railway all the way to Shillong, you should be able to do some bits of the journey by rail. There are roads, I hear, good roads to Shillong, but from Shillong there's a two-mile walk to the Old Mission Church, St Jude's, which can be reached from Dubri or Shillong. You have no other option; possibly a bullock cart ride, if you're lucky to find one.'

'We'll manage. Oh, dear God!' I suddenly remembered. 'Esther! Does she know?'

'She will, if the Mission has informed her. If not, she will in a fortnight. I've written to her. That's how long it takes for letters to get to England. I had, was given, her aunt's address.'

'Sir, may I see Gupta now?'

'He's not in at this moment... gone into town to buy a strong pair of shoes. He said he'll be back in an hour or two.'

'In that case I'll go back to Motiganj. I expect the Mazumdars already know about this, but I need to tell them of Gupta and my plan to travel with him to Shillong. Aaron, that's Mazumdar, has given me one of his newly produced bicycles. I'll return on it. May I leave it in the shed?'

'Of course. There's this letter for you. Possibly the last one Jacob wrote before this terrible, this awful tragedy. I apologise for opening it, but I had to, just in case there was something in it that would be helpful for me to include in my letter to Esther. I hope you don't mind.'

I shook my head.

'I'll leave you to read the letter in peace.'

I nodded mechanically.

'But before I go, tell me, have you decided on taking up a job with Aaron Mazumdar?'

'I haven't decided.'

'The prospects are good. His commercial businesses are going from strength to strength.'

'Right now, I'm even more undecided. I can't think clearly.' I opened the letter, and putting it down, slumped forward and covered my face with my hands.

'There, there, Michael, be strong. I'm hopeless in such situations. I don't know what to say.'

Unable to control myself, I cried out, 'he was a father to me!' And wept.

'Be brave. Dear boy, only you can face this out. Maybe a good cry will help. I'm going now, when you get back from Motiganj, you and I and Gupta will have tea and something together.'

'Sir, don't be surprised if Gupta declines.'

'I see. He wouldn't say no to a cup of tea, surely?'

'Maybe not, but he would to the something.'

'Well, thank you for reminding me. Vegetarian? I'll take the cooks advice. I'll also get hold of a map, so we can work out the best route to Shillong and from there to Mission Headquarters in Dubri. It would be wise to take their advice on how best to get to St Jude's. They may even have a dog cart. After all St Jude's is on their circuit. Dr Rivers, as you know, didn't note down place or date in his letters, but this one has certainly been sent by the Mission, because they have sealed the envelope and written Dubri on the back. Sadly it also means that their letter to me is lost. Chin up. I'll see you later.'

I wiped my tears, took a deep breath and read:

"Dear Michael, There's little news of interest to give you. Sister Agnes and I work from day to day visiting and preaching Christ to the two villages in our charge. Sadly there is little heart-warming response to our work. The tribal population regard us with some suspicion, but seem to tolerate us, although the hostility between the two village headmen is increasingly unhelpful. We tread carefully and don't press anyone into becoming converts. Compulsion is not the way of Christ. As sowers we sow the seed and leave it to take root.

"I have been keeping in touch with Das Gupta. I should have told you earlier. He's had to work at St Thomas's longer than for the few months he expected. The Bishop's choice of his successor failed to turn up and they have had to search for a new man. Those waiting months became the best part of a year. Now, for the past four years, Gupta has settled in Gaya, where he lives in a Buddhist monastery. That monastery is worth a visit. I did some years before I took charge of St Thomas's Mission school. It is a haven of tranquillity.

"I'm afraid I have not heard from the Nawab but I gather he tried to see you. Hollins told me about the gifts he left for you. Good. He is generosity personified.

"Reading through this letter I fear I have been rather negative about our tribal work. I am sorry for that. In truth I've learned a lot from those simple folk. They are not savages as some governing bodies imagine. People of simple language don't have simple thoughts. They merely lack the vocabulary to express them. In their thoughts, desires, nostalgia, joys and sorrows, in common with all humanity, is a democracy of feelings. That is why we need writers to unlock the thinking of the illiterate. I'm not being merely philosophical, I do sincerely wish people like you, with brilliant minds, will take up this challenge, even if, as a worthy task, it is but a thankless one. I think of you often and in quiet moments hope, one day, I'll see you again.

"We regularly have good news of Esther and miss her terribly. Hopefully we will be together again in the not too distant future. As ever, Jacob & Agnes Rivers."

I carefully folded the letter, returned it to its envelope and put it into the inner pocket of my cotton jacket; and as I walked briskly to the College Gates and awaiting buggy, the evil treachery with which the innocent trust of two saintly beings was savagely betrayed, angered me deeply.

ELEVEN

*T*he years had wrought little change on the lovable Das Gupta. He could not have been a day under sixty, yet I saw before me a Gupta healthier than the one I knew at St Thomas's. I said as much as I shook his hand and embraced him warmly, though his immediate reaction to my compliment surprised me. With a wry smile he shook his head. 'You see, Dr Hollins, my dear friend Michael has turned into a veritable Englishman. Consequently he is shedding all his Indian heritage behind him. But he is blameless. He was but an infant when he came under the spell of English culture.'

'Why, Mr Gupta, Michael's compliment was an open and, I'm sure, an honest one.'

'Indeed, Dr Sahib, but an Indian would have paid his compliment by saying the opposite.'

'You mean he would... oh, I understand. Is this about *nazur?*'

'Yes, Dr Hollins, so as to prevent the casting of the evil eye... but no matter. I have lived long enough to know all that is a lot of nonsense. So, my dear Michael, I thank you, and let me say my good health is the direct consequence of a peaceful life in a monastery and a vegetarian diet, plentiful in milk and pure *ghee*. And may I return your compliment in double measure. I see before me a fine specimen of a young man. Dr Hollins, I must say, Michael is blessed with his father's good looks. He could play the leading role, as his father once did, in the enactment of the *Ram Lila.*'

'Indeed, Mr Gupta, I'd say, wherever Michael finds himself, he'll be the cynosure of all eyes.'

I raised my hands. 'And I shall do my best not to believe either of you.'

'There, Mr Gupta, need we say more, not only handsome, but gifted with the intelligence of the wise. But now to serious business. I've a chart of the Khasi hills and also a map of Assam. But I'm afraid,' added the Dr Hollins, 'these are several years old. There have been transport developments, in rail and road, since then. Nevertheless they will help in the planning of your journey, which will involve all kinds of transport and plenty of walking. You two face a long and arduous trip.'

'What must be done, will be done,' I said quietly.

'I've been thinking, we may be able to work out a route to Dubri that could save you having to go via Shillong. It may not be necessary. And I believe it will be wiser to take the train from Howrah to Bhagalpur. Then hire a tonga or any horse cart prepared to take you up north-east.'

'If we can get to Lalgoda,' said Gupta, 'that's one option, and set out east from there. As you say, I believe, much on this chart has changed. Recently the Government has encouraged the building and extension of the railways.'

'I'm sure you're right and by using ferry crossings you'll speed up your journeys by choosing to take the railway whenever you can. Now, Michael how has Mazumdar taken the news?'

'He expected I would do this journey. A pilgrimage he called it; and he will help in every way he can. He too suggested Howrah to Bhagalpur as a starting point. The gateway to Assam he called it. More than that, he insists on giving me, what he calculates to be sufficient funds for the journey. By that I mean, Guptaji, money to cover most of our expenses.'

'I thought he might do that,' said the Don. 'So, you will have no problems in that quarter.'

'Then he will be thrice blessed,' Gupta said with a solemn shake of his head.

'Yes, he is also arranging with his Accountant to provide some of that money in a bag of four and eight anna coins.'

'That, Michael, will be most useful,' said Gupta. 'I have endeavoured to make a collection of copper coins as well. It will be most useful for paying ferrymen, tonga*wallas*, as well as for hiring of bullock-carts. It will save a lot of haggling and lame excuses for not giving back change. Your friend Mr Mazumdar is obviously a man of practical experience.'

I nodded absently. 'Well, he is a successful businessman.'

'In that case, Mr Gupta,' said Dr Hollins, 'I suggest you and I study the charts and make a list of place names you may need to mark your route. And we'll let Michael return to Motiganj for his final arrangements with Mr Mazumdar. Michael, is that not what you need to do?'

'Yes sir. And I realise I won't need to cycle back here, as I know Aaron Mazumdar will drive me to Howrah Station.'

'Good. I'll be there waiting with Mr Gupta. Just remember the train from Howrah leaves at half past nine this evening.'

'I won't forget. I'll meet you there, Guptaji.'

'Michael,' said Gupta, 'before you go, I want...' and his voice sank to a whisper.

'What is the matter,' I asked, rushing up to him. He was shaking violently. I put my hands on his shoulder and held him firmly. 'What is the matter, Guptaji?'

He took a deep breath and sat back in his chair. 'They were the kindest people I've ever had the good fortune to know. Saints. You know Dr Hollins, they respected me and all my strange ways. And when they had to hand over charge of the Mission... I pressed them to go back to England. I... you see doctor sahib India is a land of many peoples. Some of the most civilised and some of the most savage... and Assam has...' He stopped abruptly.

I looked up at the Don. He nodded. 'Mr Gupta,' he said, 'you don't have to tell me about Assam. Harry, my younger brother worked there for a while, on a tea plantation. He came here to Calcutta on his way back to England and told me about the tribal peoples there and their customs. It wasn't a pretty account. He found life on the plantation impossible.'

'Dr Hollins, there are tribes and tribes, all savages... some far worse... have you heard of the Khonds of Orissa and West Bengal? Until recently they made human sacrifices to their gods.'

'Yes, but the British Raj has put a stop to that.'

'For which, dear sir, you and they have my eternal respect. It is why the murder of my dear friends breaks my heart, and I shall constantly offer prayers to Lord Buddha to receive them in the peaceful realms of Nirvana.' Mr Gupta stood up. 'Come Michael let me walk with you.'

I wheeled my bicycle between us as we walked together silently towards the College Gates. There he took my hand in both his. 'Michael,' he said, 'trust me.'

'I would trust you with my life, Guptaji!'

'I will get you there, to Dubri and to that Church safely. As a native of this ancient land there are things I know that no Englishman can ever know however long he lives here. So, smart as you look in British style shirt and trousers, it would be helpful to us if you travelled in *kurta* and pyjamas kurta, Muslim style, like what I am wearing.'

'Yes, and why it took me a moment before I recognised you. I always remember you in your white dothi and black waistcoat. Why the Muslim style?'

'Because the dothi is not for long distance travel and much of East Bengal is Muslim, so we shall blend in and not draw too much attention.'

'But all I have is three sets of shirts and trousers, a night shirt, and a grey suit.'

'Leave the suit behind. That is sahib fashion, which is not necessarily a disadvantage.'

'I will certainly not carry that with me.'

'Just carry one spare set of your shirt and trousers; and when we get to Bhagalpur I will buy you two sets of *kurta* and pyjamas. I'll take you to a local tailor and have you measured. Those are fast workers. Overnight he will have them ready.'

On my way back to Motiganj the chain of my cycle came undone and I had much difficulty getting it to function again. I decided it would not do to mention it to Aaron, but as my hands were black and greasy, I went first to my quarters to wash them before entering the Mazumdar bungalow. Soon after my arrival the family gradually and solemnly gathered in the sitting-room and offered their condolences before sitting down. Then taking their cue from Aaron, Monica and Philip joined in advising me on how to tackle my trip to Assam till it tried Aaron's patience.

'Stop, stop! Phil, Monica, this is a long and serious journey and there is little any of us can tell Michael what to do. Michael and his friend Mr Gupta are going to have to solve problems on the spot. The most important and only help Michael needs will soon be here in a minute… and there, as Holmes would have put it, is the very man we need.'

Framed in the doorway was a tall man in a black pill-box cap, looking at us over steel-rimmed spectacles, and smiling benevolently.

'Arrey, Brijpal,' cried Monica, 'what are you doing here?'

'Patience, my love,' broke in Aaron. 'You'll soon find out.'

'Sir, I have managed it,' Brijpal's smile grew even wider. 'Phifty-phor rupees in coins. Also I have managed to acquire a military leather pouch belt, to keep change safely on person.'

'Shabash, Brijpal. Come in, don't stand there, leave the belt with me, then go to the kitchen. The cook will give you some tea and cake.'

'Satya,' whispered Monica, as Brijpal left the room, 'what is he going to do with cake?'

'Arrey, darling, these people love cake, especially cherry sponge cake. I've told the cook.'

'Da, it is still a good policy to make a list of things to watch out for, here Michael.'

I took the piece of paper Phil handed me and gave it a quick glance. 'This is far too much… I mean all the bits and pieces on this list. I couldn't carry all this with me. I must travel light.'

'But Michael,' chimed Monica, 'you need to eat.'

'We have a lot of walking to do. Having to carry a basket of foodstuffs will slow us down.'

'There Monica, I told you.' Aaron gave one of his brief laughs. 'Carrying food is an added burden. It also saves time to live off the land.'

'But Satya, Michael has to eat and in the wilds of Assam he may not find cooked food easily. Most of the food in that basket would last a week or more.'

'Please, Mrs Mazumdar, it is kind of you to think about this, but my companion Mr Gupta is a strict vegetarian and a Brahmin.'

'I see. Then eat what you want and give the rest to some poor beggar. Always there are a few about. And if this fellow...'

'Mr Das Gupta, Monica dear...' Aaron interrupted with another of his brief chuckles.

'If he's so fussy, Michael, let him eat on his own. At least for the first few days you'll eat well. I really believe you won't find much in that wild country.'

'You'll need an umbrella; rains quite a bit in Assam, if you remember your Geography.'

'Yes, Phil, I certainly remember that.'

'What about one for Mr Gupta, as well, umbrella I mean?'

'Mr Gupta never ventures out anyway without an umbrella, you can be sure of that.'

'And what about good strong shoes, boots. I've placed a pair next to the leather suitcase the Nawab sahib gave you.'

'Thanks Phil.'

'I'd keep you company, Michael, but I hate wild places.'

'Come now, enough talk,' said Aaron, 'time for action. You've less than two hours to pack and for dinner before we set off for Howrah Railway Station.'

'So what about this food basket, Michael, are you going to take it?'

'I'd rather not, Mrs Mazumdar.'

'But I want to have helped. Oh, Lily, fetch my plain brown shawl. As it is *pashmina* its very light and morning and evenings can get chilly. Also it will hide your money belt.'

'Thank you, it will be a great help, Monica. May I call you Monica?'

'Yes, for heaven's sake. That is my name.' Her daughters and Phil laughed in unison.

'Now off you go.' Aaron clapped his hands. 'I'll bring the shawl and this to you when you're ready.' Aaron held up the pouch belt. 'Oh, that's heavy.'

'Which reminds me, Aaron, how do I wear that pouch belt?'

'Soldiers wear it like a cross belt, from shoulder across the chest, but wear it round the waist.'

'I don't know how to thank you.'

'Don't mention it. I'll also give you something extra for emergencies. Lighter, in notes.'

'There really is no need. Very kindly Gupta had come ready to meet my expenses.'

'Good heavens, Michael. You don't want to take that man's money. Dr Rivers was a father to you, now I'm taking over that job. Who else can you turn for help?'

'Thank you again, though I fear Gupta is determined to make his contribution. Before we parted he told me he was going to get a tailor to make me two sets of *kurta* and pyjamas, Muslim style, those were his very words, when we get to Bhagalpur. It's how he would like me to travel.'

'Very wise, indeed. You're in good hands.'

Half an hour later, Aaron turned up at my chalet carrying an oil-skin sailor's jacket. 'That's for you when the rain gets too heavy. Tuck it in your bedroll. There, I'll help you with it.'

When it was done he stood up and we faced each other.

'Sir,' I said, 'why are you so kind to me? I'm helpless before such generosity? I really have nothing to give in return.'

'Yes you have,' he said, looking at me directly. 'You are going to marry Lily. You are going to be my son-in-law.'

I stared for a moment quite speechless.

'Phil tells me that you love Lily. He asked you and you said so.'

'Yes,' I said, speaking slowly and deliberately, 'That is the truth. I love your daughter, from the very first moment I set my eyes on her.'

'Then that's settled. When you have completed your mission, come back to Motiganj. And thank you. I am proud to have you as my son. Phil's a strange lad. I like him, but, and I don't mind saying this, he's a strange one. I know I can rely on you. All is well that ends well. Right, now I'll leave you and return with the gharry. I'll be driving you myself.'

He left and I sat down on my bedroll overwhelmed. So much had happened in such a short time and the pressure, from the weight of feelings within me, was exhausting. Then again, it was one thing to be in love, but the idea of marriage was too novel to handle with equanimity. And so I decided to dismiss all thought of it. This was no time for mental debate. Besides, I had given my word.

TWELVE

I cannot think what I would have done without Gupta's cool presence and ability to switch, as occasion demanded, from Bengali to Hindi. Above all his wisdom coupled with his canny ways of seeking out and gaining admission into temple complexes, where we found food and lodgings for the night, was achieved by an assumed priestly authority. And in preparation for that role he changed into a saffron coloured, loose, knee-length *kamiz*, and took great pains to emphasise his caste mark, on his forehead.

'You see, Michael,' he had said, as our train from Howrah approached Bhagalpur, 'your idea of sleeping out in the open may sound simple, but apart from the danger of being robbed, a risk of catching malaria is very probable. You see, my friend, the food served in the hostelry may be a simple fare, but it is prepared by Brahmin cooks, who are meticulously clean, while the priests in charge of the temples do make sure that the temple premises are kept clean. Apart from a covered well, there are no open ponds or drains for mosquitoes to breed. Besides, as an extra precaution I carry with me a plentiful store of *agarbatti* and a box of safety matches.'

'*Agarbatti*, like what my *Daadi* would light in front of the image of Ganesh?'

'No, no. Those are joss sticks. These are not sandalwood spice or highly scented things like that. It is stronger stuff. A green, coil you light up and the smoke from it drives insects away.'

However, after the first night of sniffing its smoke I found sleep difficult and next day tried to tactfully tell Gupta that he need not go out of his way to search for night lodgings. 'You know,' I said, 'in all my years I have never had a day's illness.'

'Hush, Michael,' he scolded, 'you must never talk like this. Do not tempt the gods, who may want to teach you a lesson. They dislike human pride.'

I was tempted to say I was a Christian and that by now the gods would have given up on me. But as the pressures of any sort of religious belief played little part in my life, it was of no great importance to say anything that was likely to hurt Gupta's sensitivities.

'Very soon, Michael, you will get used to the aroma and enjoy the thought of its protection.' And the truth of what Gupta said was proved on the second night. I slept soundly.

Our plans to continue our journey the next day had to be postponed because the Bhagalpur tailor needed a little more time for my *kurta* and pyjama suits. Consequently we asked the chief priest to let us spend another night at the hostel of the Lakshmi Narayan Temple and my gift of two eight anna coins was gratefully received. Early that afternoon the tailor arrived with the suits and Gupta asked me to try them on. Nodding his approval, he paid the tailor and then turned to me. 'You look very smart. Chiefly for being blessed with the physique of a Greek God.' He grinned and rolled his head. 'But now I must leave you to make arrangements for our onward journey. First I shall bathe then change this saffron robe for my white *kurta*.'

'What are these arrangements?'

'There is no point telling you unless I succeed.'

'You will, you always manage to succeed.'

'For no special reason, except I know my country and its peoples. I would take you with me, but now you have the style and manners of a sahib. For instance, now, when I go to make this arrangement, after I bathe, I shall not wear my Hindu caste mark on my forehead.'

'Why, Guptaji?'

'Because the people I will be talking to are mostly Muslims. If I succeed, we will be joining a caravan going to an animal fair, to sell camels, horses, goats... The fair happens to be near where we next want to get to, Lalgoda.'

'How did you learn about this?'

'The tailor told me. It will be an early start tomorrow, if they let us join them, and a free ride on a bullock-cart. Have you ridden on a camel? No? I get you a ride. You will enjoy that.'

And so I did. It took some getting used to, but after a while it was great fun, although a trifle uncomfortable and, as soon as I could without hurting the cameleer's feelings, I dismounted and waited to join our bullock-cart, to find Gupta asleep with the goats. I tried getting on but a large billy goat with translucent grey eyes butted my every attempt to do so. I quickly gave up, more for the sake of not waking Gupta. But he opened his eyes. 'I need to rest,' he sighed. 'When we get to Lalgoda, there will be almost a mile's walk to catch the train.'

We had joined the caravan at break of dawn and when the huge procession of men, women, children, horses, goats and ill-tempered camels set off from Bhagalpur, I feared then if the long walk to their camp, a distance greatly underestimated by Gupta, had not already taken its toll on him. Now my fears were realised.

'Yes,' he said intuitively, 'I'm fifty-nine. But I will do my best not to slow you down.'

'You must not put a strain on yourself. There is no urgency to get there.'

'Thank you friend, but rest assured we will get there. It will be less than a mile's walk to the railway station from Lalgoda. I know this for sure, no mistake this time.'

'Yes. But before we get to Lalgoda there is a halt for lunch, when the women prepare the meal. So, by the time we set off again it will be dark before we reach there. I know this because I had a talked to the cameleer. By the way, he's not Muslim.'

'You mean the fellow with the big red Rajput turban? Of course he isn't, he is a Marwari and the boss in charge of this Muslim gathering. You know, when this fair comes to an end, and the people disperse, he will make a lot of money. Marwaris are great businessmen. He is also the auctioneer, and gets a commission on each animal sold.'

'He said, trains leave twice a day from Lalgoda for Sangsak and Dubri, one very late in the evening the other soon after nine the next morning. We may be in time for the evening train, but he will give us shelter for the night, so we could catch the morning train. Why not rest today and after a good meal and a good night's rest, you will recover your strength for the morning.'

'No, no,' Gupta said, as he struggled to sit up, 'I could easily walk to the station. It is a slow train. So I will get all the rest I need in our wagon and hopefully recover my strength.'

'If that is what... ah, here is Arjun Singh, the man himself.'

'Ram, Ram! Namaskar!' Gupta greeted Arjun with folded his hands.

'I've heard all that you and the old man have been talking about.' Arjun shook his head. 'It is madness. Lalgoda is at the foot of the Khasi Hills and dangerous country. After sunset, wild animals are about. It is tiger and leopard country.' He shook his head again. 'It is wild country. I mean jungle wild. Rest the night, after a good meal with us, then set out refreshed at dawn.'

'I must admit I did not think about that, about the wild animals, I mean.' Gupta rolled his head thoughtfully. 'But, if it's so dangerous at night what about where you camp?'

'*Arrey bhai*! I've three licensed *shikaris* with rifles; and they keep three fires burning all night. Those fires not only keep the beasts away, they also discourage insects,' Arjun laughed. 'Except moths... Listen, if you stay the night, I'll get one of the *shikaris* to wake you. I will even lend you one of my wheelbarrows to carry your suit cases and bedrolls.'

I was glad Gupta did not obstinately persist. 'That will be most kind,' he said.

'You could leave the wheelbarrow at the Railhead with Madan, one of the coolies, who works for me, or if you miss him, with Victor Mason, the stationmaster,' Arjun said to me.

I offered to pay for the hire of the barrow, but he waved his hands. I thanked him profusely. He left, and I walked alongside the grindingly slow, lurching bullock-cart. I was pleased to see Gupta lie back and shut his eyes; pleased but not without some anxiety regarding his health.

I need not have worried. I was woken, having slept well but much bitten by mosquitoes, by a solemn looking sentry, to find Gupta sitting up, cross-legged, like a yoga with his eyes shut.

'You see, Michael,' he said, opening them, and peering over his spectacles. 'This is how I gather up my strength. You should try it, should you need to. Shut your eyes, concentrate on your navel and say a prayer to your god.'

'Guptaji, it is good to see you looking well,' I sighed with relief.

At the railhead I bought the tickets for Dubri, found Madan, the porter I was to look out for, and handed over the wheelbarrow, reminding him it was the property of Arjun Singh. He said he knew that and I tipped him a whole silver rupee. The grateful man wheeled our luggage to the end of a waiting train. The last wagon was different from the other passenger compartments and while we waited for Gupta to catch up and join us, Madan explained this was the guards van. It was divided into unequal halves. The smaller rear half was open with a lookout balcony. The larger front half was a rather austere compartment separated by a brown, wooden partition and a connecting door. Inside, opposite a long wooden bench was a table and an upright, cushioned armchair. Madan assured us this was the train to Dubri and Sangsak and the guard's van was entirely at the railway guard's disposal; and that for this trip the railway guard was an Englishman of the old school, one of the heaven-born, named Reginald Brown.

'He is an old friend of mine,' Madan said as he left us and returned soon after, precariously balancing on his head a small, solid-looking, black steel trunk, which he supported with a raised right arm while his free left hand carried a large railway oil lamp. Not far behind him was a large man with a double-barrelled gun under his right arm and a military swagger in his gait.

Mr Brown waived any introductions, appearing content simply to study us briefly and with a low grunt placed the gun on the table. Then perfunctorily, he directed Madan to take the railway lamp through the dividing door and into the open, rear half of the guards van.

'That is a rather frightful weapon,' remarked Gupta aloud, with a solemn shake of his head.

'This?' inquired the big man, unloading the gun and examining the barrels. 'No, it's perfectly harmless,' he added, unsmilingly. 'It fires blank cartridges. You will hear loud bangs every now and then, just to scare the wild animals away. We are in wild, jungle country.'

'Then you are doing a noble service of duty on behalf of protecting your passengers,' said Gupta. 'My name is Das Gupta,' he stretched his hand forward.

The big man ignored it. 'And mine is Reg Brown,' he grunted.

'I am pleased to meet you, Mr Brown. But how do you know when to fire the gun?'

'When I hear jackals howling... a sure sign of tigers or panthers on the prowl.' He turned to me. 'So, young man, I gather that you aim to get St Giles? Is that so?'

'Yes, sir,' I replied and at once realised Gupta must have told Madan about our pilgrimage.

'But you also mentioned something about Shillong. Why do you need to get to Shillong?'

'To make inquiries there, about how to get to St Giles Church and cemetery.'

'You don't need to go out of your way to Shillong. You can get to St Giles from Dubri. I've been there, many years ago. I even know a chap in Dubri who will help you to get there. You could even get there from Sangsak, but you're more likely to get a tonga or cart from Dubri.'

'Thank you, sir.'

'I see you are wearing an old Cavalry Officer's cross belt. Don't tell me, I don't want to know about how you came by it but, when we get to Dubri, remind me about St Giles and I'll give you the name and address of this chap who could help.' He opened the door, side-stepping to allow Madan to pass through, then he went in and from behind the partition picked up two flags, a red and a green one, and rolled them up with meticulous care. 'We're off in thirty-five minutes,' he said, adding as he kicked the door shut, 'it will still be light when we get to Dubri.'

Madan gestured me to meet him outside on the railway platform. I did.

'You see, good sahib, all those people.' Then switching into Hindustani, he continued with a roll of his head. 'Those passengers are mostly village folk, setting out with their baskets of fruit and vegetables. Not so good, yes, so very uncomfortable to be sitting with them… with all their pushing, shoving… But you and old man no worry. Here, no such problem. No one allowed here. I make request, Brown sahib, to let you in here.' He looked at me searchingly. Then in English he added: 'You see, good sahib, because he is old friend.'

I was expecting this overture and, although prepared for it, hesitated a moment.

'So, good sahib, do I have your permission to leave?' He regarded me with sad anxiety.

I delved into my trouser pocket for the eight anna piece I set aside for this very contingency.

Madan took it with profuse bowing and salutations. I climbed back into the van and joined Gupta. 'Ah, dear friend, did you have to part with another tip?'

I nodded.

'Well, it is worth it. I know what it's like to travel in crowded compartments. But it would be wise not to draw attention to your money belt.'

'Yes. I always take the precaution of keeping some loose change in my trouser pocket.'

'Nevertheless, when you move about, the coins in your belt jingle like a *nauch* lady's anklet.'

'I can't help that. But I'm ever alert and I shall protect this belt with my life.'

'Well, you look *pailwan* enough to discourage anyone.'

'*Pailwan*? What's that?'

'Have you forgotten? A *pailwan* is a strong man. No man will try to rob you without fearing he might suffer for his pains.'

I laughed. 'Actually, it's a word I should know. Uncle Ganesh was a wrestling champion.'

'Indeed, I remember him. Talking about heroes, how are you getting on with the book Dr Hollins lent you for the journey?'

'*King Solomon's Mines*? I should have finished it but it gets left behind shut in my suitcase. Do you remember, years ago, you gave me a book.'

'Yes, I remember, *Tom Brown's Schooldays*.'

'I enjoyed it, with some help from Father Jacob.'

'Oh, God!' said Gupta, and stood up. 'Will I ever be able to forget that terrible crime?' He waved his hands as if to drive away a mental cloud. 'Let me walk down the platform. I'll find something for our lunch. No hawkers will dare to come here. They are all up there among those passengers. I'll buy fruit, just fruit, to keep us going.'

'We'll have too. While he was wheeling our luggage here, Madan said Mr Brown objects to food being consumed in his van.'

'Yes, I heard him. When we get to Dubri we'll find a clean hotel and have an early dinner, hence my suggestion of fruit.'

'Quite right, too!' A voice boomed as the partition door opened a crack. 'And *jaldi, jaldi*, while you're about it. We move in less than fifteen minutes.'

'Indeed, sir. And may I get you something?'

'The memsahib gave me a big breakfast at *bara hazari*. Well, maybe a banana or two.'

Gupta liked to be the one who bought the food and I always deferred to his wishes. So, after briefly watching him striding as fast as he could towards the fruit vendor's cart, under the round, railway clock, I opened my suitcase, took out my book, found my place in it, lay back against my bedroll on the wooden bench and started to read.

When Gupta returned with guavas and a bunch of bananas in a basket, he was breathless.

'You didn't have to kill yourself, old boy,' said Brown startling me by his sudden presence. 'I wouldn't have left you behind. But, ta very much for the bananas... I hope you haven't got that spicy, smelly, powder they use for the guavas? Too much cumin... can't stand the stuff. No? Good. I'll save the bananas for later. Is that all you have for yourselves? Anyway, you won't go long without sustenance. We'll be in Dubri soon after four this afternoon.'

Just then we lunged forward with a violent jerk, which was accompanied by a loud bang.

'Oh, what was that?' Gupta and I exclaimed in unison.

Reginald Brown burst out laughing. 'You should know by now. That's the engine, shunted in and coupled.' He went in, collected his flags, stuck a whistle in his mouth and stepping down on to the platform blew on his whistle. The engine's steam whistle blew a long and urgent blast, as if in acknowledgement. 'That will send any stragglers scuttling in,' he added, grinning widely as he spoke through the open window and held out his red flag.

I studied his granite-like profile as he waited staring at his pocket watch. 'Nine-thirty on the dot... yes, we could be in Dubri by four this afternoon, if the engine does not expire.' He turned to me. 'We have a two Eurasians manning it. Driver and fireman… stout fellows.'

'It's been a fine, cool morning,' I said, feeling obliged to say something.

'That's because it rained last night. You'll soon feel the heat. Leave that window open.' He put down the red flag, waved the green one, with another blow on his whistle and climbed back into the compartment. There was another clang and a shudder as the train moved forward and soon picked up speed. 'Well, good luck,' he said and disappeared behind the dividing door.

'He was quite open and friendly then,' said Gupta, adding with a confidential whisper: 'How very English and taciturn to start with.'

'Probably had a tiff with the memsahib,' I smiled. 'Anyway you broke the ice.'

'It is not in my nature to give up. Eventually life will give up on me but I'll never give up on life.' He looked at me quizzically, then found a space on the bench and sat down. 'I've heard of Rider Haggard and something about that book. But it's too recent for me.'

'You know, Guptaji,' I said putting the book down. 'I'm curious about your command of the English language. Where were you educated, because you know a lot about English literature?'

'I'm from a village, not far from Calcutta. My father was a Pandit and Hindu scholar, who made me study the Vedas from an early age. Neighbours kept pestering him to send me to the famous Hindu College in Calcutta. Like people said of you, they said of me too, "the boy is a genius" and that I could be a babu and get a good job in service of the Raj.'

'You once told me how much you love English literature, especially Dickens.'

'Indeed! I had the good fortune or rather the Hindu College had the good fortune, of having Professor James Stuart, as Head of the English Department. A kind man and a brilliant scholar totally dedicated to the enlightenment of his students.' He sighed and stared out of the window. 'He had such high hopes for me, but I'm afraid my father decided to curtail my education and learn all he could teach me about Hinduism. But, within a year of taking me out from College he was dead and at seventeen I was alone in the world. Well, not quite, a friend of his, also like him a Pandit, who became disillusioned with Hinduism, took me under his wing. Together we both turned to Buddhism. We were that close,' he joined the palms of his hands, 'for fourteen long years till his death.'

'But you left Calcutta and also the Buddhist ashram in Gaya and ended up in Gujarat.'

He nodded. 'My Panditji friend was a Gujarati. Together we made the long journey across India from Calcutta to Aurangabad. In those days the only transport was bullock cart. It took us almost a year. We didn't mind, treating it like a religious duty. You know Buddhist monks are mendicants, told to beg for food and shelter. We shaved our heads and wore saffron.'

'And how does the Mission come into all this?'

'After Panditji's cremation—you know he returned to Hinduism, leaving me quite confused—I made a pilgrimage to the Buddhist caves of Ellora... Do you know of them?'

'Only what Aaron Mazumdar... no, not much... oh, he mentioned Thomas Daniell's etching or some sort of illustration of the Ellora Mountain.'

'I was in cave 10 and the only other person was an Englishman. We talked about how old the rock images were then sat on a rock taking in the rather wild landscape. He seemed quite impressed by me and before we parted he told me of the post for an accountant in the Mission near Pultanpur, and gave me an address to apply for it. Did one have to be a Christian, I asked. He said, they would be more interested in my ability to do Maths and to communicate.'

'We are slowing down,' I said, leaning out of the open window.

The door opened and Mr Brown stuck his head out. 'We are approaching Nagong for a ten minutes stop. It will be a long run after this. So if you've have some quick business to do, now's your chance. It's a small station and I wouldn't use its facility, it's filthy. Use the bushes.' As the door shut, I heard him mumble: 'The whole bloody country is one big lavatory.'

We did. We had no option. As we climbed back I said to Gupta, 'I wonder what he does?'

Before Gupta could speak, Brown peeped out. 'I have a corner,' he said, 'the funnel goes straight out on to the rails. I only use it when the train's on the move. Soon each compartment will have that sort of lavatory facility. I've been nagging the authorities.'

When the train continued on its journey, I begged Gupta to pick up where he left off.

'Where was I?'

'You applied for the post.'

'Yes, and got the job as Munshi at St Thomas and found a place close by to live.'

'Rambagh.'

'Yes. Mind you, I scraped through by a single vote, three for and two against. The Bishop, yes, the same Bishop, had someone else in mind. But

Doctor and Mrs Rivers, and one other, I forget, might well have been Miss Tolly, supported me.'

'For a Brahmin, I'm surprised you feel quite at home with the English.'

'Not in a servile way, but with a touch of admiration. Remember about the caves, in Ellora? I might never have seen them if it wasn't for the Brits. There's a story about how in that area of Ellora two Englishmen out hunting got lost in what apparently was impenetrable jungle. So they rode their horses to a view point and looked across dense jungle, till one of them picked out, through a gap in the trees, what looked like a man-made cave, with smoke rising from it. It led to the discovery of what is the eighth wonder of the world, the frescoes in the caves of Ajanta.'

Gupta paused a moment to take in my reaction. I didn't disappoint him.

'It's a story,' he continued, 'confirmed by the name of John Smith scratched on the wall of one of the caves. A story, but I believe it. Indians are not curious people. We are not ones for researching and recording, though now some of us want to follow the example set by the Brits. The Civil Service have been studious and given back to us much of our culture and civilization.'

'Aaron Mazumdar told me a similar or near similar story about the discovery of the Hindu Sun temples of Orissa.'

Gupta opened his hands and raised them. He need not have said more.

'But,' I asked. 'What about working for and in a Christian community?'

'As long as I can be myself, it has never troubled me. I have a great respect for Christ. If my memory serves me, in the Vedas there is mention of a Redeemer, who will be the Tenth *avatar* of Vishnu. Besides a Buddhist is basically an atheist. A unique atheist with a serious outlook to live a life governed and guided by rules of conduct.'

'I see.'

'Why are you looking at me like that?'

'You had a choice, Guptaji, I had none.'

'Michael, see it this way. You are honouring your father. From any point of view, Hindu or Christian, that means you are blessed.'

I took in a deep breath. 'You know, Guptaji, when the train stops next, I'll get one of those earthen cups of hot sweet tea, which the *chaiwala* sells.'

'Get two, I shall join you. I don't believe Mr Brown will object to that.'

'Call me Reggie,' said a voice through the partition. 'Make it three.'

THIRTEEN

*D*ubri Railway Station was at one end of a broad street with market
stalls on either side. At the other end, almost a mile ahead, a Bailey
bridge went over a river, where high on a bank was a Hindu Temple, with
steps leading down to the waters. Half-way down these steep steps were
ghats flanking the Temple, where two funeral pyres were in full blaze.
The Temple bells rang intermittently and in the late afternoon light the
townsfolk seemed to be out in full force, and a number of its women, in
clinging wet saris, were bathing in the river.

Brown handed me a piece of paper. 'That's my name and this is the
name of my friend Ali.'

I thanked him. He smirked and turned to Gupta. 'Your young friend
is terribly English in reserve. Anyway, what's this trip about? One does not
set off from faraway Calcutta without a damn serious reason?'

Gupta told him in detail. Obviously he must have rehearsed an
extended version of the one he told Madan, for Brown was visibly moved.
'Sorry, old boy,' he said to me. 'Truly, I'm sorry for your loss. I did hear
something about a murder of white folk in the hills. Bloody shame.'

'I would have told you if asked or if it was necessary,' I said shakily.

'Quite right too! It's none of my business.'

'I didn't mean it that way. Will you be returning on the train?'

'Yes, this very evening.'

'When the wilderness comes alive?'

'Indeed, you'll probably hear the first few reports from this,' he smiled
as he patted the gun under his right arm. 'Well, my condolences and good
luck. I suggest you both dine here at the Station Restaurant. Before that,
while Gupta stays with the luggage, go ahead, find Ali. He is Ali to me,
but I've written down his full name, Hamid Ali. I've drawn the route to
the blacksmith's workshop. Take directions from him. Both he and Ali,
the man you want, are Mussalmans, so you won't have to cross the bridge

into the Hindu quarter. Ali has an Oil Press Factory away in the outskirts of the town.'

'The blacksmith, does he have a name?' I asked.

'I forget his name, but you can't miss the smithy. You can't see it from here, but just before you get to the bridge, there's a narrow dust lane that goes down to it. Can't miss him either, he's a big man with big muscles. Tell him I sent you and you want to meet Ali. He can read English but I've also written my name and Ali's in Hindustani, just in case. He'll take you to Ali himself, but that may not be today. Spend the night here. I suggest you do it here at the Station. I'll tell Victor, the stationmaster to allow you to do that... another Eurasian, but a decent Johnny.'

Gupta attempted to seize Brown's free left hand with both his but Brown stepped back. 'If Ali is not around you may have to fend for yourselves. The blacksmith will give you a lift in his pony trap, at a price. He won't know where St Giles is, but you can pretend you do. I know it's about three miles due East from here. Ali may remember. And after some distance you should be able to see the Church spire.'

'We may need to spend a few days there,' said Gupta, 'will that be possible?'

'Should do, can't have a Church all by itself. It may be little more than a chapel but the small village of Kulla is ancient and also one of the early Scottish missionary outposts. There is a Dak Bungalow, but you can't use that, as you know. But there will be a resident Minister or Pastor serving a slim congregation. Seeing you both were close to Dr Rivers and his wife, he'll certainly help find you food and shelter.'

'Thank you again for all your help and advice,' I said, 'we were fortunate to meet you.'

'In India, there is always someone ready to help. It is not a God forsaken country. I've lived here since the day I was born and I shall die here. This strange country fascinates and irritates me, almost in equal measure. Well, bon... Oh, when I was there some years ago, I was told the Church also kept a farm, with a farmhouse by a well.'

'Then they will have bullocks,' Gupta said.'

'True. In that case hang around and join any party that sets out from there back to Dubri. Now I'm off, about my business. Cheerio!'

We were in luck. Hamid Ali was happy to take us to Kulla, as he had to transport two five gallon canisters of pressed groundnut oil for sale in Lumi, the larger neighbour of Kulla. We set out in the pouring rain, but kept fairly dry under the tent like construction Ali raised to protect his merchandise and by covering our protruding feet with our open umbrellas.

On arriving at Kulla, which turned out to be a pretty village of much greenery and undulating grassy hillocks, we made straight for the Church, left our luggage in the porch and were about to enter into the open west door, when Gupta held me back and pointed to the woman we had missed seeing. She was squatting by the wicket gate behind a large basket of marigold and white jasmine garlands. 'You wanted flowers for the graves,' he said. 'This is the next best thing.'

I bought two garlands and I noticed that the woman wore a blue and white bordered sari and round her neck a plain silver cross held by a twisted jute string. Assuming she was Christian and likely to understand simple English, I remarked on the freshness of the flowers.

She gave a broad toothless smile. 'I also having nice, nice white roses... all gone into Church for...' she hesitated, 'for makin' pretty. Tomorrow Pentecost.'

'Pentecost? What is that?'

'I can just about answer that, Guptaji, but don't test my knowledge of Christianity too much. I had to take it on without protest as part of fate. I also now realise I have lost count of the days. Today has to be Saturday. Pentecost is a great Church Festival. Memorable to me because it has another name: "Whitsunday", that is "white" Sunday. When Jesus was taken up to Heaven, He promised His disciples He would not forsake them, but would send down upon them the Holy Spirit to help, guide and comfort them. Hence it is a sort of birthday of the Church.'

'I see. There are echoes of that in the way Buddha sent his disciples into the world, but in a more desolate way. He sent them without a God, so in time, they turned him into One.'

'Come, let us go in and find somebody to tell us where the graves are.'

We entered the Church. Facing us, in the centre at the far end was an altar covered with a plain white sheet and on it a simple brass cross flanked by two unlit candlesticks. On the left of the altar was a raised wooden pulpit, while in front of the altar was a small bald headed man in a white cassock raising his voice as he gestured directions to two loin-clad brown men in faded red turbans. They were carrying a bamboo ladder, appearing to be confused about where to place it. Next to the bald man in the cassock stood a woman in a long white dress, holding a basket of red and white roses.

Gupta folded his hands and bowed. 'That man,' he said, 'is speaking fluent Bengali, but with a British accent, which is why the men are having difficulty understanding him.' At that moment the two minions carrying the ladder pointed to us: 'Padre sahib! Padre sahib! Dekko sahib!'

The man in the cassock turned round and walked down and stood in front of us. He studied Gupta, opened his mouth but did not speak. Then he looked at me. 'Can I help you?' He said in English, and I realised why. I had changed into my light grey, gabardine suit, in honour of my dear friends. 'We are looking for the graves of Father Jacob Rivers and Sister Agnes,' I said.

'Paul, Paul dear!' cried the woman who had dropped the basket of roses and rushed down to join us. 'The letter, dear, the one I showed you three days ago. You must be Michael and Mr Gupta?' We nodded. 'Yes, we've been expecting you. Dr Hollins wrote about you to us.'

'Yes, of course,' said her husband. 'I'm pleased to meet you. I'm Pastor Bill Mackay. This is my wife Judith. Come, I'll take you there, follow me. Not graves, just the one. They were interred in the same grave.'

The woman, I registered as rather pleasant looking with large grey eyes, said something to the men carrying the ladder, which they promptly laid down and ran out through the vestry door on the right. When we got to the graveside I saw them again. One was on his knees bent over a gravestone, while the other, standing over him, splashing it with water from a small bucket.

They then moved away, very respectfully as we approached.

I stared down at the wet, flat white marble slab. Lying flat at the very top of it was carved a small cross and below it was inscribed:

In memory of
Jacob & Agnes Rivers
Well done, Good and
Faithful Servants
Enter into the Joy
Of The Lord

Gupta took one of the garlands from me, placed it at the foot of the grave, folded his hands, bowed in prayer, moved to a spot away from us and sat down on the grass, cross-legged, closing his eyes in meditation. I glanced at him briefly, placed my garland on the gravestone, knelt and as I stroked their names an electric current pass through me. I stood up, shaken, helpless and inadequate. Prayer never came to me naturally. 'There are no dates,' I said.

Paul MacKay shook his head. 'You'll see the dates when you sign the book of condolences. There for the record. I resisted having them inscribed in stone. Dates mark a time span. But they are not here or even dead. Christ said: Those who live, believing in Him shall never die.'

'My husband chose the inscription,' whispered Judith.

'Thank you,' I said. 'It's very apt.'

'Both of you,' she said, as Gupta joined us, 'must rest now. Come back with us to Church House. We have no spare bedroom, but there's enough space in the veranda. You won't mind sleeping on the floor?'

'Not at all, for the past many days that's what we've been doing.'

'And for supper, I hope a Bengali fish curry and rice will do.'

'That is most kind, though I do believe Das Gupta will pass on that.'

'Indeed,' Gupta rolled his head. 'Just a glass of milk will suffice, if that is possible.'

'There is always plenty of milk. The Church runs a farm, you know. Dr Hollins warned that you are a Brahmin. But surely a glass of milk is not enough?'

'Madam, I'm carrying my ration of dried fruits.'

'Paul, take them back to the house. I'll stay on to do the decorations. Oh, your things.'

'In the Church porch,' I said. 'We'll collect them.'

'I have also noted, Michael, you have a money belt under your jacket.' Paul raised his brows.

'Indeed, sir, and we will, of course, pay for our board.'

'We wouldn't know what to charge. But we're well provided for. Many family members in our small community bring us meals in tiffin carriers. You could give something for the upkeep of the Church,' he smiled. 'But, Mr Gupta, as you may have to spend a few days here you can't live on just milk and dried fruit.'

'Then, maybe a plain *chappati* and pickle will do. Or maybe some *dahee*, that is curd.'

'We'll do our best. Judith are you sure you'll manage on your own?'

'I'll have finished in half an hour.'

'Why don't we stay here till you're done and then set out together,' I said quickly.

Paul sighed with relief. 'That, Judy, is a good idea. And, as our place is some distance away, we'll get Chootu and Bhillu to carry their luggage.'

I had said the right thing, but more importantly I was anxious about Gupta's health. He had, in the past two days, shown signs of physical exhaustion. 'Guptaji, we'll sit down in one of the pews, there at the back of the Church. First, I'll bring our stuff in from the porch.'

On our way to Church House we passed the Dak Bungalow. It was big, within a large walled compound and looked shut and deserted. Behind it were two out-buildings. I guessed aloud.

Paul nodded. 'Yes, you're quite right. The kitchen and the *khansamah's* quarters.'

'A waste of good accommodation, you could have been comfortable there,' said Judith.

'It's not for the likes of us,' I smiled. 'Whites only.'

'Well, you could have chanced it, if you were older and an officer in the army or the Civil Service,' said Paul. 'But I hope this sort of thing will soon end.'

That night, as he lay on the floor, Gupta covered himself up to his neck with the thin saffron shawl that he wore when negotiating with temple priests for food and lodgings. 'You too, must take all precautions, Michael. Sadly, I've used up all the *aggarbatti* I brought with me.'

I squatted next to him. 'We'll see if we can buy some more. Till then I'll survive. I don't expect there'll be too many mosquitoes in this open country.'

He reached out from under his shawl and took my hand. 'You must not worry about me. I am a little tired, that's all. Rest and meditation is all I need to recover my strength.'

'Then promise to rest here. We don't have to go anywhere for a day or two. Paul was saying that in a couple of days a friend of his will take us in his pony cart to Dubri.'

'You do that, Michael. I don't want to return to Calcutta. I live in Gaya and getting there via Calcutta is the long way. I'll go to nearby Lumi. Hamid Ali told me there are many Buddhists there, who travel as pilgrims to Gaya. I'll go with them. We got here together safely. You don't need me, now. Allow me to go with your blessing.'

'I will. Let me at least give you some money. I've quite a bit left, even after I've kept enough to cover my journey. Mazumdar won't expect me to return any of it.'

Gupta turned his head. 'Tell me, Michael. I sense you're a little troubled. Confide in me. We have shared so much together.'

'When I get back to Calcutta and Motiganj, I'm marrying Mazumdar's daughter Lily.'

'And you have not as yet a salary earning job. Is that it?'

'I'll be working for Aaron Mazumdar. There's no worry about that or money or a house to live in... and I love her... I don't see any problem. Yet I worry.'

'Is this what you want?'

'Yes, and yet...'

'I care for you. But I'm in no position to help or give advice. Most people will envy you.'

'And yet… but please no more of this. I'm fortunate, truly fortunate. I must stir myself.'

In all our time together Gupta was always up before me, doing his light yoga exercises and meditation. So I was surprised to find him still asleep the next morning. I touched his forehead and I asked him if he was well. 'Michael, I can't understand why, but I feel feverish.'

'I don't think it's fever. But stay where you are and rest. I'll get you some tea.'

I returned with two mugs of steaming sweet tea and two buttered *chappatis*. 'Now, I'm going to insist you eat these. Freshly made by their cook, such a clean looking village woman, I don't believe she's low caste. There's also a piece of jaggery to go with them.' To my surprise he sat up without protest, crossed his legs, folded his hands, said a short prayer, in words I could not understand, and started to eat and drink.

'Bless you, Michael,' he said. 'Give my apologies to the Padre sahib. I'll rest here awhile.'

'I'll stay with you and read.' I looked about me and spotted two cane chairs, a low table and a stool. I moved them to where we were. 'I'm sure they won't mind, but we will both be more comfortable if we sat on these. The stool is for you to put your feet up after you've eaten.'

He did exactly as I told him, then remembered what day it was. 'Oh, Michael, put that book down. Go to the Church. I'll be fine without you attending to me.'

'Before they left, Judith asked if you need to see the local doctor.'

'Please, Michael that is the last thing I want. Now go, or you'll be very late.'

'When I get to the Church I'll visit the graves. I'll be away for a couple of hours.'

He nodded. 'I shall be well by then.'

At the point of leaving, I asked him to give me a prayer I could say over the grave.

'My prayer is the universal Buddhist prayer, which is repeated again and again: *Om mani padme hum*, the jewel in the sacred lotus flower. But why not say the Lord's Prayer? You must know that, or one of the Psalms? Even my Hindu father knew one or two of those.'

I nodded. 'What did you make of what Paul said about them not being dead?'

'I did not find it odd. It's the wheel of life.'

'But what would modern science say?'

'Ah, dear Michael, always remember science may teach but it does not learn.' An American lady told me that, when she visited the Monastery in Gaya. She had a great love for India and is writing a book after her travels here and in Ceylon.'

'It's very Shakespearean and reminds me of what Hamlet says to Horatio. There are more things in heaven and earth than are dreamed of in your philosophy... or words to that effect.'

'Shakespeare! What a man!'

'I better be off. Thank you Guptaji, about the prayers, it's a great help.'

'It's quite a walk.'

'You know I love walking. Judith says when they have enough funds they'll build a vicarage near the Church. Manse, she calls it. I've never heard that word before.'

'Hurry now. Take good care of yourself. I have and will always remember you in my prayers. They may not be Christian ones, but every prayer said with a pure heart transcends.'

On the way to Church, I looked at the Dak Bungalow. Unlike yesterday there seemed to be a lot of bustle and activity. Fascinated I stopped and stood by the gate. Standing in the veranda was an Englishman, rather indistinct apart from his military moustache. We greeted each other, I rather defensively to cover my embarrassment for having been caught staring.

'Off to Church, are we?'

I smiled, waved and hurried away.

When I arrived at the Church they were singing the last hymn with naïve gusto; and though I could not make out the words the tune was familiar or at least one I had heard before. Then as the congregation filed out of Church and shook hands with Paul and Judith, she signalled me to stay. So I entered the Church and studied the two black boards with the Ten Commandments written in gold letters. They had been cleaned and raised again with a border of white roses.

Quite sometime later Paul and Judith joined me and we walked through the Church into the graveyard and stood by the grave. Paul was wearing his stole and held a prayer book.

'Michael, I did not invite you to join in prayer yesterday because Mr Gupta was present. But, in his letter, Dr Hollins said, you were dear to the Rivers, and that he, Dr Rivers, was like a father to you. Now, we three here present will say a few prayers for the souls of our dear faithful departed.'

We returned to the bungalow together. Gupta had gone. A short note left on the table, next to where I had left him sitting, filled me with despair. It was written down, like a list, in his firm copper-plate handwriting:

> *First, apologise to Paul, on my behalf, for using his stationery.*
>
> *Next, thank them for their hospitality and give them the two silver rupees as a gift to the Church.*
>
> *It was kind of you to offer me money, but I came prepared to bear your expenses.*
>
> *I go to join the pilgrims in Lumi. Together we will be fed and cared for. So I need to carry little more than what I am wearing and my umbrella. Kindly dispose of my bedding and any surplus articles. Maybe Paul will know of some destitute who will find a use for them.*
>
> *Finally my dear Michael, God speed, and may your future life be thrice blessed.*
>
> *Shortly, the Railway network will cover the whole country. When you have the time and opportunity, come to Gaya. I may still be around.*

I handed the note and money to Paul and sank into my cane chair, fighting back my tears.

FOURTEEN

*L*ate the next morning, Judith asked me to join them in their sitting-room where they were entertaining a prominent *Zamindar* or landowner of the Kulla and Lumi district. 'He's a good friend to the Church. He sends two of his *malis*, twice a week, to tidy up the Church cemetery.'

Paul stood up as we entered the room and introduced me to Mr Joyti Basu, who remained seated. 'This is the young man I've been talking about.' Mr Basu was a fresh-looking, full-faced and rather stout middle-aged man.

'Okay, no problem now. Now room enough to take him to Dubri Station.' Joyti Basu spoke with a very rounded, strong Bengali accent.

'Thank you, Joyti *bhai*,' said Paul. 'There you are, Michael, tomorrow, my good friend Joyti is driving his pony and cart to Dubri and he will take you there. He will pick you up from here, early tomorrow morning, at six.'

'Thank you, I am most grateful,' I said.

'Come, Michael,' said Judith. 'Sit down and join us for tea. Mr Basu has brought us a box of very fine Bengali sweets.'

Still a little distracted by Gupta's sudden decision I found it hard to make light conversation. It seemed not to matter. The irrepressible Judith chatted away, drowning my silence and giving me time to wonder if Gupta had removed himself to make it easier for me to get to Dubri... To make sacrifices was very much in keeping with the character of my unworldly friend. I waited for a moment when it was a good moment to make a decent exit, thanked everyone in the room again and bowed out.

'Michael, don't forget lunch at one,' Judith called out after me. 'That's an hour from now.'

'I won't Mrs Mackay. I'm just going to collect Das Gupta's things and—'

'Take them to my study!' Paul interrupted.

After lunch, I said to Paul and Judith that I would like to make one last visit to the grave, was told it would be cooler after five o'clock and invited by Judith to play a round of Carom.

'You'll have to guide me,' I said. 'I'm not sure of the rules.'

'Never mind, as long as you don't win,' she laughed. 'I'll cheat anyway.' But in fact we spent much of what remained of the afternoon talking, or rather me listening to the history of the fifty year old St Giles Church and of the dozen or more years of the Mackay tenure.

I left soon after five and on my way to the Church kept to the far side of the beaten track to avoid being seen from the Dak Bungalow. I heard voices as I went past but resolutely looked away, quickening my pace till I stood in front of the Church. I gazed long and hard, knowing, as a lump rose in my throat, I was unlikely ever to see it again.

It was a pretty little brick church with a low spire built above a hollow tower in the forlorn hope of someday installing a clock within. Consequently there was no belfry or even a bell; and volunteers marked the start of each Service by striking a piece of iron rail strung up in a corner of the porch. I smiled and moved on. But the thought of never again seeing the grave of a dear friend, who had done so much for me, made me weak in the knees.

I decided not to go through the Church but instead to walk round, etching in my memory the image of a neat cemetery and a tall neem tree casting its caressing shadow over a simple grave... And then I froze. Kneeling with her back towards me was a young woman, young from the fact of her rich auburn hair, hurriedly tied in two luxurious plaits. I gasped: 'Esther!'

She squeaked and turning round fell back on her hands. 'Is it you, Michael?' She sprang up and ran to me with open arms, leaving me no option but to hold her in mine. 'Oh, Michael, Michael you came!' And she broke down, sobbing bitterly.

'I'm sorry, Esther, I didn't mean to startle you.'

'You did, but it is wonderful, wonderful to see you.' She freed herself, wiped her tears with the sleeve of her light blue shirt and stood back to regard me.'

I offered her my handkerchief. She laughed, shook her head, took her own from the front pocket of her navy blue skirt, dabbed her face and blew her nose. 'It was sweet of you to come.'

'How and when did you come?'

'Oh, Michael, we had such a long and tiring journey. I thought it would never end.'

'We?'

'Uncle Graham, he's in the Church finishing the sketch he made of the grave. We were here in the morning. But when did you get here?'

'I came with Gupta. We arrived on Saturday.'

'Gupta? Is he also here?'

'He was, but now he's disappeared. I think he's decided it would make it easier for me to get back to Calcutta without him around. Did you come here via Calcutta?'

'No, Graham thought it would be quicker to get off at Bombay instead of sailing all the way round to Calcutta and travel by the railways.'

'Where are you staying?'

'Almost opposite here, what they call the Dak Bungalow. And you?'

'In Church House, with the Pastor, he's not happy to be called Father or Reverend, Paul and Judith Mackay. I believe I've seen your uncle. Has he got a moustache?'

'No, that's Captain Jock Forsythe, an old school friend of his, now stationed in Jampur. He was a great help getting us here and arranging for us to stay in the Dak bungalow.' She took my hand, walked round the grave and looked down. 'Oh, Michael! Poor, dear, sweet mum and dad, why? Why did they do this?' And she bit hard on her handkerchief.

'Madness, a fit of madness... But Esther, your father and mother would have known the risks they were taking. Gupta said they were, heart and soul, the very essence of sainthood.'

She moved her head towards me and was about to speak when an urgent voice called out to her from the direction of the Church. 'Esther, Esther! Who are you talking to?'

Esther dropped my hand. 'That's Graham,' she said quickly, then called back. 'Graham, it's Michael, a very dear friend of dad and mum; and mine.'

'I see. One moment, I'll roll up this sketch. Come over and introduce him.'

As we approached, I looked from the fine featured Esther to the heavy looking, stoutly built man. 'How are you related?' I whispered to her.

'Graham Smith is uncle by connection. But unlike my aunt Hannah, he's a sweetie.'

'I see, quite the Indian Apollo,' he said, offering his hand and giving mine a hearty shake.

'Yes, Graham, the most beautiful man in the world.'

I raised my hands with a wave in protest. 'Please Esther! I'm pleased to meet you, Graham.'

'And I you. I see, Esther has already mentioned me.' He picked up the rolled paper, which rested on the sundial. 'Michael, keep us company to - to the Circuit House as Jock calls it. We must get back. It's surprising how soon it gets dark here after sunset. And Esther, we mustn't let Michael become part of a tiger's diet,' he laughed. 'Have you far to go?'

'Michael is staying with the Mackays,' Esther piped in.

'Give the young man a chance to speak. That's the trouble with teachers... ever ready to speak up for others!'

'Teacher! Esther, a school teacher. Is that what you are?'

'Yes, Michael. In Uxbridge. About to start... my first year.'

We reached the gate of the Dak Bungalow. 'Well, Michael, do we see you tomorrow?'

'No, Graham, I'm afraid I'm leaving early tomorrow morning.'

'Oh,' gasped Esther. Her eyes widen as her beautiful lips parted.

'I'm getting a lift, to Dubri Railway Station, and then I go on, back to Calcutta.'

'Well, goodbye, and my condolences. Alas, to meet at such a sad time.'

'I don't know what to say.'

'You, don't have to say anything, Michael. Come Esther.'

They turned and walked towards the bungalow. I waited to see them go indoors. Then I saw Esther grasp her uncle's arm and they stopped. He bent towards her, listened and nodded. 'I'll wait for you in the veranda,' he said. She turned and ran towards me.

'Michael! Michael!' she called. Spontaneously, my hands reached out towards her. She took them in hers and we regarded each other for a while. 'Why are you looking at me like that?'

'Your hazel eyes are golden in this evening light,' I said. 'So you're all grown up.'

'Yes, and I have a home of my own.'

'You mean, you're married?'

'No, silly.' She looked at me long and hard. 'I don't think I ever will.'

'Why ever not?'

She looked away and shook her head. 'I wish you were staying on. Michael, please come to England. Please come and see me.'

I gazed at her sweet face in silence and wondered if I should tell her about Lily. I decided not to. 'What is there for me to visit England?'

'Am I not good reason enough?'

'Of course you are, I didn't mean it that way... oh, clumsy of me!'

'You could stay at The Rose Inn, a ten minute walk from me. And England's worth the visit. It's a free country. Just come. Michael, please, please come! Promise me you will.'

'I promise... as soon as I can.'

'And you will write. Dr Hollins has my address. I answered his letter.'

'Yes, I will,' I said, at once realising that sometimes news is best conveyed in writing.

'And I can hold you to your promise?'

I nodded.

'Then kiss me, as a seal of your promise.'

I did, very lightly, on her lips.

FIFTEEN

At Dubri Railway Station I wondered if I would meet Reggie Brown again. I paid the coolie to stay with my luggage and walked down to the end of the platform, peeped into the guards van and to my delight there he was, seated in his cushioned chair, cleaning his double bore gun. He looked up, without betraying the slightest surprise. 'So, young'un, still alive.'

'Yes,' I said. 'And I hoped to see you.'

'Good. Hoping to cadge another lift in my van? You can, first buy your ticket. There'll be plenty of time, we're not moving till seven this evening.'

'Then I'll write a letter to tell my College Professor in Calcutta I'm on my way.'

'That's a waste of effort. You'll get there before he sees your letter.'

'Then I'll see Hamid Ali, and thank him again.'

'Wait a moment, I'll come with you.' He went through the partition door, unlocked a panel, and put the gun away. 'Right, tell me,' he said, locking the panel and pocketing the keys, 'have you seen a tiger in the wild? No, well, I'll point one out, if we're lucky, from the safety of our moving train. We'll be passing at least two watering holes, where the wild beasts come to drink.'

We began to walk towards the Station exit, when he stopped. 'Where's your stuff?'

'There, as you see, the coolie is faithfully keeping an eye on it.'

'And, I see you have your cavalry cross belt and money.' He turned to shout at the coolie, '*oi, saman lehjah udder guards van mein*. There, I've told him to put your stuff in the van.'

'Yes, I heard, and many thanks for this and for putting us on to Hamid Ali.'

'I like you, Michael. You're a pleasant sort of chap, vastly different from the average native. By the way, you must have a surname.'

'I do. It's Balaram. Krishna Balaram.'

'A high-caste Indian name. So they've tagged on a Christian one. Don't see the point of it. You're still the same Johnny. Oh, I suppose it gives them a sense of having achieved something. Something to show, how else can they separate the sheep from the goats?' And he slapped his chest and roared with laughter. Pulling out his handkerchief, he dabbed his eyes and blew his nose noisily. 'Did your trip to St Giles go well? Good. But you've lost your companion.'

'Das Gupta? I believe he's attached himself to a band of Buddhist pilgrims on their way to Gaya. Shall I buy my ticket now?'

'Get it on our way back. Not a cheap third class one. Travelling with me is "First Class", so pay up.' And again he guffawed and smacked his chest in response to a coughing fit.

Three days later I was back in Calcutta and the Christian College and I thought the Don was looking rested and particularly well. He asked about Das Gupta and wanting to know all about our expedition invited me to afternoon tea at his office.

I had decided to rest a couple of days, to appear more presentable, before visiting Motiganj, and asked if I could have a bed in the dormitory.

'You can have Philip Mazumdar's room for that time. He's left the College. In a month or so he'll be on his way to Oxford.'

'Then maybe I should go there tomorrow. Actually, when Aaron saw me off on the train, he told me to come over to Motiganj on my immediate return.'

'Yes, and I know why, but that's no longer the case. Aaron Mazumdar has confided in me. About a fortnight ago matters took a disastrous turn, and Philip has told me to tell you never to come again to Motiganj.'

I stared in astonishment. 'But Aaron told me to come straight back to my chalet.'

'I'm sorry. Firstly Aaron is not in Motiganj and Philip asked me to tell you plainly not to visit the family. It's not for any wrong you have done. You are entirely blameless. They've stressed that. They just want to avoid embarrassment, or as Philip put it, family shame. You see Lily has disappeared... according to Philip, eloped.'

'I see.' I took a deep breath. 'I suppose there is nothing more to be said or done. If Aaron is not in Motiganj... then?'

'He's somewhere in the Punjab, making inquiries. Poor man, it's a wild goose chase. I hear the man she's eloped with, a much older man, was her tutor and they have covered their tracks. And if Philip is right, Lily's twenty-one, the same age as you, an adult.'

I stood up. 'Did you say at four?' He nodded. 'I'll see you then.'

'Michael, I have to say you're taking the bad news remarkably well.'

'In the circumstances, it is all I can do.'

He looked up at me. 'Good, I look forward to our tea and gossip.'

'Yes, there's quite a lot to say. Oh, I'll just say this, quickly. I met Esther, but you might have guessed that. She said she answered your letter.'

'Yes, she did. What a journey they must have had… from one corner of India to the other.'

'Maybe better than ours made from Pultanpur to Calcutta; more of theirs was by railway.'

'Hmph, now are you sure you're all right? Philip was concerned, though he said he tried to warn you off, that Lily meant a lot to you.'

I said nothing.

'Well, at four then.'

I started to leave but stopped at the door. 'Philip and I were close friends. I'm surprised he did not think of talking to me personally.'

'Michael, forgive me. I should've… Philip did say he would be here next week to meet you. Right now he's away in Lucknow. I simply forgot to tell you. Put it down to old age.'

'That reminds me. As you know, Aaron covered all my expenses and there is quite a bit of money left. Sir, I'd like to return what's left.'

'I don't know what to say. Ask Philip, he's the best person to deal with that.'

When we met for tea, I told Dr Hollins in much detail about our journeying and the days we spent trying to get to Dubri; about Gupta's invaluable resourcefulness and our good fortune in bumping into Reggie Brown and Hamid Ali; then about St Giles Church, the grave under the graceful neem tree, the Mackays and Esther, her uncle Graham, finally about Esther's invitation.

'Esther's right. England's an open country. It will be a good experience for you to have. Do give it serious thought. It could take you out of yourself and give you a new outlook.'

'After working a year or two, I should have saved enough to pay for my fare. But this break with the Mazumdars puts me back to square one. Where will I find a job?'

'Don't despair. It's part of this College's remit to find work for our leavers. No rich pickings but enough to get by--jobs with the Anglican Mission or even here, as an assistant. When I retire next year, I'll certainly highly recommend you to my successor. You've certainly made quite a mark in Literature and Mathematics. But do you really believe Aaron's completely given up on you? He genuinely had a high opinion of you.'

'I don't know.'

'Dear boy, don't let this get you down. I know you've been deeply occupied writing down life as it happens around you. Keep at it. You are never without your note book and pencil and your fertile mind will be your reprieve. Here,' he stood up and handed me a key. 'This is the key to Philip's room. It's all right. Philip knows about this and his room has been vacated.'

I took the key. 'I suppose a time will come when there are no more upheavals in my life.'

'You know, Michael, I'm not one for sermons. I see no point in them. Life is learning to live with oneself. If in that exploration you find a partner with whom you can mutually reach that goal, then you have found what it means to be content.'

I stood still a moment, tempted to ask if at any time he had found such a partner.

He smiled. 'I know what you're thinking. Yes, I did not find a human partner and so not the sort of contentment I outlined. But I found Philosophy and consolation between the covers of books. Someday, get hold of a copy of Boetius' *The Consolation of Philosophy...* but I know you'll find the ideal partner. Now I must leave you and bicycle to the Hindu College. Professor Wilks has taken our boys there to watch a Cricket match.'

'I see, I did wonder where they were.'

'Now, while you're here, you could help Wilks. Relieve him from some of the Mathematics. I'll see if I can pay you eight rupees a week... a little something to build up your kitty.'

In the week before Philip came to the College to see me, I decided to shut out thinking about anything else other than a concentration on my writings. In doing so I noted a change had crept into my style alongside a desire to read poetry. Increasingly I began to wonder if this turn was due to my constant preoccupation with Esther. The days, which first seemed to drag at a snail's space now raced to the clumsy moment when Philip and I faced each other.

'You needn't say anything you don't want to,' I said. 'I know how things stand.'

'I did warn you, Michael, remember.'

'Yes, but your father was so sure, that I felt pressed to give my word. Where is he, now?'

'At home, back from all his excursions. He's done all that a father can do, before accepting defeat. He is too embarrassed to have to face you.'

'But he needn't be. I'm grateful for all he's done for me.'

'How was your trip to Assam?'

'You were right. It rained a lot and our journeys were frequently interrupted by having to seek shelter under all sorts of cover.'

'But it's warm rain, not the type to strike one down with pneumonia. Tell me more.'

'I will, I really will, but not just now. Right now I'm concerned about the fact that I have a good bit of the money left out of what your father gave me.'

'Keep it. Father doesn't want to be reminded of it. In fact he has asked me to give you a fair amount of money for you to bank with the College. I don't agree with this, but my father is as obstinate as he is superstitious. But as he's agreed to send me to Oxford I'm in no mood to argue with him. Anyway, since he is determined to get rid of this sum, you more than anyone else may as well keep it. It's in this brief-case. I'll leave it on the table. It's in cash, notes.'

'And you say he's getting rid of it because of a superstition.'

'Yes, five thousand rupees; it was to be your wedding present. He's convinced it will be bad luck to keep it.'

'What am I going to do with it?'

'You astound me Mike. Give it to the Don to keep it for you, till you decide. In case we don't meet again, one last bit of advice. You're brilliant and have the looks of the average Greek god, but you need to shake yourself; positive action. You said you were in love with Lily, but you sat on your hands. You did nothing about it, not even a single letter. I'm not suggesting it would have made a difference in the case of Lily. But for the future... the chap who said faint heart never won fair lady, knew what he was talking about. Mike, come now,' he opened his arms, 'embrace me, set the past aside and be friends again.'

As I did, I whispered: 'sorry about Lily.'

'She wasn't worth it, Michael.' He put an arm round my shoulder. 'Come and see me in Oxford, someday.'

'You know, Phil, I'll do that.'

SIXTEEN

I did not waste time. In less than two months of receiving Philip's letter from Balliol College, Oxford, I arrived at Southampton, where he met me.

'I'm a new man,' I said laughingly.

'I knew the moment I saw you. Such a loss otherwise... What are your immediate plans?'

'Find lodgings in London.'

'I've done that for you. It's on Grove End Road, St John's Wood area, very central, belongs to a friend of dad's. But you know him, rather of him, Bill Tolly. Retired and settled in Stoke Poges, but stays there when he comes to London. He knows about you and he'll warn you of his arrival if you still happen to be there.'

'Thanks, that's a great help. I no longer hesitate to use all the help I can get. Dr Hollins gave me a name and an address of a second-hand bookshop owner, who might give me a temporary job with a small salary, a Mr Alfred Watson. His shop is in Primrose Hill, near some Park.'

'That's a stroke of good luck. I'm beginning to know London well and Primrose Hill is near Regent Park. You won't have far to go. There's a Cricket Ground in fairly open country and a Chapel nearby. W G Grace famously scored many runs...'

'And, not many years ago, Ranjitsinghji, so the Don told me, before I set out.'

'Quite,' Philip pursed his lips. 'And did he tell you that Primrose Hill was a famous duelling ground and where Blake had his vision of the Heavenly Host?'

The mention of William Blake made me think of Esther and wonder what happened to her first letter, the one James handed to me, till I abruptly realised that Philip was speaking.

'Sorry Phil, could you say that again.'

'Bookshops are shut on Mondays. With Sunday that gives you a long break at the end of each week. Spend some of them in Oxford. I'll show you around.'

'I'll certainly do that but not immediately. I've plans... some serious wooing to do.'

'Wait, let me guess. Esther, Esther Waters.'

'That's the name of a novel, published last year. You mean Esther Rivers.'

'Ah, yes. Not far off. You're lucky she was still available when you met her again in Assam. Now I see why your long letter about that trip was so lyrical. You know, bookshop owners know about publishing. Get a few addresses for your manuscript. You write well.'

'Thank you, I'll... why are you looking at me like that?'

'I'm glad you've come prepared and got yourself a warm suit. It's been dry and sunny these past few days, but even April can get unexpectedly chilly. Get yourself an overcoat or at least a raincoat to start with. This woollen grey suit is good. I remember the grey gabardine.'

'The trousers had to be lengthened. Enid Wilks did that, but now sadly it had to go. Enid also knitted a blue woollen pullover for me. She has been quite sweet and motherly.'

'Not to us parlour boarders. She said we put on airs, a ridiculous thing for her to say. There always were Indians aristocrats long before the British were around.'

'Did you tell her that?'

'No, I'm a coward.'

On the train to London Phil talked about the deal he made with his father. He would, after his time in Oxford, return to Motiganj to work with him and finally take over from him.

'I think you've made the right decision. It's wonderful to be here, but India needs us.'

'So what will you do when you succeed with Esther?'

'Marry her and take her back with me to make what contribution we can for our country.'

'And if you can't?'

'Go back. There won't be any point in staying on here. But I've seen possibilities, to use the Don's favourite phrase. I was slow at first, but now signals from her make me optimistic.'

'Well, she's a woman who can't resist...'

'Stop, I don't want to feel too... let humility and perseverance be my guide.'

Phil turned away to look out of the window and I saw a slight smirk reflected on the glass.

I touched his arm. 'Back to future plans. You know India's going through a bad time. Right now, a plague in the Bombay area and famine in central India... the Don said disease epidemics and famine almost invariably go together.'

'And Victoria is now Empress of India.'

'You can't blame Britain for a failure of the monsoon.'

'But I hope they'll stir themselves to do something about the famine.'

'I hope so too. They are the Government.'

'You've come here at an auspicious time. In a couple of months there'll be celebrations to mark Queen Victoria's Diamond Jubilee.'

'Yes, in June. Hopefully, I'll join in some with Esther. I'm certain she'll want to.'

'The grandest bits will be at St Paul's in the City. That's the usual focus.'

'You'll join us, won't you? Bring a friend.'

'By that do you mean a lady friend? You know women are not high on my list. But I'd like to meet Esther. I'll play the role of an elderly relative. I feel quite protective for-of you.'

I laughed. 'I forget how old you are, but you have to be younger than her. She's about four years older than me. But a very young looking twenty-six.'

'You speak of her as being independent, but she will have relations in England. It might be a wise move to marry in India.'

'That occurred to me. Winning Esther is one thing, having also to win them over is... well, I mean, one obstacle is enough.'

'See, what women do to men. Marriage is like taking a voluntary walk into prison, locking oneself in, and throwing away the key.'

'Cynic, it was you who advised about faint hearts.'

'Now, I'll stay the night and then I'll have to get back, tomorrow. I've had four days leave. One is not free if you are living in... they call it something else. There's a lot of Oxford jargon to pick up.'

Following Phil's directions I got to London zoo, walked to Primrose Hill and turned into a side street. It had no name, but it was impossible to miss the bookshop. A.G. Watsons was on the ground floor of a Victorian terrace between Solomon, a very open greengrocer and Mullens Limited, a very closed ironmongers shop. I looked for a bell outside the door of the bookshop and finding none, gingerly pushed it open. A bell rang. I entered a dim room with its labyrinth of bookshelves. 'With you in a minute,' a voice called. I looked in its direction and saw a man's corpulent figure bent over a pile of books stacked on a table in front of him. He was bald with hoary sideboards and a pince-nez at the end of his nose. As I approached he looked up. 'Yes, how can I help you?'

'Mr Alfred Watson?'

He stood up and nodded. I held out Dr Hollins note. He took it and sat down. 'Ah,' he said, 'I know what that will be about. Let me see.' He had a deep voice and spoke with great deliberation. I waited as he appeared to study the note thoroughly.

'My cousin speaks highly of you. You come at a good time. A guinea, twenty-one shillings, every Friday... When can you start?'

I was taken by surprise. 'T-t-tomorrow? Will that do?'

He sat back, removed his pince-nez and beamed. 'Good. I would never turn away a friend of David. Besides, as I said, it is a good time. Gives me a chance to have a holiday. Years since I've had one.' He beckoned me to sit down by removing another pile of books on a stool next to him. I did. 'Now write your name and address in this book. You have an address? Good. Couldn't give you the keys till you... that's fair handwriting... Grove End Road, St John's Wood, ah then you could walk that distance and save money. Yes, if you like walking.'

'I do. I can walk for miles.'

'Then I'll draw a map. Show you a short cut through the Park.'

'Thank you. And thank you for the job.'

'And not too hard a job... prices are clearly marked, inside book covers. Just take the money and put it in this cash box. I'll be here for the next three days. Watch me lock up. I always give the keys of the shop to Solomon the greengrocer. You do the same. He's an old friend and he keeps an eye on my shop. He and his wife Jessica live in the rooms above their store. And, oh yes, I'll tell him to give you the pound and one shilling every Friday evening.'

'What time tomorrow?'

'Half past nine. That's Tuesday to Saturday. It remains shut Sunday and Monday.'

'Indeed,' I said. 'It is all very clear, and once again thank you.'

'Then I'll see you tomorrow.'

I booked Sunday night at The Rose and Crown in Uxbridge and discovered it was one of six Georgian cottages in a quiet street called Elm Tree Road. The charming young woman at the counter smiled and tried hard to hide her curiosity. 'Just the one night?'

I nodded.

She turned a register towards me. 'Please write your name and address.' I did. She read it aloud. 'Michael Balaram, is that Spanish?' I shook my head. 'Sorry, you look Spanish.'

I smiled. 'I gather there's a Fern Cottage nearby.'

'Yes, it is the last of the five cottages next to a Victorian Terrace. But no one lives there.'

'Surely there has to be.' I looked at the clock behind her. 'I'm invited for afternoon tea, an hour from now.'

'Never seen no-one there.'

'Is there a problem, Sarah?' A voice called from behind the swing doors as a jovial looking, buxom woman came out and joined her.

'Na, no problem mum. The gentleman is visiting Fern Cottage. I said no one lives there.'

'Silly child. Yes, love, a young lady lives there. Rather pretty young thing. Keeps herself to herself, which is why we don't see her. Lives with her maid. Is she someone you know, young sir?' She looked down at the register. 'Michael Balaram, sir?'

'Yes, I knew her when she was a girl of twelve, in India.'

'Funny... Sarah, help dad with the... Yes, funny you should mention India. I knew of the couple who lived at Fern Cottage some years ago. They worked in India, returning every year or two for a holiday. I remember now, it was last year I caught sight of the three of them. So this young lady must be a relation.'

'I wouldn't know about that.'

'Well, none of my business. Mustn't keep you. Any way we can help, just ask.'

'Actually, could you tell me where I can buy flowers, roses preferably?'

'You're new here. Or you would know, it being Sunday. But we have roses in our garden. I'll tell Sarah to get you a bunch. Sit in the lounge, she'll bring them to you.'

I rang the bell and waited nervously, transferring my bunch of red roses from one hand to the other. Someone was pushing open the gate behind me. I turned to see a petite woman in a blue cape, hurrying up towards me. At that moment the front door opened silently and I heard a squeak and her voice. 'Oh, Michael!' And I found myself looking straight into a happy face that now meant the world to me. But before I could speak the girl in the cape slipped past me.

'Sorry, madam, I'll get the tea.'

'That's all right, Bella, there's no hurry.'

I offered the roses to Esther. 'There,' I said and paused to think what to say next. 'Press at least one in a book, to remind you forever that I kept my promise.'

'I certainly will. Please come in quickly. Always there are eyes searching for a scandal.'

I followed her awkwardly, again searching for something to say. 'Do forgive me.'

'There's nothing to forgive. What is there to forgive?'

'Me! For being me.'

'I can't do that. I like you being you.'

The memory of the way she had looked at me at the gate of the Dak Bungalow and the soft kiss on her lips, returned. 'But you must forgive the fool I have been, who let my pearl of great price slip through my hands.'

She stopped and turned to face me. 'But now, I am in your hands.'

'I should have given you more. More time, more appreciation.'

She drew near and quickly stepped back. 'Yes Bella? Bring the tray in, when you're ready.'

Esther turned, walked to a chair opposite a highly polished, plain rosewood table and sitting down invited me to take the chair opposite to her. I did, gazing into her twinkling but strangely sad face and realised I was really seeing her for the first time. The luxuriant auburn hair was tied into a loose bun behind her slender neck and the figure below her high lace collar was full.

'I have been blind and foolish.' The borrowed literary phrase at last lent me an eloquence that was sincerely meant. 'But all that is in the past. Can I make a fresh start?'

'Do. I'm all for fresh starts.'

We laughed as Bella brought in the tea and left. Esther leaned forward, picked up a spoon and stirred the tea in its brown china pot.

Emboldened I blurted out. 'But I am tired of beginnings. I want to make an end.'

'Then marry me. Michael will…'

I jumped up. 'I will, yes! A thousand times yes!'

'Hush, Michael. Sit down. You'll frighten poor Bella.'

I sat down in a daze and trembling with excitement. 'But, Esther, do you mean it?'

'Oh, Michael, I could never forget you. From the moment we parted in Calcutta you have haunted me. It's those eyes of yours, they're so-so penetrating.'

'But you were so quiet, and-and, indifferent.'

'I wasn't well.'

'And I thought you were thinking of going back to England, to the new School, and staying with your aunt… Is she the wife of your uncle Graham?'

'Yes. They live in Kent.'

'And this house? I was told that a middle-aged couple live here. Or rather, they returned here from India for the holidays.'

'Yes, my aunt Margaret Mackay. Dad's cousin, the headmistress of the school I went to in the Hills of Panchmarhi.'

'I remember now. A tall lady. Any relation to the Mackays of St Giles?'

'No. Not that I know of. Aunt Margaret is not Scottish or Scotch. Her husband could be. They let me move in here with Bella their maid. The maid is around to avoid all wild gossip that would stick to a young woman living alone.'

'Anyway,' I said, confident and in full control of my emotions. 'We mustn't lose sight of the most vital turn of events. If I don't marry, I shall burn…' I laughed as I recalled Phil's advice. 'My friend Philip Mazumdar will be astonished at how fast I achieved what I came for. He said we should marry in India.'

'Wise advice. Let's return to India, together, at once.'

'But what about… you said you are a teacher.'

'I had applied, but I did not take up the job offered. When you gave your word, I decided to wait till I knew what move you were going to make.'

'Do you want to wait to see the Jubilee Celebrations?'

'No,' she said, quite simply.

The End

Characters & Glossary

(the glossary omits those foreign words where
the meanings are clear from the text)

Devnath – a "god" title of respect that the Hindu wife uses to address her husband. Traditionally the wife does not call her husband by his first name.

Krishna – there is no prohibition in Hinduism to name boys and girls after gods and goddesses. Krishna or Hari Krishna is the most popular incarnation of god Vishnu. It was later discovered that Krishna had been secretly baptised and given the name Michael.

Daada & Daadi - grandfather and grandmother on the father's side of a family.

Karam Chand – name of the stationmaster.

Laxman – name of *Daada's* elder brother. Laxman was the brother of god Rama. Rama was the incarnation of Vishnu, before Krishna.

Ramoo & Ganesh – uncles of the boy Krishna.

Hira & Noti – names of the bullocks.

Munshi – title severally applied to a tutor, clerk and accountant.

James – name of the Bhil young man given charge of the orphans in the hostel.

The Revd./Father/Dr Jacob Rivers – Head of the Mission Orphanage and School.

Esther Rivers – daughter of the above.

Sister Agnes – mother of the above.

Pandit Motiram – village teacher at Pali.

Walid Khan – the big Pathan ***chowkidar*** or watchman.

Namdeo – tonga driver and syce. **Tonga** – a basic and light Indian horse-drawn carriage.

Mohan – son of above and milkman to the orphanage.

Husain – cook at the orphanage.

Das Gupta – name of the Bengali Munshi who also teaches Arithmetic.

Mrs Mackay – cousin of Dr Rivers and Head of Tara House, Esther's school.

Rosie Almeida – Esther's erstwhile **ayah** – i.e. Indian nanny.

Noel & Luke – names of two of the twenty-five orphans.

Nawab – titled Indian nobleman. A title adopted by the Eighteenth Century Anglo-Indians but corrupted to *Nabob*.

Nawab Ali Baig – close friend of Michael's father and Dr Rivers.

Sorab Ali Baig – son of the above.

Gulab – Sorab's mute horse-carriage driver.

Yusuf – Sorab's personal servant and guardian.

Bishop Cyril Robinson – powerful committee member of the Christian Mission in his diocese.

Revd. Mark Hastings – named to take over from Dr Rivers.

Farouk – coach driver employed by Nawab Ali Baig.

Sher Ali – another employee of the Nawab, detailed to escort the Rivers family to Calcutta.

Pastor Erikson – Swedish missionary who worked with the Bhil tribes.

Rumi (Ronny) – the cook, also in the Nawab's employ, who produced meals for the Rivers family, when they broke their journey en route to Calcutta.

Denis Hay – Eurasian railway stationmaster at Allahabad.

Dr David Hollins – Dean of the Christian College in Calcutta, respectfully and affectionately referred to as "the Don".

Professor Derek Wilks, **Bill Foster** (Friar Tuck) **& Dr Arthur Collins** – colleagues of the above.

Philip Mazumdar – close college friend of Michael.

Aaron & Monica Mazumdar – parents of Philip.

Muni & Lily – sisters of Philip.

Manju – horse-carriage driver to Aaron Mazumdar.

Brijpal – accountant in the employ of Aaron Mazumdar.

Shikari – armed huntsmen hired to keep guard.

Arjun Singh –**Marwari** merchant and leader of the camel fair. Marwaris are from Rajasthan.

Madan – *coolie*, i.e. porter at Lalgoda Railway Station and close acquaintance of Reggie Brown.

Victor Mason – Stationmaster of Lalgoda Railway Station, a Eurasian.

Professor James Stuart – Head of English Department in Gupta's Hindu College.

Reginald (Reggie) Brown – a railway train guardsman an Indian domicile Englishman.

Hamid Ali – another acquaintance of Reggie Brown.

Paul & **Judith Mackay** – Scottish missionaries. Paul is Pastor of St Giles Church.

Chootu & **Bhillu** – menial labourers of St Giles Church.

Mr Joyti Basu – friend of Paul Mackay.

Lightning Source UK Ltd.
Milton Keynes UK
UKOW04f1048270116

267199UK00001B/104/P